Tishomingo Bingo

The Life and Times of Theo Son of Mann

A novel by Jeffrey L. Sakas

Published by:
Maudlin Pond Press, LLC
PO Box 53, Tybee Island, Georgia 31328, USA

Layout and Design by: Lauren Clackum

ISBN: 979-8-9857239-7-7
eBook ISBN: 979-8-9857239-8-4

Disclaimer: This book is a work of fiction and any incidental reference to any person living or dead is unintended. While the events depicted are similar to those events depicted in the Gospel account of the life and ministry, death and resurrection of Jesus Christ as written in the first four books of the New Testament of the Holy Bible this book is a fictional account of a character who is completely fictional.

Scripture taken from the Holy Bible, New International Version© NIV©. Copyright 1973, 1978, 1984, 2011 by Biblica, Inc™. Used by permission of Zondervan. All rights reserved worldwide. www.zondervan.com The NIV and New International Version are trademarks registered in the United States Patent and Trademark office by Biblica, Inc.™

This book is dedicated to 马嘉欣 with whom
I am most pleased. I hope her faith is
restored by these words.

Preface

When I first began to write this book, I had a different set of ideas that I wanted to pursue about the gaming industry in Mississippi. I thought about the relationship between the small bingo parlors and the tribal gambling interest in Tunica and the casinos along the Gulf coast. As I started to gather information and research the gaming industry, something was prompting me to go in another direction.

One night as I was praying it came to me that a different setting for the New Testament might be of use in the understanding of the life and ministry of Jesus Christ and might be useful to those who have been reluctant to read and study the Gospels. This book is my effort to put the story of Jesus in a new setting. The Northeast corner of Mississippi and Middle Tennessee was familiar to me from my college days and the time I spent with my daughter during the Covid pandemic. That location and a desire to explore again the ministry of Jesus prompted me to write these pages.

I do not intend to add to or take away from the truth of the Holy Bible. Everyone should read and study the Bible as the inspired word of God. This book is only intended to be a fictional account of a man that I have named Theo Mann. (There is an attorney in Newnan, Georgia with that name with whom I am acquainted, and I apologize for any confusion caused by the use of that name.) While I have intended to choose a name for the main character that is in close proximity to the Son of Man as I could think of, Theo Mann is still a fictional product of my inadequate mind.

There may be controversy concerning my writing from any number of sources including the churches that I have been a member of over the years. I grew up as a Southern Baptist because my mother and father were members of Southern Baptist churches. I found as I grew, and we moved from place to place that there was a wide diversity of belief within the ranks of the churches that we attended. My father was in the United States Navy until I was 13 years old, and we lived along the East Coast of the U.S. from Jacksonville, Florida to Quonset Point, Rhode Island. We eventually moved to Clarksville, Tennessee and then to Nashville while my father pursued an EdD. I graduated from high school in Nashville and graduated from college at Middle Tennessee State University before going to law school at Tulane University in New Orleans.

The Southern Baptist Church that I attended in New Orleans (St. Charles Ave.) was nothing like the churches in Tennessee. I eventually moved to Atlanta and the churches I attended in the Atlanta area were not like the others that I had attended in other locations. The last church that I regularly attended seceded from the Southern Baptist and joined what I like to refer to as the Jimmy Carter Baptist (it is actually the Co-operative Baptist Fellowship).

While it is not my intent to create controversy in the writing of this book and I do not intend to add to or take away from the Gospel account of the life, teachings, ministry, death and resurrection of Jesus Christ. I believe the Gospel account of Jesus are accurate and should be carefully studied for the truth that the Gospel of Jesus Christ contains. It is my hope and prayer that this book will encourage those who seek God to study for themselves the ministry of Jesus Christ, my Lord and Savior.

Tishomingo Bingo

The Life and Times of Theo Son of Mann

A novel by Jeffrey L. Sakas

Table of Contents

Introduction

Tishomingo County is located in the northeast corner of the state of Mississippi. To the east is the Alabama State line and to the north is the Tennessee State line. Just over the Alabama border is the city of Tuscumbia, Alabama the birthplace of Helen Keller. A little further to the east is the city of Muscle Shoals, Alabama which is famous for its Fame music recording studio. Across the northern boundary of Tishomingo County is Hardin County, Tennessee that is the site of the Shiloh National Military Park where a great Civil War battle took place early in the war to end slavery in the United States. The battle of Shiloh was a major Civil War battle that made the reputation of General and later President U.S. Grant.

The county seat of Tishomingo County is the city of Iuka that was also the scene of a Civil War battle. To the West by roughly 12 miles from the western county line is the city of Corinth, Mississippi. Corinth is the county seat of Alcorn County and Corinth was also the site of two Civil War battles that were fought because Corinth was a rail hub that served southern interests during the early part of the 1860s.

Tishomingo County, Mississippi is different from the delta region of the state. The topography consists of rolling hills and in some cases rocky ground. Even though geographers contend that the northeast part of Mississippi is made up of lowlands, it appears different to me. Tishomingo State Park is very rocky and has limestone outcroppings that are found in no other location in Mississippi and can be seen as one drives within that park. Near Iuka is the highest point in Mississippi, Woodall Mountain, that has an elevation of 806 feet above sea level. While the Mississippi delta is flat and alluvial the elevations in that part of the state are nowhere close to the elevations found in Tishomingo County. Tishomingo County more closely resembles the foothills of the Cumberland Plateau found in middle Tennessee. It has small mountains that have more or less flat tops. Because of the topography Tishomingo County has many small family farms that did not lend themselves to the plantation culture of the delta during antibellum times. As you go further West from Tishomingo County, towards Memphis, the land flattens out and the rolling hills give way to the Mississippi alluvial plain.

The population of Tishomingo County is overwhelmingly white with 97% of the county being made up of non- Hispanic white people. The black population that is normally found in the Mississippi delta and in other parts of the state cannot be found in Tishomingo County. The black population in Tishomingo County is small, and in the schools, there are also very few black children as opposed to the black population of Corinth's schools where the black population is substantially greater.

At one time prior to white settlement in northeast Mississippi, Chickasaw Indians inhabited the area in and around Tishomingo County. The county is named for a famous Chickasaw chief. The name Tishomingo is Chickasaw (Tishu Minco) meaning warrior chief. Tishomingo was an actual Chickasaw chief who fought along with the United States against other Indian tribes further to the north and west of northeast, Mississippi. Chief Tishomingo was given a medal by President George Washington for his services to the United States.

The Chickasaw Indians were displaced from northeast Mississippi by the Treaty of Pontotoc Creek on October 20, 1832. In 1832 the state of Mississippi declared jurisdiction over the Chickasaw tribe (without their consent) and outlawed tribal self-government. The Chickasaw tribe eventually moved to the Indian Territories that now forms part of the state of Oklahoma. The migration of the Chickasaws and other Indian tribes to Oklahoma became known as the Trail of Tears because many of the Indians that were forced to move in that migration died along the trail from Southeastern states to the Indian Territories.

The Mississippi alluvial plain is part of the Gulf Coastal Plain that 40 to 70 million years ago was covered by the Gulf Coastal Embayment. The Mississippi alluvial plain is a river floodplain composed of unconsolidated sediment from as far away as the eastern slopes of the Rockies and from the western slopes of the Blue Ridge Mountains. While the Mississippi alluvial plain can be seen from the western edge of Tishomingo County, the county is quite different from the rest of the state because of its topography, history, and population. At one time the making of bootleg whiskey was a thriving business in Tishomingo County. The consumption of illegal alcohol was a sport that was engaged in by both men and women in this very rural part of America.

Just over the Mississippi line in Tennessee are a series of TVA dams that harness the Tennessee River and form lakes that allow the residents of the conjunction of Mississippi, Alabama and Tennessee many forms of water recreation. The Tombigbee Waterway emanates from the Tennessee River travels through Tishomingo County near the city of Burnsville and traverses the border between Mississippi and Alabama until it hooks up with the Tombigbee River and empties into the Gulf of Mexico at Mobile Bay. On the northern edge of Tishomingo County is a lake formed by the Pickwick dam. Pickwick Lake crosses the state line between Tishomingo County, Mississippi and Harden County, Tennessee. A marina is located on the state and county line that allows fishing enthusiast to launch their boats and store their boats at that location.

People from the northeast Mississippi region engage in all sorts of sport fishing. Even high schools in the area have competitive fishing teams that compete with other high schools and engage in fishing tournaments. The high school students that participate in competitive fishing seek to earn scholarships to colleges that also have competitive fishing teams. In and around Tishomingo County there are bass fishing tournaments that are open to the public or more precisely to fishing enthusiasts who pay an entry fee in hopes of winning the prizes offered.

These privately owned fishing tournaments require that the fishermen pay an entry fee from which prize money is awarded to those who catch the most fish by weight and to the angler who catches the biggest fish. The most popular fishing tournaments involve fishing for large and small mouth bass. Professional fishing tournaments are sometimes held at the lakes formed by the TVA dams in which professional fisherman compete for cash prizes awarded to the individual that catches the most fish by weight during a pre-set time limit at a particularly designated lake. Just like in other sports, professional fisherman that enter into bass fishing contests are sponsored by purveyors of fishing equipment and boats. It is not unusual for the top professional fishermen to earn substantial money from the cash prizes and endorsements.

People in northeast Mississippi enjoy boating. As one drives along the country roads in northeast Mississippi, northwest Alabama and the adjoining parts of Tennessee, it is not unusual to see a boat parked in someone's yard or in their driveway. For the most part these boats are used for fishing.

There are, however, pontoon boats that can be seen both in driveways and on the waterways. Pontoon boats can be used for fishing, but it is more likely that the pontoon boat is used for cruising and partying while on the lakes and rivers. In order to engage in fishing tournaments, the fisherman needs a more powerful boat that can maneuver more easily into the desired fishing spots. Fishermen in northeast Mississippi are always looking for the best boat to give them an advantage in finding and catching fish. Those that are serious about sportfishing in this area of the country, equip their boats with trolling motors, sonar apparatus, depth finders, and other equipment that will give them an edge in catching not only the most fish but also the biggest fish.

Once a person becomes infected with the fishing fever, that person will engage in lengthy conversation about the type of boat they have, the equipment that the boat is outfitted with, the type of bait or lures that will be used in catching any particular fish species. Men often talk about the best places to go fishing, and when they can next get out on the lake or river. When men and women gather for holidays or other family gatherings, fishing and fishing equipment is often a major part of the conversation. It is not unusual during family gatherings for a man to show off his boat to other family members or friends. Discussions often revolve around the make of the boat, the manufacturer of the motor, the horsepower of the motor and the maneuverability of the boat.

In addition to the equipment that is discussed, a fisherman will brag concerning the fish that he has caught, or the big one that got away. Interestingly, while actually engaging in fishing the fisherman is incredibly quiet and concentrates on his casting and placement of the lure or the bait at the exact right spot to entice a fish. In contrast once the fisherman returns home there is a lot of discussion concerning everything that went on during the fishing trip or tournament.

The Natchez Trace was originally a path created by bison and other animals in seeking salt licks (especially located near Nashville, Tennessee) and was used by Native American Indians in their pursuit of these animals. The Natchez Trace Parkway is a national limited access two lane road that is 444 miles long. It runs from Natchez, Mississippi, that sits on eastern bank of the Mississippi River, northwards through the Mississippi delta, northeast Mississippi, northwest Alabama into Middle Tennessee with the northern terminus near Nashville. Largely following a geographic ridgeline, prehistoric animals followed the dry ground of the Trace and were pursued by tribes of Indians that were prehistoric indigenous people. There were Indian settlements along the Natchez trace including the 2000-year-old Pharr Mounds of the Middle Woodland period, located near present day Tupelo, Mississippi.

Starting out in the delta region of Mississippi where it is flat and straight the Natchez Trace Parkway heads north into the Cumberland plateau region of Middle Tennessee. The Parkway is under the control of the National Park Service, and it is very well maintained. The Trace climbs steadily in altitude as you go northward until it becomes steep and winding. Along the way there are many historical sites and geographic points of interest. Not far into Tennessee from the Alabama boarder, is the burial site of Merriweather Lewis, one of the leaders of the Lewis and Clark expedition that explored the vast American West shortly after the Louisiana purchase in 1803. The land that made up the Louisiana purchase more than doubled the size of the United States and caused this country to shine from sea to shining sea. Mr. Lewis was killed close to the site of his burial.

The two largest groups of Native American tribes (among several other smaller tribes) that inhabited northeast Mississippi were the Chickasaw Indians and the Choctaw Indians. The Choctaw Indians were a much larger tribe than the Chickasaws. While the Choctaws were more agrarian, the Chickasaw Indian tribe was more war-like and aggressive. The Chickasaw Indians subsisted as hunter gathers and relied on hunting and fishing the forests and streams and rivers of northeast Mississippi. During the Seven Years War (1753 –1760) between the English and the French that became known as the French & Indian War in North America, the Chickasaws sided with the English and the Choctaws sided with the French. Both the Chickasaws and the Choctaws engaged in making slaves of conquered people whether they were black, white or Indian. The Chickasaws sold Indian slaves to the English settlers.

The Chickasaws and the Choctaws share a common language, Muskogean, indicating a common origin of the two tribes. At one point in time both Indian groups were united but somewhere along the line there was a falling out between the two tribes. The Chickasaws and Choctaws engaged in war with each other that resulted in each tribe separating themselves and engaging in different methods of keeping the tribal governance separate and at odds with the other tribe. When the English supplied guns to the Chickasaws as the sales price for the slaves, furs and deer skins they exchanged, the balance of power between the warring tribes swung to the Chickasaws and remained that way until the French supplied guns to the Choctaws.

The Chickasaws fished. Prior to encountering European traders, the preferred fishing method of the Chickasaw men was to throw a poison made from Buckeye or green walnut hulls into a deep hole in a stream. This concoction would temporarily paralyze any fish that might be affected by the spreading poison, and the men would catch the fish by either spearing them or grabbing them by hand when the fish came to the surface. After contact with Europeans in the 1600s, the Chickasaws traded animal skins for knives, guns, metal pots and fishing hooks. The territories that the Chickasaws used for hunting and fishing stretched from northeast Mississippi through Tennessee and Kentucky and all the way to the banks of the Mississippi River.

When European settlement pushed from the East Coast into the interior of southeastern United States including Northeast Mississippi, the Indian hunting grounds and fishing areas began to diminish. It became harder for the Chickasaws to support themselves as hunter-gatherers. The Chickasaws and the Choctaws were compromised by war among the tribes and the incursion of more European settlers in the lands of these indigenous people. By the early 1800s the Choctaws made the strategic decision to begin the process of moving to the Indian territories in what is now Oklahoma. By the 1830s the Chickasaw tribe because of increased pressure from white settlers and the reduction of their hunting and fishing territories, also agreed to move their tribe to the Indian territories. The Chickasaws purchased land from the Choctaws and set up their tribal headquarters in Ada, Oklahoma. However, the Chickasaw Indian tribe (Chickasaw Inkana Foundation) maintains that their true ancestral home is in northeast Mississippi. The Chickasaws have established a presence in Tupelo, Mississippi for the purpose of maintaining their cultural link to their native lands and to offer those who want to know, a glimpse into their culture and history.

There are about 100 churches in Tishomingo County. For the most part the churches are Protestant with almost equal numbers of Baptists and Church of Christ congregations. The congregations are typically small with a few exceptions. There is a smattering of Catholic churches, but it is the Baptist and Church of Christ churches that predominate this mostly white southern landscape. As with the Chickasaws and Choctaws, the Baptist and Church of Christ are similar to each other in their belief in the authority of the Bible but broke from each other somewhere along the way. Some Baptists contend that the two denominations were the same denomination of fundamental Christians until the Church of Christ under the leadership of Alexander Campbell broke off from the Baptists.

Alexander Campbell according to some Baptist historians was the pastor of the First Baptist Church of Nashville, Tennessee. Campbell felt that the Baptists beliefs were not fundamentally sound, and he formed the Church of Christ. Some say that pastor Campbell stole the pulpit from the First Baptist Church of Nashville and took it to the church that he formed several blocks away. While the historical account of the formation of the Church of Christ differs from some Baptist historian's point of view, members of the Church of Christ are sometimes referred to as Campbellites.

Both the Baptist and the Church of Christ denominations are considered congregational rather than hierarchical in their church governance. Congregational churches are governed by members of the local church rather than an ecclesiastical hierarchy that governs a group of churches. Baptists churches are governed by the Board of Deacons while the Church of Christ call their governing board, Elders. Both deacons and elders are elected by the congregation to serve in that capacity. In Baptist churches in which the congregation is black, church governance can be quite different from that of predominantly white churches.

One of the major differences between Baptist and Church of Christ congregations is that the Church of Christ does not allow the playing of musical instruments in church. When the congregation sings hymns, the leader of the singing starts out by hitting a proper note on a pitch pipe. The women of the Church of Christ congregations dress very modestly and traditionally did not wear make-up or jewelry. Church of Christ women do not follow the latest fashion and are prone to wear dresses below the knee. On the other hand, Baptist women, are more fashion conscious and can be seen in church services with very stylish clothes, jewelry, and make-up and on occasions hats.

There are generally three church services in both the Baptist and the Church of Christ denominations during the week. There is a Sunday morning service, a Sunday evening service, and a Wednesday evening prayer meeting. For many years Baptist churches had a Wednesday night supper, but because of the pandemic and other economic conditions the Wednesday night supper has gone by the wayside. Usually, prior to the Sunday morning service there is an hour-long Bible study that is referred to as Sunday school. During Sunday school the congregation is divided by age into small groups. Children are taught Bible stories. Adults that attend Sunday school engage in a more detailed study of the scripture.

Politically Tishomingo County voters overwhelmingly support Republican candidates. The county voted for Donald Trump by wide margins in both the 2016 and 2020 presidential elections. Voters also cast their ballots in favor of Cindy Hyde Smith in the last Senatorial election despite her status as the least effective senator in congress. Her opponent was a black congressman from the Delta, and he did not stand a chance in Tishomingo County.

Tishomingo County has one of the least vaccinated populations in Mississippi, when it comes to the COVID vaccine, having only 26.68% of its population vaccinated. Even with a low vaccination rate, only a few people wear face masks even when they go into the Walmart store in Corinth. As far as the people who attend churches in Tishomingo County, they act as if the pandemic had never occurred.

Chapter 1

The Bingo Parlor on Highway 72

Highway 72 is a four-lane divided highway that runs from East to West across the northern counties of Mississippi. The first Mississippi county that one comes to from the Alabama state line is Tishomingo County, Mississippi. Highway 72 is a limited access highway and the first exit from the highway is that of the city of Iuka, the county seat of Tishomingo County. One of the first roadside attractions that a traveler will see while traveling to the West from Iuka is the Tishomingo Bingo Parlor. The Tishomingo Bingo Parlor is housed in a two-story building with a covered area so that when it rains people can exit their cars without the use of an umbrella. The building is white with large red letters proclaiming that it is in fact the Tishomingo Bingo Parlor.

The Tishomingo Bingo Parlor is on the north side of Highway 72 and sits back from the highway behind a parking lot that can accommodate nearly 100 cars. Bingo games are held on Sunday nights and Wednesday nights and are in direct competition with the local Baptist and Church of Christ congregations in the area. Anyone can see a large number of cars parked in the Tishomingo Bingo Parlor parking lot if one is traveling on Highway 72 when church services are going on at the Baptist and Church of Christ churches. The bingo game sessions also just happened to coincide with the time set for Sunday night and Wednesday night church services.

While the congregations of the Baptists and Church of Christ churches in the area are singing hymns and praying for the sick and the souls of the lost sinners in the community, a room full of Bingo Players are closely paying attention to their bingo cards as letters and numbers are being called by "The Caller" employed by the bingo parlor owners. The numbers and letters that correspond to the letters B, I, N, G, and O are cried out over a loudspeaker by the caller who has complete control of the Bingo parlor while Bingo is being played.

The loudspeaker crackles, as the "Caller" announces "I, 27" and all the serious Bingo Players search their bingo cards so they can take their markers, that emit a transparent color so as not to mask the appropriate entry and mark their cards.

Just inside the entrance to the Tishomingo Bingo Parlor is a table set up from which Bingo Players can buy their bingo cards and marking devices. Bingo players can buy single cards for each game session or multiple cards that come in five-card packs. A five-card pack is more economical than buying single game entry cards especially for the clientele of the Tishomingo Bingo Parlor.

Most of the bingo players are what one would call the blue hair crowd because the ladies of the group have white hair that turns blue as bright light shines on it. The men in the group are generally less enthusiastic about bingo playing than the women and are there to uphold their end of the bargain in which the wife preforms homemaking obligations, and the husband agrees to accompany the wife to the bingo parlor. In other words, if the husband wants to eat and have his clothes washed, he must accompany his wife for the multi-weekly bingo sessions at the Tishomingo Bingo Parlor. During game breaks the men huddle together and talk about fishing, their boats and college football during the football season.

The Bingo Players after entering into the bingo hall sit at standard vinyl tables that one could purchase at a Sam's Club for around $30.00 each. The chairs are set around the playing tables and are also standard straight back folding chairs offered for sale at Sam's Club for less than $15 apiece. The chairs are arranged so that all the chairs are facing the podium at the front of the hall. The bingo players all face in one direction so that the players can not only hear the numbers being called but can also see the Caller that is actually drawing the numbers from a revolving hopper. "N, 44" is called and the men and women in attendance look over their cards as the Caller continues to rapidly call numbers and letters in a seemingly endless stream that sends players into action studying their cards to match the numbers and the row on their cards with the numbers and letters being called over the loudspeaker. The bingo players compete against each other for money and prizes at the Tishomingo Bingo Parlor.

Bingo has an interesting history. A form of bingo was played as early as 1530 in Italy. The game was called "Lo Giuoco del Lotto D' Italia." The American version of bingo has 75 numbers as opposed to English bingo that has 90 numbers. Edwin Lowe is credited with the modern bingo game in America. A precursor to bingo, referred to as Beano was being played at a carnival near Atlanta in the 1920s. Mr. Lowe took the game to Pittsburgh and hired Carl Loffler a Columbia University math professor to do the mathematical formulas regarding the odds and statistical evaluations needed to make the game competitive. Bingo was copyrighted in 1933.

Bingo came to the interest of church groups in the late 20s and early 30s and spread across the United States by the 1940s. Eventually, states started passing laws prohibiting gambling but made exceptions for church and fraternal organizations in their use of bingo as a gaming method. Generally, it is illegal in a bingo operation for a bingo player to play against the house, while in most cases it is legal for a bingo player to play against another bingo player even if the winning player receives a cash reward from the bingo parlor.

The Federal Indian Gaming Regulatory Act (FIGRA) has changed the playing ground for bingo in the United States because gambling is permitted on Indian lands. In Mississippi the casinos in Tunica, Mississippi is on Indian owned land and there are exceptionally large gambling businesses located there. Because of FIGRA bingo can be played on the internet and can be played in many locations simultaneously.

In some bingo operations there are digital bingo cards and electronic posting of bingo numbers. With the advent of gambling casinos controlled by Native Americans, bingo parlors can be electronically joined so that cash rewards for a winning bingo player can be more substantial.

The bingo operation in Tishomingo County is not owned or operated by Indians. State of Mississippi law related to bingo parlors relegates non-casino bingo operation to churches, fraternal organizations and 501(c) and (d) non-profit organizations. Mississippi limits the amount of money that may be made at such a bingo operation and the prizes that may be awarded. Employees of the bingo parlor are limited to a salary of $600 per bingo session and sessions are also limited by state law. All money collected by the bingo operation must be deposited into a trust account and the money that is left after paying expenses and salaries must be donated to the charity that operates or is affiliated with the bingo parlor.

Bingo Players need to have sufficient room at each table in order to spread out their cards so that when the numbers are called, they can quickly look over the line and number called. Not very often, but sometimes turf wars can happen at the bingo parlor. When one bingo player believes that their space is being compromised by some other bingo player, and they are likely to let the other player know about it. Squabbles over the seating arrangements at the bingo parlor are short lived because Bingo Players are more interested in making sure that they are adequately marking their cards as the numbers are being continually called and because that is the method that a player determines if they have won any particular bingo game.

There are prizes awarded to the person that meets that game criterion for that round of play. In some games, all that is necessary to win is that a complete line, either horizontal, vertical or diagonal is filled in on in a bingo card. Some games require that the whole card be filled in, in order to win and in some games only the corners of the card need to be filled in to claim BINGO. There are many variations in the type of games that can be played and the criterion for winning a single game is determined by the Caller. There are also progressive games in which the Caller continues to call letters and numbers until the whole bingo card has been filled in completely. When the session comes to a close bingo players count up their prizes and engage in greeting and conversing with their neighbors and friends. Prizes range from inexpensive trinkets to substantial amounts of cash.

When a player has met the criteria for the game that is being called, they will cry out BINGO. The game then stops for the person in charge to verify that the game criteria has actually been met by the person claiming to have won. Sometimes the stoppage in play can take a few minutes for the authorities to determine whether the player has actually met that game's criteria. On rare occasions the administrator of the game determines that the game criteria have not been met and the person claiming to have won is returned to their seat in humiliation amid catcalls and snickering. Usually, because the people that are playing bingo are seasoned veterans of the games and are among a group of individuals that regularly play bingo together whenever the bingo parlor is in session, care is taken to make sure that when BINGO is called the Bingo Player has correctly filled out their card and has successfully won that round of Bingo and has qualified for the prize.

Numbers and letters are not officially registered until it is called by the Caller. Sometimes, especially with the advent of electronic methods of selecting numbers and letters, a number and letter will be posted on a television screen prior to the time that the number and letter is actually called. If a Bingo Player calls BINGO prior to the official call even if that number appears on the television screen in the bingo parlor the Bingo Player may be disqualified and lose their prize.

Chapter 2

Zack's Extraordinary Closet Meeting

In the mid-1980s, there was a great divide developing in the United States. It was not so much a physical divide or even a divide among people because of their economic condition, but there was a great spiritual divide among people. People who would ordinarily be persons of goodwill to each other but, for some reason began treating anyone, who did not believe as they did, with contempt and that had far ranged consequences.

In Murfreesboro, Tennessee a man named Zack Waters, one of the leaders of the Southern Baptist denomination lived near the campus of Middle Tennessee State University. It was Mr. Waters job to drive the 35 miles, on a daily basis, from Murfreesboro to Nashville where he worked at the Southern Baptist Sunday School Board as an editor of Sunday school material offered for sale to Southern Baptist churches throughout the denomination.

Normally, during the week Zack Waters who was in his early 50s got up with his wife, Betty, had breakfast, and got into the morning rush hour traffic on his way to the Sunday school board offices in downtown Nashville. Zack and Betty had no children but the couple and especially Betty had always wanted to have children. Betty had almost given up all hope that the couple would become parents. Betty was 45 years old.

Zack and Betty lived a comfortable life in Murfreesboro. Both of them had grown up in Middle Tennessee and were well acquainted with the ends and outs up their hometown. Murfreesboro was in the exact geographic center of Tennessee and had been the scene of the battle of Stone River during the Civil War. Murfreesboro sits in a natural bowl with the Cumberland plateau's higher peeks surrounding that part of Rutherford County.

Betty had tried to get pregnant throughout the early years of her and Zach's marriage. They had even gone so far as seeking the advice of fertility doctors in order for Betty to get pregnant. This all seemed to be of no avail and now Betty was closer to 50 than to 40, and the couple remained without children. While Betty and Zach were members of a larger family group including cousins, aunts and uncles, and all forms of other relatives, they were often not included in family outings because they did not have children.

At Zack's place of employment, it was the usual custom for there to be a Friday morning prayer meeting that was mandatory for all Sunday school board employees to attend. From time to time, Zach would be called on to lead the prayer meeting and to pray for the missions that the Southern Baptist were engaged in at that particular time of the year. When Zach was called upon to lead the prayer meeting, he would usually sequester himself in a small closet just off the stage at the Southern Baptist headquarters building for the purpose of collecting his thoughts and preparing to pray before the large group of employees.

Zach had driven from Murfreesboro on Interstate 24 and had gotten off at the exit near the football stadium at which the Tennessee Titans play their home games. This was not the usual route that Zack took to the office but on that morning when he was to lead the prayer meeting of the Sunday school board employees, his mind had been filled with thoughts about his wife and their inability to have children. Betty had become increasingly distraught, and Zach on several occasions had found Betty somewhat depressed, and he attributed that to her inability to have children.

When Zach entered the closet just off the stage at his office, he usually sat in the dark for a few minutes collecting his thoughts. On that Friday morning, however, the most unusual thing occurred. Zach found himself face to face with a man dressed in a gleaming white linen suit looking intently into Zach's eyes.

"Who are you and what are you doing here?" Zack blurted out as he fumbled to control his fear because he had never encountered anything quite like he was encountering at that particular moment in that particular closet.

"I'm here to make some of your dreams come true young man." Came the reply from the man in the bright white suit. "You see, my boss has heard your prayers and I'm here to fill you in on the details."

But for the fact that Zach had just gone to the bathroom he probably would have peed his pants because of the fear that overcame him. "Quit playing with me and get out of here because I need some time to get ready for the prayer meeting."

"I'm not playing with you, I am being very serious, and because you have an attitude, you're not gonna be able to talk until all that I'm about to tell you is completed."

Zach tried to reply but found that just as the man had said he could not utter a word.

"Zach don't be afraid because what I'm about to tell you comes straight from heaven. When you go home this evening Betty will be waiting for you and she will be very happy to see you. She will have made you your favorite dinner treat, and when you go to bed, she will be receptive to your sexual desires. Nine months from now you and Betty will become the parents of a baby girl. You will name this child Jonnie and she will become a remarkable person. She will proclaim good news to many people and will be a blessing to all who listen. Jonnie will be as strait-laced as they come, refusing a glamorous life for that of a naturalist, who desires to live rustically and without rich food or fancy clothes. She will usher in a time of spiritual awareness that has been long overdue."

As soon as the visitor had finished his speech he was gone. Zach was left alone in the now darkened closet unable to speak and still frightened beyond belief. It took Zach several minutes to come back to his senses and to quite shaking in his boots.

When he left the closet, he was immediately confronted by the Secretary of the Sunday School Board who wanted to know what was going on in the closet because Zach had been in there for a long time and the prayer meeting was ready to start.

"Zach, what were you doing in the closet? You look as white as a ghost. Are you ready to lead the prayer service?"

Zach could not reply. He tried to speak but nothing would come out. Zach wanted to explain to the Secretary that he had just had the most remarkable experience, but he could not get out a single word. Finally, somewhat exasperatedly, Zach found a tablet and a pen and wrote out as best as he could explain what had just happened to him. After reading what Zach had just written, the Secretary shook his head and asked if Zach had been on the sauce because none of it seemed to make any sense.

The Secretary told Zach that he had to go home, "because he wasn't gonna have anybody with that big of a fairy tale hanging around the Southern Baptist headquarters, while the good employees perform their duties and keep their odd stories to themselves."

When Zach got home it was late morning and Betty had gone out to the grocery store. Betty had decided that she wanted to give Zach a treat for dinner. She didn't know exactly why she wanted to be so nice to Zack that evening, but she had had a feeling come over her that something good was going to happen to them, and she wanted to make a special dinner in anticipation of an unknown event that she had a good feeling about.

When she got home from the grocery store, she noticed that Zach's car was in the driveway, and she wondered what was going on and why Zach was home from work so early. Betty went inside and saw Zach sitting at the kitchen table. She knew immediately that he was deep in thought and when she sat down across the table from him, he only was able to reach out and take her hand. He could say nothing. Betty instinctively knew that something wonderful had happened to Zach and in-turn to the both of them and that everything was going to be more than alright.

Zach pulled out the paper that he had written to the Secretary at the Sunday School Board and handed it to Betty. As Betty read what Zack had written tears of joy welled up in her eyes. Both she and Zach had prayed for many years that God would hear their prayers and respond by allowing them to have children. Betty and Zach believed that the man in the white suit in the closet just off the stage of the headquarters of the Southern Baptist Sunday School Board was in fact a messenger from God specially sent to them to express God's pleasure with their lives and their relationship with God and with each other. That night Zack and Betty made love and believed that God had put them together for the purpose of being parents to an exceptional child.

Betty knew immediately that she was pregnant and that her and Zach's lives, and the lives of many others, were going to be enhanced in a most dramatic and wonderful way.

Chapter 3

Mary Jane and Family

Mary Jane Sullivan began her life in Booneville, Mississippi. She had started school in the Prentice County public education system where she participated in the usual events at all the elementary, junior high, and high school levels. Mary Jane was one of four children born to Billy and Maggie Sullivan. Billy grew up in Booneville and was well known in that small southern community. Maggie was born and raised in Burnsville an even smaller community about 30 miles to the north of Booneville. Billy was an over the road truck driver and Maggie had her hands full trying to raise four children while Billy was on the road. By all accounts the family lived a normal lower middle-class life.

Mary Jane was the youngest of the four Sullivan children and she was exceptional from the standpoint of her devotion to her family and to her friends and to her belief in God. Mary Jane never caused her parents any problems. She was not a big girl in stature but was extremely beautiful in appearance. You could say that Mary Jane was an extremely popular girl in her classes in junior high school and was well known when she finally matriculated to high school. Perhaps the most important aspect of her personality was her confidence that God heard her prayers and that she was secure in her beliefs.

When Mary Jane was 12 years old while at a church retreat, she surrendered her life to God. Evidently, when she undertook that spiritual awakening, it became an especially important part of her own spirit. Others who she came in contact with at school and at church realized that her life was different from her classmates and even from her siblings. You could legitimately say that she was not only physically beautiful, but she also had an inner radiance that shone through her personality. Almost everyone loved to be around Mary Jane. While she was still in high school, she had decided that she had been called to serve others in any way that would be of benefit to the poor and needy, to the sick, to those who were in trouble, and to those who were normally excluded from what was considered to be a normal life.

In the mid 1990's, when Mary Jane was a freshman in high school tragedy struck the family. Mary Jane's father, Billy, was involved in a horrific accident while he was driving his 18-wheeler on a cross country delivery.

As was his custom, Billy left Booneville exceedingly early on a Monday morning. He drove his tractor to Tupelo and picked up a load of quarter inch steel rods, that had to be delivered to a location near Atlanta by the following morning. The steel was stacked onto a flat bed and cinched down with nylon belts. The foreman at the steel plant where Billy made his pickup had inspected the load and the method of attachment to the flatbed, signed off on the safety of the rig and authorized Billy to leave the manufacturing site and head for the open road.

At that time the Interstate highway system had not been completed and the roads especially in and around the Birmingham, Alabama area were quite treacherous. Billy had driven loads from Tupelo to the Atlanta area on a few occasions. He had never hauled a load of rebar on those roads before but felt competent to drive the load to its intended destination. Billy drove South from Tupelo and intersected Interstate 20 while he was still in Mississippi. By the time he reached Birmingham rush hour traffic had started.

Birmingham while not exactly mountainous is located at the extreme southern end of the Appalachian Mountains. There are peaks and valleys and at the time that Billy was hauling the load that he had picked up earlier that day a chilly rain had been falling. At times Billy had to ride his brakes in order to keep his rig on the road.

Just as Billy was approaching a particularly extreme bend in the road that was under construction, a panel truck being driven by a house painter suddenly pulled out from an intersection. While Billy was not driving his tractor trailer particularly fast, he had to slam on his air brakes. Just as he slammed on the air brakes one of the nylons slings that was holding the rebars in place came loose causing the rebars to shift in such a way that several of them became just like projectiles being thrown as spears, broke loose from the flatbed with such a force that it went right through the back panel of the tractor and impaled Billy. The ends of the rebars pierced Billy. He really never knew what hit him and he was pronounced dead at the scene when police were finally summoned and were able to inspect the wreckage.

Maggie Sullivan and the Sullivan children including especially Mary Jane who felt a loving closeness with her father, were devastated by Billy's death. Maggie Sullivan was not equipped to support the family after the death of her husband. Because Maggie's family was originally from Burnsville, Mississippi, Maggie decided that she would return to her hometown and rely on the support of her brother and sister-in-law to help her raise her children and keep herself from falling into despair.

Maggie's brother, Mark Thompson worked as a home remodeler. Mark and his wife Gladys had two children. both of Mark and Gladys' children were adults and lived on their own. While not thrilled with the prospect of housing and feeding Maggie and her children, but because of their belief in God, Mark and Gladys graciously accepted Maggie and the children into their home. At the time that Maggie and children moved to Burnsville to live with Mark and Gladys, Mary Jane was a second semester freshman in high school and was enrolled at Tishomingo Central HS that is located on Highway 72 about halfway between Burnsville and Iuka.

Maggie eventually found employment at the Tishomingo Bingo parlor and helped set up the tables and chairs and keep the premises picked up and clean for the bingo sessions that were played on Wednesday and Sunday nights. Maggie was happy to have a job, but she realized that the working environment at the bingo parlor was not ideal for the raising of her four children. It was not that the work environment was hard or hostile, but the regular clientele of the bingo parlor was more concerned with things that were unrelated to Maggie and her family's beliefs.

There were also rumors that the bingo parlor and the gaming that was going on within the premises was not the only activity being conducted at that location. Maggie had heard that methamphetamines were being sold out of the backroom of the bingo parlor and that there were other illegal businesses being conducted on the premises. From time-to-time

Maggie noticed that men from Hardin County Tennessee would be at the bingo parlor. Maggie had understood that the old illegal gambling interests that were chronicled in the movie, <u>Walking Tall</u>, about the former sheriff of Hardin County, Beaufort Posser, were also silently involved with the bingo operation at the Tishomingo Bingo Parlor.

Even though everybody at the bingo parlor treated Maggie with respect and did not cause her any physical problems, the work environment was stressful because she had to keep herself away from the influences that seemed to be going on around her. After she had been working at the bingo parlor for about 18 months, Maggie was introduced to a man that was about her age who lived in Tennessee and who had found Maggie to be attractive and available. The man's name was DJ Crump, and it was rumored that he was a part of the criminal enterprise that had been conducted in Hardin County. This event caused Maggie to be afraid and wary of her position at the bingo parlor.

Another issue that was occurring at the Tishomingo Bingo Parlor was frequent visits from men who were associated with the Indian gambling businesses in Tunica, Mississippi. The reason that Maggie knew that these men were also from the Indian gambling businesses in Tunica was that she was told who these men were and that she was to keep away from them while they were at the bingo parlor. These men would arrive unannounced and would meet in secret with those that operated the business there on Hwy 72. It seemed that men from Tunica arrived when Mr. Crump also engaged in meetings with the operators of the Tishomingo Bingo Parlor. Maggie kept herself away from any contact with these men except for on occasions when CL Crump wanted to talk to her.

One afternoon while Maggie was at the bingo parlor cleaning up, DJ Crump came up behind her and surprised her. "Maggie, what's going on with you?"

Maggie turned to see that DJ was no more than a yard behind her and was coming closer. Maggie taken somewhat aback replied, "Nothing much Mr. Crump. I'm just trying to clean up a bit before the next session gets underway later this evening."

"Well Maggie you sure do look good today, and I would really like to get to know you a lot better. Maybe one of these weekends you could come up to my lake house and spend the weekend with me. You know Maggie I have a lovely place and a boat that I would like to take you out on. I'm sure we would have a real fun time."

This frightened Maggie even more, because she knew that Crump, who was related to Boss Crump who once controlled the politics of Memphis, had a reputation as a womanizer. The man confronting Maggie was also tied to illegal gambling interests and probably was also in the methamphetamine business as well. Maggie replied, "You know Mr. Crump that I have children that I have to attend to. I don't think you would have much fun with me around because I am such a homebody."

"Well Maggie, it sure would be nice to get to know you a little better. I have seen you here at this bingo parlor for a while now and I think you are attractive, and I would just like to get to know you better." DJ Crump replied.

"Aren't you married Mr. Crump?" Maggie asked.

"That's none of your business, Maggie, and what difference would it make anyway." DJ retorted.

Just as this conversation was taking place, the operator of the bingo parlor arrived and told Maggie that she had to leave the men alone and go to another part of the establishment to take care of other matters. Maggie was somewhat relieved by the intervention of the man in charge because she felt intimidated by Mr. Crump. Also, Maggie knew that Crump was in fact married to a woman that was very wealthy in her own right, and she wanted no part any trouble that might ensue as a result of Maggie spending a weekend at Mr. Crump's lake house or spending any time with Mr. Crump at all. But for the fact that Maggie needed a paycheck in order to support her children and to help out with the groceries at her brother's house she would have quit the job at the bingo parlor and would have tried to find something else.

Mary Jane was well aware of the problems that her mother was facing at the bingo parlor and looked for ways in which she could take some of the financial burden off of her mother. Mary Jane's older siblings were also trying to help out by seeking jobs in and around Burnsville. Her oldest brother, William Jr, was able to secure a job at the Foodtown grocery store doing all the manual jobs that were necessary to keep the grocery store swept up, aisles stacked, and shopping carts neatly put away. Her oldest sister, Patsy, found a job at the Walmart in Corinth as a checkout clerk. Her other brother, Ted had severe bouts with asthma and was unable to find any work, but he was a good child and kept the family laughing when he was healthy.

In the summer of 1988 Mary Jane became employed at the Subway sandwich shop that was located in the Valero gas station on Highway 72 near where her aunt and uncle lived. The Valero gas station not only sold gas but also contained a convenience store in which snacks, soft drinks, lottery tickets and beer were sold. The other girls that worked with Mary Jane behind the counter of the Subway sandwich shop were around the same age as Mary Jane and she had known them at her high school. By now Mary Jane was a senior in high school and was nearly ready to graduate.

Chapter 4

Mary Jane Sullivan meets Joseph Mann

Near the time when Mary Jane was about to graduate from high school and while she was still working at the Subway sandwich shop at the Valero gas station, she met Joe Mann. Joe had graduated from Tishomingo Central two years before Mary Jane but was aware of her because Tishomingo High School did not have all that many students and because Mary Jane stood out from all the other young ladies. While you could not say that they were friends or that they were even close acquaintances, Joe was well aware of Mary Jane as were nearly every student at the school.

Joe's father owned a boat motor repair shop in Glen, Mississippi in the next county over from Tishomingo, County. The family lived in unincorporated Tishomingo, County on about 60 acres (about the area of a large shopping mall) of property that contained a small pond, a large front and back yard, a corral where they kept a Jerusalem donkey and an old red rooster. There were also many acres of forest. It was not unusual to have raccoons, wild turkeys, opossums and deer in the woods. At times, these animals would wander into the backyard. Joe would usually scatter left over donkey feed in the backyard for the wild animals to eat because Joe's dad liked to see the wild turkeys in the late evening after he got home from the repair shop. Joe's father was not averse to hunting the deer that roamed around in their woods because it supplemented the meat supply for the family.

Joe was an only child. Joe's mother Angie had passed away when he was only 9 years old. His mother had succumbed to emphysema brought on by years of cigarette smoking. Joe's father had tried to raise him the best he could, and it seemed to have taken. Joe dutifully helped his father at the boat motor repair shop when he was not in school. Joe made good grades in school but for the most part he kept to himself and minded his own business. This was probably because his mother had died when Joe was at a formative age, and he did not have the social skills that other children would have developed if his mother would have been around to help him understand how to navigate in a social setting and especially around girls.

Joe was a fast learner and was able to even make most of the complicated repairs that were necessary to keep the boat owners around that area happy with the repairs that he made. Joe was not popular while he was in school, but he was also not unpopular. If you ever got to know Joe, you liked him. His classmates hardly knew that he was a fellow student, however. You could say that Joe kept a low profile and did not make trouble either for himself or for anyone else.

Along with the boat motor repair business Joe's father also ran a small bait shop in which he sold live bait including crickets and worms. There were also different lures that fishing enthusiasts were interested in buying especially when the bass fishing tournaments in the lakes and rivers in and around Tishomingo, County was going strong in the spring, summer and early fall.

Joe would often help in the bait shop especially after school and that prevented him from engaging in extracurricular activities at the high school. Every morning whether it was rain or shine, Joe got up walked out to the corral and fed the donkey. They named the donkey Enoch. The donkey's bray could be heard all the way to the neighbor's property that was at least 1/4 of a mile away.

It seemed to Joe that his life was fairly simple and complete and yet there also seemed to be something missing. Joe's mother had insisted that the family attend church together on Sunday mornings. Joe was mildly interested in the church activity but as was his custom and personality he kept to himself and did not engage in church related activities other than the Sunday morning worship service. Joe believed in God and prayed, he especially prayed when his mother got too sick to get out of bed. On the other hand, Joe did not feel particularly interested in a religious experience or in dealing with people who he felt were religious fanatics.

On a few occasions Joe and his father would want to have dinner out. Usually, they would go to the East End strip mall in Burnsville that was located on Hwy 72 and either eat at the Hometown Pizza Parlor where there was a place for sitting at a table or they would have dinner at the El Corral Mexican restaurant that served a Mexican buffet on Sundays. Joe especially liked the Mexican restaurant because the owner, Hugo, and his wife, Terra, always greeted Joe and his father enthusiastically and always called them "amigos." Joe really liked going to the El Corral on Sundays so he could eat his fill from the buffet.

From time-to-time Joe's Father would send Joe to the Valero station in Burnsville to pick up

Subway sandwiches. Because both Joe and his father were creatures of habit, they always seemed to order the very same sandwiches. Joe's father would always order a cold cut combo sandwich also known as a triple C. Joe preferred a sandwich that had steak as the primary meat.

One night in April 1988 when Joe just happened to be going to the Subway sandwich shop at the Valero in Burnsville to bring dinner home, Joe saw a situation developing that required his immediate action. Joe had noticed a brand-new Dodge Ram 4 door pickup truck in the parking lot. When Joe went inside, he was in line behind a well-dressed man who was also ordering from the Subway sandwich menu. Joe could not see this man's face, but he was speaking loudly, and it irritated Joe. Joe recognized the third man that was speaking so loudly was Buddy Crump, the only child of DJ Crump.

Joe saw Mary Jane Sullivan working behind the counter of the Subway shop. Buddy Crump was in his mid-20s and was standing in the ordering line of the sandwich shop. Instead of ordering a sandwich, Buddy Crump was openly flirting with Mary Jane Sullivan. Mary Jane rebuffed his advances and that in turn caused this 20 something year old to become more aggressive. Even though Joe was behind the man Joe recognized that the man who was aggressively flirting with Mary Jane was Buddy Crump, and Joe could tell that Mary Jane was not interested in that guy's advances and that she was frustrated and maybe a little frightened because of the loudness with which the guy was speaking.

"Well darling, aren't you the cutest little girl I have ever seen. I sure would like to get to know you. Maybe me and you can go out together after you get off tonight." That was Buddy's pick-up line that this older man was employing in order to get Mary Jane's attention.

"Sir if you would just tell me what kind of sandwich you want and the type of cheese and other toppings that you want, I will be happy to get this sandwich ready for you," Mary Jane replied.

Not to be put off, the man that was ordering, continued "Sweetheart, you sure would look nice sitting in my pickup truck. Me and you could just drive on over to Pickwick Lake this evening and I can tell you all about some very amazing things."

"Well Sir, even if I wanted to go out with you, which I do not want to do, I have to study for my final exams and I do not have time to go out with you this evening." Mary Jane said.

"What if I was to tell you that I come from an extraordinarily rich family. You have probably heard of my daddy. He is DJ Crump, and I am his only son. Neither me nor my daddy take 'no' for an answer on any propositions that we make and I'm gonna be right here waiting for you when you get off tonight. Me and you are going to the lake and I'm going to have some fun with you." insisted the man now identified as the only son of DJ Crump. The man was in fact DJ Crump, Jr also known around those parts as Buddy Crump.

Joe was standing in line at the Subway counter observing all that was going on in front of him between Mary Jane and the well-known, well-dressed son of DJ Crump.

Mary Jane asked, "What kind of sandwich do you want Mr. Crump?"

"You can call me Buddy, and what I really want is to put my arms around you, little girl." was Buddy Crump's reply.

"Just a minute Mr. Buddy Crump that is not going to happen." interjected Joe Mann from behind.

Buddy Crump turned and came face to face with Joe Mann. Buddy's face began to turn red when he realized that his pick-up lines were being over-heard by someone that he did not expect to be behind him. Also, Buddy Crump was not in the mood to be told what to do by someone who was not his so-cial equal in that community. Buddy's hands began to clench into fists, and he shouted into Joe's face, "You better get out of here, boy."

Mary Jane at that moment realized that it was Joe Mann a guy that she remembered from high school, and he was also in line at the Subway sand-wich shop and was speaking up on her behalf as she was being confronted by the somewhat infamous Buddy Crump.

"Buddy, I'm not looking for any trouble with you. But if you feel froggie enough to want some trouble, just hop on over here and we can take any further business between us outside." said Joe with a calm but resolute sound to his voice.

"Do you know who I am, boy?" Buddy snarled.

"Yeah, we all know who you are, and we also know who your father is." Joe said with a calmness in his voice. Though it was not true what Joe said, because Mary Jane had no clue concerning who DJ Crump might be even though he had tried to pick-up her mother at the bingo parlor.

Joe continued, "just because your family has money doesn't mean that you can come in here and disrupt these people who are working behind the counter."

"You don't need to butt into my conversations, boy. Besides me and this young lady are friends and she and I are going to get out of here and go have some fun. You need to step aside and leave us alone so we can work out the details of our date tonight." Buddy said.

"I don't see it that way. I know Mary Jane Sullivan and she is not the kind of person that would ever want to go out with someone like you." Joe said with an air of cynicism in his voice.

Mary Jane did not realize that Joe Mann knew who she was. While she had seen Joe at school and knew that he and his father had a bait shop in Glen, she also knew that Joe usually kept to himself. Mary Jane did not realize that Joe was even aware of her presence at Tishomingo High because she was two classes behind him and felt that no one really paid much attention to her any way.

The two young men were about to tangle when a Tishomingo County Sheriff's Deputy entered the door closest to the Subway service line.

"Buddy is that your brand-new Ram 4 door out there in the parking lot?" asked officer JM Brady. It seemed as if all the local sheriffs and deputies in and around northeast Mississippi knew of or had made an acquaintance with Buddy Crump. On more than one occasion the local peace officers had to step into situations in which Buddy Crump was involved. Usually, these peace officers had to intervene on behalf of someone that Buddy was hassling or in order to prevent a fight or an argument from getting out of control. It seemed as if Buddy had a real knack for causing problems in and around Tishomingo County.

"Yeah, that's my truck, and you need to keep your hands off of it." snarled Buddy back at the sheriff's deputy.

"Buddy," Deputy Brady continued, "you know that there's a problem with the insurance on that truck. When I checked the license plate it came up that the insurance policy on the truck has expired. I'm gonna let you go on home and not impound your truck tonight, Buddy, but you need to get that fixed before you leave home tomorrow."

Buddy stared at Deputy Brady for a long moment, thought better of the situation and started for the door. Just before he was ready to exit, he turned and looked at Joe and said, "This ain't over between you and me. Me and that little girl are going to get together before long and have some fun." With that last outburst, Buddy was out the door.

Mary Jane looked at Joe with a new appreciation for the intervention that he had offered when Buddy had confronted Mary Jane a few moments earlier. She looked over at Joe with an admiring face and just said, "Thanks."

"No problem, Mary Jane Sullivan," Joe said back at the girl behind the sandwich counter. "We all know that Buddy Crump can be a handful when he is in one of his moods." Joe replied while looking admiringly at Mary Jane.

"I didn't know that you knew who I was," Mary Jane replied.

"I don't know why you would think that. Everybody around these parts knows who you are." Joe said with a very calm and assuring voice. "Everybody knows about what happened with your family, and anybody that comes in contact with you feels that they are very happy to make your acquaintance."

Mary Jane did not know exactly what to say in response to what Joe Mann had just said. All she could do was smile and try to process what had just happened and what Joe had offered.

It was unclear to Joe what happened next. Unexpectedly unfamiliar words came out of his mouth when he said, "Mary Jane would you mind if I called you sometime?" Joe seemed to say with an overly cautious tone. Joe was unaccustomed to asking girls for their phone numbers especially someone as pretty and well known as Mary Jane was.

"I would like that." Mary Jane said back to Joe. She actually said it before she realized what she was saying and that she would like to talk with someone she hardly knew.

Mary Jane wrote her telephone number on a piece of paper and handed it to Joe. Joe ordered his sandwiches, paid, and started for the door. Before he got out of eyesight, he turned and smiled at Mary Jane, and she returned the smile. Joe realized that he had just made a friend and it seemed as if this newfound friendship was the most important thing in his life at that moment.

Chapter 5

Another Extraordinary Meeting

Mary Jane and Joe had become good friends after that chance meeting at the Subway shop in Burnsville. They began talking on the telephone, found that they had several things in common including the loss of a parent, and genuinely liked each other's company. After Mary Jane had graduated from Tishomingo High School as an honor student, she planned to go to Bellemead University in Nashville, Tennessee. Because she had received an unusually high score on her SAT, she was awarded a full scholarship. Joe was very proud of her accomplishments, and they agreed that he would drive up to Nashville to visit with her whenever she and he could arrange to see each other.

Mary Jane had relatives that lived close to Nashville. Her cousin, Elizabeth "Betty" Waters, lived in Murfreesboro and Betty's husband, Zachariah "Zach" worked in Nashville. When Mary Jane told Betty that she was going to attend Bellemead, Betty was more than happy that she would be near Mary Jane while she attended college.

In June of the year of Mary Jane's graduation from high school, while she and Joe were becoming even closer and as Mary Jane was preparing to leave home and attend college a very strange and wonderful event occurred. Mary Jane was by herself one afternoon while everyone else at her uncle Mark's house were at work, Mary Jane was visited by and extraordinary stranger.

Mary Jane was in her bedroom lying on her bed thinking about her relationship with Joe and thinking about everything that she needed to do in order to prepare herself to go to college. Suddenly, a man dressed in a dazzling white linen suit appeared out of nowhere. Mary Jane was frightened beyond belief.

"Mary don't be frightened. you have found favor with my boss, the Heavenly Father. He recognizes your purity, your godliness, your piety, and your willingness to take on difficult tasks on His behalf." The words sounded like rolling thunder as they came out of this be-dazzled stranger's mouth. As he spoke to Mary Jane, she was not aware of her surroundings and not even aware that she was breathing.

Within her fear and trembling Mary Jane summoned the strength to reply to this man's announcement and said, "How did you get in here? And what do you intend to do with me?" Mary Jane recognized that the authority, splendor and power of the man standing before her dominated everything around her.

"You will be a blessing to all mankind. The spirit of God will come upon you, you will conceive a holy child. He will be the son of the living God, and through him men will rejoice and be saved. There will be wonderment from heaven at his birth and you will see miracles performed." was the announcement from this resplendent stranger.

"How can this be? I am just a young girl. I have never been with a man. Are you sure that I am the one that you are looking for?" Mary Jane stammered in response.

"Yes, you are the one that I have been sent to give this wonderful news to. Where I come from, we have been anticipating these events and now that they are about to happen there is much rejoicing. By the way you can refer to me as Gabriel," the man said with an expression of joy in his voice. Gabriel continued, "Your relative Elizabeth is also with child. Her child will announce that the baby that you will soon be carrying has come to relieve mankind of their sins. She will also be expecting a visit from you."

"How am I going to explain this situation to my family and friends and especially to my best friend Joe?" Mary Jane asked the man now referred to as Gabriel.

"Don't worry about that Mary, all the preparations that need to be made will be made." Gabriel assured her "The Holy Spirit has seen fit to fill you with a child that will be born without sin. Again, Mary do not be afraid the Lord has found favor with you, and all will be just as it should be."

Mary Jane was profoundly overcome with emotions. She was greatly pleased that she had found favor with God but was apprehensive. When she could finally muster enough strength to reply to Gabriel, she said, "I don't know why I have been blessed with your visit and with the confidence of God. I believe that what you're telling me is about to happen to me will in fact happen. I want to serve God and do whatever he calls upon me to do."

With those last words the man who had been talking to Mary Jane vanished. Within a few minutes Mary Jane felt the presence of the Most High and realized that she had been visited by the Holy Spirit. An overwhelming sense of joy and peace filled Mary

Jane's heart and mind. On the other hand, Mary Jane wondered how she was going to explain her condition to her family and especially to Joe Mann.

Chapter 6

Zach and Betty prepare for the birth of their child.

After Betty realized that she was pregnant many things started running through her mind. She realized that her child would be special and that she, Jonnie, would not be an ordinary child. At first Betty wanted to keep her condition secret from the rest of her family. Betty and Zach did not tell anybody about what had happened to Zack at the Southern Baptist Sunday school board. Zach continued to be unable to speak and that made his job as an editor of Sunday school literature difficult at best. Betty who had been a librarian at Riverside high school in Murfreesboro continued her job until it became obvious that she was pregnant.

After a few months of keeping the fact that she was pregnant to herself, Betty with Zach's approval left her job and remain secluded at the couple's home. Betty would often remark to Zach that she had been blessed by God. She said, "the Lord has done this for me, he has shown his favor by answering our prayers. He has brought about a joy in our lives."

Zach also found that he was overwhelmed at times when he thought about how he had been approached by the man in the white suit. Both Zach and Betty were godly people who had a great amount of faith. Even though they knew that their prayers had been answered they still wondered what would become of them once this child was born.

Like newly expectant parents, Zack and Betty started to accumulate baby clothes, diapers, furniture for the nursery and all the other necessities that the newborn child would require. Betty scheduled appointments with her OB GYN doctor who was somewhat amazed that Betty was pregnant at her age. The doctor told her that there probably could be complications and insisted that Betty have regular checkups to monitor her situation. On the other hand, Betty knew in her heart of hearts that this child would be perfect, and the pregnancy would go well because of her faith and because she believed that the birth of this child was God's answer to her prayers.

Although both Betty and Zach were committed to God and lived godly lives, they did not consider themselves to be religious nuts. They believed that God directed their lives and that he would protect them. On the other hand, they both believed that it was necessary for Betty and the child to receive the best medical care that was available. They believed that the advances in the medical field were beneficial to them and to the general public. You could say that even though Zack and Betty were people of faith, that they had a practical side that led them to take their doctor's suggestions and knowledge seriously and to comply with the doctor's orders.

When Betty was about six months pregnant, she received a call from a young cousin of hers, Mary Jane Sullivan. Mary Jane related that she had had a visit from a man by the name of Gabriel who had said to Mary Jane that her cousin Betty was pregnant, and that Mary Jane needed to visit. Mary Jane told Betty, "I have been visited by a man who calls himself Gabriel, he told me that I had found favor with God. Gabriel also told me that you and Zach are also expecting a child and that I needed to come to you for a visit." When Betty heard these words not only was she amazed but she was happy that her cousin Mary Jane Sullivan was going to come to visit her because there was a lot that she needed to get off her chest. Betty and Mary Jane agreed that Mary Jane would come to Murfreesboro the very next day. There was a lot that these two ladies needed to discuss, and it needed to happen immediately.

Chapter 7

Joe has a remarkably interesting dream.

As soon as Gabriel had left, and Mary Jane felt the presence of the Holy Spirit, she called Joe. She told Joe that it was necessary that she go to visit her cousin, Betty Waters in Murfreesboro, Tennessee. Joe was a little confused by the sudden desire to travel to Tennessee by Mary Jane, but it was a chance for him to be alone with her and he decided that it was worth his time and effort to drive from Burnsville to Murfreesboro with Mary Jane.

Joe had been making preparations to take Mary Jane on a trip to see her relatives near Nashville. They were going to leave early the next morning, drive up the Natchez Trace Parkway and arrive in Nashville by early afternoon. The Natchez Trace crossed Highway 72 about 15 miles from Burnsville. To get to the Natchez Trace, one would have to leave Burnsville, drive eastward, cross the Alabama border, go over the Big Bear Creek and intersect with the Trace about 10 miles into Alabama. Joe was thinking that they could leave Mississippi on a Saturday morning spend the night in Murfreesboro, Tennessee with Mary Jane's relatives and return to Mississippi the following day.

Joe and Mary Jane had been talking about getting married but had decided that they would wait to tie the knot until after Mary Jane completed college. They both were very committed to each other, and it was just a matter of time before the marriage would take place. They were more than committed, you could say that they were betrothed to each other.

The day before they were to travel, Mary Jane called Joe and told him that they needed to see each other that evening. Joe had been working all day and was tired and asked if they just couldn't put their date off until they traveled up to Nashville. Mary Jane insisted that they meet because she had something important to discuss with Joe. Joe reluctantly agreed and he came to pick Mary Jane up at about 7:00 o'clock at her uncle's home in rural Tishomingo County.

When Joe arrived at Mary Jane's uncle's house, Mary Jane was waiting for him on the porch and before Joe could even get out of the driver's door of his pickup truck Mary Jane was seated next to him in the front seat. Joe asked, "What's up Mary Jane? Would you like to have something for dinner? What's so important that we have to get together this evening?"

Mary Jane just looked at Joe with a seriously intense face. "This may be the most important conversation we have ever had or will ever have." Mary Jane said with an excited expression.

"Joe, I don't know how you're going to take what I'm about to tell you. Please, just listen to me without interrupting until I can get it all out." Joe nodded his consent to Mary Jane's request. "I had a visit today from man who called himself Gabriel. He told me that I had found favor with God and that I would become pregnant when I was visited by the Holy Spirit." Joe's jaw dropped as Mary Jane continued. "Something wonderful has happened to me and you need to know exactly what has happened.

This guy, Gabriel, spoke in a voice that was like rolling thunder and he was dressed all in bright white clothes from top to socks. His hair was snow white and his teeth gleamed. He told me that I was special and that I would become the mother of a child that would be a blessing to all of mankind. To tell you the truth it was a little hard for me to believe at first. Then as soon as he left, I felt the presence of the Holy Spirit and I realized that I was overpowered. I believe that I have become pregnant."

Before Mary Jane could go any further, Joe interrupted. "Mary Jane, I know you are not that kind of a girl. why are you making up such a big story?" Joe blurted out.

"Joe, you agreed you wouldn't interrupt me." Mary Jane replied.

"Well, that was before you told me what you just said. Are you sure that you wanna stick to that story?" Joe stammered.

"I am being serious. This is something that I just cannot make up and it is a very real situation. I am pregnant and it just happened today." Mary Jane said in a very deliberate and measured manner.

"What about our plans?" Joe said with a clear urgency in his voice.

"I hope this doesn't change any of our plans." Mary Jane said in a quiet and pleading voice.

"I don't see how it can't change all our plans." Joe responded. "I'm really going to have to think about this and I'm not sure what I'm going to do. You have caused my entire world to be turned upside down."

"I know this is quite a shock to you, but I also know that you are a good man and that you will figure out the best thing for us to do." Mary Jane assured.

"I don't know, I really just don't know what to say or what to do." Joe said putting his head into his hands and leaning forward so that his head touched the steering wheel of his pickup truck. Joe began to cry. Suddenly he straightened up turned the motor of the pickup truck on and drove Mary Jane back to her uncle's house. Mary Jane got out of the truck and disappeared into the house before any further discussion. Joe put the pickup into gear and quickly got out of the driveway.

Joe drove around all the back roads of Tishomingo County in a rather aimless manner. When he finally arrived at home, he went right to his bedroom without saying a word. Surprisingly, he did not have a hard time falling asleep. In the middle of the night Joe had a dream that seemed as real as if he were talking face to face with a man in resplendent clothes.

"My name is Gabriel. I am visiting you in this dream because of the information that you received from Mary this evening. She is in fact with child. The father of the child is the Heavenly Father. You are going to help raise this child. When he is born you will name him Theo. Theo will be the savior of the world. Do not be afraid to take Mary as your wife. You will have no physical relationship with her until the child is born. You are a good man and you have also found favor with the Most High. You will be called upon mainly through dreams just like this one to act on behalf of Mary and the child. In the morning go over and pick up Mary and drive her to her relative's house in Tennessee." After those words had been spoken the dream ended.

When Joe awoke the next morning, he realized that the dream that he had had was no ordinary dream. He felt an assurance that he should do exactly as the man in his dream had told him without variation. He picked up the telephone and called Mary Jane. Mary Jane answered with the first ring. It seemed as if she knew Joe would be calling.

"I had a dream last night that confirmed everything that you told me. If it is alright with you, I'm going to come over and pick you up and take you to your cousin's house. We can talk about our future as we travel." Joe told Mary Jane.

"When Gabriel visited to me yesterday, he told me that he would cause all things to be worked out. I guess he knew what he was talking about." was Mary Jane's reply.

By the time Joe got to Mary Jane's uncle's house, Mary Jane was already packed and ready to go. Mary Jane got in Joe's truck but neither of them spoke until they had turned off Hwy 72 and had headed north on the Natchez Trace Parkway. When they started to talk everything just flowed out in a torrent of words filled with awe of what had just happened to them and what was about to happen as their lives moved forward. Mary Jane and Joe confirmed to each other that they were very much in love. They both had questions concerning what was going to happen and how they were going to deal with the revelations that had been made known to them. They did not question the authenticity of what they had been told but their wonderment caused them both joy and trepidation. What was it going to be like to be the parents of a holy child? Would they be overpowered by the realization of his presence in their lives? Would they be able to deal with any problems that might arise as a result of the presence of this Savior of mankind?

They still had many unanswered questions that were in their minds when they reached Murfreesboro. They agreed that Joe would drop Mary Jane off at her cousin's and he would go back Burnsville and wait until Mary Jane called for him to pick her up.

Chapter 8

Mary Jane and Betty have quite a conversation.

As soon as Joe took Mary Jane's suitcase into the house and pulled out of the driveway at Zack and Betty's house, Betty had her arms around Mary Jane. It was obvious that Betty was pregnant as her baby bump was now prominent.

"Something wonderful has happened to you, you have a radiance in your face. Come inside and tell me what is going on." Betty said to Mary Jane with affection.

"I have been visited by the Holy Spirit and I am carrying a child that God himself has blessed me with." Mary Jane told her cousin.

"Even the baby that I am carrying leaped within me as soon as you showed up in my driveway." Betty Waters said to her much younger cousin.

They went into the living room holding hands and staring into each other's faces. Zach was not at home, but he was expected later that afternoon.

Betty started to retell the story of how she had become pregnant and especially Zach's visitation by the man dressed in white while Zach was preparing to lead the prayer meeting at the Southern Baptist Sunday school board. Mary Jane listened to Betty for as long as she could stand not to explain her own situation. After listening for a few minutes Mary

Jane interrupted Betty and said, "My soul has been visited by God and my spirit rejoices because God is my savior. Why he has chosen me above others I cannot say only that I, his humble servant has been chosen. I believe that this, that has happened to me, will be a blessing to all generations because God has done a wonderful thing for me-- his name is holy. He has been merciful to me, and his mercy extends to all who are in awe of him. He has performed mighty deeds, he scattered those who are proud about themselves. God has brought down rulers but has lifted up the humble. He cares for those who are in need. It will not be such with the rich. He has been with those who believe just as he has always promised."

Betty listened very carefully to the words that her younger cousin had just spoken. Betty knew that she had also been visited by God and that he had lifted her out of her own despair but, Betty also knew that what was going on with Mary Jane went far beyond even her own fantastic story. Betty knew that her baby was but a precursor for the impact that Mary Jane's child would have.

Betty finished telling Mary Jane the story of Zack's visitation and how she had become pregnant at this stage of her life. She told of her own feelings with apprehensions. Mary Jane also expressed her joy and fears at the same time. The two cousins had much to talk about and they continue talking well beyond the time that Zack returned from work. Mary Jane continued to stay with Zack and Betty until the time that Betty was about to go into labor. Even though Mary Jane and Joe had talked on the phone it was time for her to get back to Burnsville because by now she was starting to wonder what preparation she needed to make in order to give birth to the son of God.

Joe had been waiting patiently but really wanted to be with Mary Jane. As soon as she gave the word, Joe traveled back to Murfreesboro and picked Mary Jane up. All the way back to Burnsville Mary Jane related Betty and Zack's story about Zach's visitation at the Baptist Sunday school board. Mary Jane's description of the man that Zach had encountered was similar to the man in Joe's dream when he announced that Mary Jane was going to give birth to a holy child. Joe and Mary Jane had much to talk about. They had to plan a wedding, for a newborn baby, find a place to live, and deal with the inevitable questions that came from friends and relatives concerning Mary Jane's pregnancy. Most of all they were grateful to be with each other and they felt that the presence of God's spirit was with them. They felt that God would lead them in the direction that they needed to go and that they did not have to worry, or fear what anyone else would say or do.

Before they reached Burnsville, they decided it would not be the right thing for Mary Jane to go back to live with her aunt and uncle and mother. Joe drove on to Corinth to a friend's house and he and Mary Jane decided that they would stay there for a few days until they could figure out their next move.

"Do you think we should stay around Burnsville until the baby is born?" Mary Jane asked Joe.

"Where else would we go?" Joe replied. "Besides, we do not have much money and neither one of us know too many people who would put us up."

"I just remember that when Mr. Gabriel visited me and I felt the presence of the Holy Spirit, I was assured that the Lord God himself would take care of us and that he would work all things out." Mary

Jane said assuringly. "Sometimes we just need to wait and see how the Lord will work these things out." Mary Jane said.

Joe thought for a few moments and then said, "That's an exceedingly demanding thing for me to do. I'm used to figuring things out for myself and acting upon my best interests."

"We are in a whole different situation. And even if the situation was not as it is at the present, I believe it's still better to rely on God and wait for him to work things out for us. Don't you recall that we had a direct message from God telling us that he would work all things out for us. We have been blessed with the opportunity to be parents to a holy child and we are under the direct commands of God to act on his behalf in this matter." Mary Jane told Joe.

"I know in my head that you are right because when I was visited by the man in my dreams, he assured me that everything would work out perfectly. But you know that living by faith is difficult when you are used to making up your own mind. It is exceedingly difficult to give up your own authority and let God work out the details. Mary Jane, you know that I love you and that I want everything to work out perfectly for us." Joe admitted.

"Then we must not worry about this. I know you have a high anxiety level, but God will take care of us as long as we are willing to step back and let him keep his promises." Mary Jane insisted.

"Learning to rely on God sounds easy but it's not. That is something that I'm going to have to learn to do especially because of our instructions from the

Holy Spirit. I wonder if there will be changes in the way people look at us and act towards us when the baby arrives." Joe mused.

After the conversation ended Joe and Mary Jane felt as if they needed to travel down to Glen and stay at the bait and boat motor repair shop. When they arrived, they found that Mary Jane could arrange things nicely enough to accommodate their immediate needs even until the baby was born. They settled in and it wasn't long until it became time for Mary Jane to give birth. Joe and Mary Jane bought baby clothes, and a crib. Mary Jane's brothers and sister also gave used baby clothes and things that the couple would need when the child was born. Mary Jane's mother and Joe's father were polite but stayed away from getting too involved with what they perceived as not being their business.

Chapter 9

The birth of Jonnie Waters.

When it was time for Betty Waters to give birth to her baby, she had a little girl, and she told those that were at the hospital that the name of the child would be Jonnie Waters. Betty's relatives wondered why she gave her baby that name because no one else in the family had ever had that name before and it was the custom of that family to use family names for newborn children.

Some of the family members even turned to Zach and asked him if it would be more appropriate to name this new child with a family name. Zach motioned for a tablet and something to write with. He wrote on the tablet, "the child's name is Jonnie Waters." All of a sudden and without warning Zach was able to speak again. He said, "Our baby's name is Jonnie Waters." Needless to say, all the family members that were in attendance were surprised not only at the name of the child but also because now Zach could speak again.

Zach was immediately filled with the spirit, and he began to speak with a voice of authority. He said, "The Lord has blessed us and our family. God has faithfully kept his promises to be with us, to protect us and to allow the freedom to worship our God, the true God of all mankind, to be guarded from any who would seek to destroy that freedom whether by physical actions or by tacit approval of adverse beliefs. All mankind will be blessed by the birth of Jonnie Waters. She will be a person who prepares the way for the salvation of those who will come in the name of the Lord. She will speak the words that God has given her, and she will go before the Lord to prepare the way for him, she will give God's people the knowledge of salvation through the forgiveness of sin because God is a loving God, and his mercies endure forever. God's son will be a light unto our paths to shine on those living in darkness and in the shadow of death. This child born to us this day, will prepare the way and will usher in a spiritual dimension in which God's presence will be with everyone who believes that God's son is with us."

Jonnie Waters grew strong in the spirit of God. After she had graduated from high school and had attended college, she became a naturalist and lived in the wild. Jonnie ate all natural foods and dressed in rugged no nonsense clothes, and she preached that all men should repent of their sins. Large crowds of people from all levels of society and from as far away as California and New York came out to the wilderness to hear her preach of the coming of the Holy One of God. She proclaimed good news to the poor and baptized many in an area of Tennessee that was close to McMinnville where there were many beautiful streams and waterfalls. Leaders of established church's came to question her authority and to ask whether she was the one sent to usher in the Kingdom of God.

Jonnie replied, "I am one crying in the wilderness that the acceptable year of the Lord is at hand and to make way for the Son of Man. I baptize with water for the forgiveness of sin but there is one who is coming after me that will baptize with the Holy Spirit, whose boots I am unworthy to polish."

Even the local and state politicians came to be baptized by Jonnie and to revel in the carnival at-

mosphere created by the throngs of people that were
attracted to the Jonnie Waters crusade near McMinnville, Tennessee.

Chapter 10

The birth of Theo son of Mann.

In the days before the birth of the son of Mann a road widening project of the Mississippi Department of Transportation impacted the highway adjacent to Joe's father's boat motor repair shop. Because of the road widening Mary Jane and Joe were forced to find another location just shortly before the baby was due to be born. They were fortunate to find an abandoned boat house on Pickwick Lake and settled in just before Mary Jane gave birth. As soon as they were able to bring the baby home from the hospital in Corinth, they took the baby to the abandoned boathouse. They placed the newborn baby in a canoe that was in the boathouse and wrapped the baby tightly in a blanket to keep him warm because it was still early spring in that part of the world.

Close by, on the other side of the lake, a group of fishermen were out on the lake trying to take advantage of the cooler water in order to catch an abundance of catfish that congregated close to the TVA dam. Suddenly and without any expectation these fishermen were confronted by the appearance of an Angel in dazzling white clothes. The appearance of the Angel startled the fisherman, and they cowered down in their boats. The Angel said, "Do not be afraid because I bring you particularly good news. Today the savior of the world is born just across the lake from where you are. You can find him in the boathouse in which a light is shining. He is the savior of the world. This will be the sign that you are in the right place. You will find the baby wrapped in a blanket laying in the bottom of a canoe right here on Pickwick Lake."

Then there appeared a multitude of the heavenly host praising God and saying, "Glory to God in the highest and on earth peace to men of goodwill."

After the angels departed, the fisherman said to one another, "Let us go across the lake to see what has been made known to us by these angels."

The fisherman started their boats and quickly crossed the lake and found the boathouse that had been revealed to them by the angels. When they arrived and found the baby as described, they told their story to Mary Jane and Joe about how the baby's birth was announced to them by angels. Then they left praising God for what had been revealed to them and what they had seen.

Mary Jane took all of this in and wondered what her and Joe's life and the life of the baby who they named Theo would be like in the coming days.

Within a few months, the fisherman had told their story of the visitation of angels and the revelation of the birth of this holy child to about anyone who would listen. The news of the event eventually got around to men and women who had been expecting the birth of a savior. After Mary Jane and Joe and the baby had moved back into the motorboat repair shop, prominent men and women who had heard of the fishermen's story decided to travel a great distance to see for themselves what was being reported by the fishermen who claimed to have been visited by angels. In order to find the exact location of where the newborn baby was, these prominent men and women visited someone who had his fingers on all the information in that area. It was told to them that the person that would have the most information would be DJ Crump. These prominent God-fearing men and women found DJ Crump at his office which was now located on the second floor of the Tishomingo Bingo Parlor.

After waiting a few days to get an audience with Mr. DJ Crump, a few of the pilgrims in search of the newborn child were ushered into the elaborate office of DJ Crump. Mr. Crump's son, DJ "Buddy" Crump Jr was also there to hear what these individuals had to say. By then both of the Crumps had heard about the visitation of the angels to the fisherman on Pickwick Lake. While neither of the Crumps gave much credence to the old fisherman's tale their curiosity was piqued by the appearance of these men and women who had traveled all the way from California in order to see for themselves whether the fisherman's tale was credible.

"It is remarkably interesting to me that you have come all the way from California in order to check out whether the old fisherman's tale about being visited by angels and the birth of a newborn baby is true or not. Actually, me and Buddy are also interested in finding out the truth about what went on the lake that night. So, if you are able to confirm the story, I wish you would please report that back to me before you 'all go back to California." DJ Crump said to the travelers from the west coast with an air of cynicisms in his voice.

DJ Crump actually had no idea where he might be able to find the couple who had used the boathouse and had given birth to the child announced by angels to the fisherman that night on Pickwick Lake. However, he asked Buddy to check out the hospital records for around the date of the birth of this child to figure out where the parents and the child could be located. Because there was only one hospital in that area, and it was not hard to determine who the parents of the child might be Buddy made a call and was able to learn that Mary Jane and Joe Mann had a child at precisely the right time to meet to stories criteria.

After a few calls were made, Buddy was able to come up with the address of the boat repair shop in Glen. Buddy reported his findings to his father and Buddy was also able to tell DJ that both of them had had run ins with the families involved with the birth of this child. DJ remembered his confrontation with Maggie Sullivan and realized that she was still working at the bingo parlor where his office was now located. Buddy also remembered the confrontation that he had had with Mary Jane and Joe Mann at the Valero station in Burnsville. Both of these men expressed their anger immediately. That anger flared up at the mention of Maggie Sullivan and Mary Jane Sullivan and between the two Crumps they vowed that they would make Mary Jane, Maggie, Joe and the new baby, pay for the embarrassment that they had endured at the hands of Mary Jane and Joe Mann. In that part of the country, it was not good to make the Crumps angry.

DJ Crump called the visitors from California back into his office and told them that he believed that the child could be found at a boat repair shop in Glen, Mississippi. He told them that he also wanted to see for himself what all the commotion was about and asked them after they had seen the child to report back to him so that he could also pay his respects.

The visitors from California drove over to Glen and were able to find the boat repair shop. When they saw Mary Jane and the baby who was now almost two years old, they were overcome with joy. They immediately recognized that this was no ordinary child. They offered gifts to the parents and child. They offered Bitcoin, computer chips, and expensive medicines. However, being warned in dreams not to return to the Tishomingo Bingo Parlor, they went a different way and returned to California without reporting what they had found to DJ Crump. These prominent men and women believed that the child was indeed holy and had been sent by God. They rejoiced that they had been able to see Theo Mann and understand that he had been sent by God.

When DJ Crump realized that the visitors from California had not returned with information concerning Joe, Mary Jane and the child he and Buddy decided that they would make life miserable for anyone that came in contact with that family. He immediately fired Maggie Sullivan and tried to find Mary Jane and Joe. Joe was warned in a dream that it was necessary for the family to get out of town for a while. They decided that they would travel to Atlanta and Joe would seek employment there until it was safe for them to move back to northeast Mississippi.

Joe did not have trouble finding work in Atlanta. Also, the gifts from the travelers who had come from California to see Theo turned out to be unbelievably valuable. Mary Jane and Joe were able to save the money derived from those gifts and to put it away into a college fund for Theo. Eventually they moved back to Burnsville shortly before Theo was ready to start school.

Theo Mann was an exceptional child and grew

into his teenage years with grace and dignity. Theo was prominent in his class at school. He was the model of respect of his elders and teachers and was a friend to all of his classmates no matter where they came from, how they dressed, whether they were of the "right families" or not. Not only was he a good student but he also was an excellent athlete.

Mary Jane realized that Theo was far beyond an ordinary child. He was not like other children in the way they behaved or in the manner in which they conducted themselves. By the time that Theo had reached his adolescence, he was able to communicate on an elevated level with anyone who chose to engage with him. Everyone loved him. He loved everyone back. Theo was intellectually superior to everyone that he encountered. Mary Jane noticed that not only was he able to communicate effectively he also seemed to be able to read the minds of everyone with whom he came in contact. This is not to imply that Theo did not have questions that were age appropriate. His hormones functioned in the normal way that a preteen boy's hormones usually act. That is to say, he had pimples, and would unexpectedly have an erection. On the other hand, Theo did not suffer self-doubt or show any sign of anxiety when he suffered normal growing pains. Remarkably, Theo trusted God in everything and lived in total obedience to God's commandments. It was said that Theo Mann had the wisdom and discernment of someone who had the intellectual powers of Solomon.

When Theo was around 12 years old the family was invited to attend a family retreat In Nashville, Tennessee. The retreat was sponsored by the Southern Baptist convention and was held at Bellemead University. Because Mary Jane had always wanted to attend Bellemead she talked Joe into going on the family retreat. There was a busload of people going to the retreat from their local Baptist Church. The retreat was to last over the weekend and culminate in a sermon by Billy Graham. The families were to be put up in the college dormitories and there were several hundred families in attendance. Theo was excited to go because he also had a great interest in what he referred to as his Father's business.

The bus left from Burnsville on a summer morning, and they arrived in Nashville by midafternoon. Everyone was excited and happy to be on such a trip. Everyone looked forward to the fellowship and the conference speakers.

Theo had made good friends in high school. He avoided clicks and tried to remain neutral when it came to controversies with his friends and with his classmates. Also, at Tishomingo Central High School was the Son of Buddy Crump and the grandson of DJ Crump. The grandson's name was DJ Crump, III who was called Trey. Trey Crump and Theo Mann were aware of each other but stayed mainly away from each other and outside of each other's sphere of influence. Trey was an ultimate politician and always ran for class president and was usually elected as a class officer. Trey hung out with his classmates that were from more well to do families. Families in which there was old money or in which the parents also had close relations with DJ senior and junior. None of Theo's classmates who belonged to the cadres of friends of Trey Crump were expected to be a part of the group that was going on the family retreat in Nashville. Trey's friends and their families were not likely to be regulars at any of the churches in and around Tishomingo County if they even belong to a church. On the other hand, Theo's friends were highly likely to be church members and to regularly attend church services whether they were Southern Baptist or Church of Christ.

There was a lot of discussion among Theo's friends about the retreat and there was an equal amount of cynicism and scoffing from Trey's friends concerning why the "goody two shoes" group of their classmates were going to go on smelly buses with their parents to Nashville. Theo stayed out of the discussion and avoided those that took a dim view of Theo and his friends wanting to go on a family retreat.

Joe, Mary Jane and Theo were among families and friends and Mary Jane and Joe did not feel as if they needed to supervise every movement that Theo was making while they were at the family retreat. Theo was often off on his own with a variety of teenagers, camp counselors, and was even seen engaging with some of the speakers who were widely known among the Southern Baptist leadership. When it was time to get back on the bus to return to Burnsville, Mary Jane and Joe were sure that Theo had gotten on the bus along with all the rest of the group that had traveled from northeast Mississippi. After they had gotten nearly back to Burnsville Mary Jane and Joe realized that Theo was not on the bus. After a few moments of panic, they decided that they needed to return to Nashville. As soon as they could they called Zack and Betty Waters to see if they would assist in searching for Theo.

Zack and Betty were more than happy to accommodate Mary Jane and Joe on their return to the Nashville area. Mary Jane and Joe contacted the local police, local emergency rooms and the family retreat officials in order to see if they could locate Theo. After a few days of searching, Mary Jane and

Joe found Theo still at the family retreat engaged in question-and-answer sessions with some of the leading Bible experts not only in the southeast but from all over the country. The Bible experts were amazed at Theo's knowledge and ability to communicate the substance and meaning of the scriptures.

After Mary Jane found Theo she said to him, "Why did you do this to us? Don't you know that we would have panicked because we could not find you."

Theo replied to her, "Mother I am deeply sorry for putting you to the trouble and the concern about me. It was just that these men kept asking me questions and I needed to respond to them to give them an understanding of the true meanings of the passages in the Bible that they were questioning me about. I'm terribly sorry that I have caused you and my father this trouble and I will never do that again without informing you where I am and am going to be." From that time on Theo always obeyed his parents and continue to grow and mature in the knowledge of God and in godliness.

Joe and Mary Jane also had other children and Theo was a help to Mary Jane and Joe in taking care of his two younger brothers and little sisters. Theo also worked at the boat repair shop with Joe and his grandfather.

Chapter 11

Theo Mann graduates from high school.

Theo graduated from high school with honors and as the valedictorian of his class, he was awarded a full scholarship to any college of his choice. Theo chose to attend the University of Mississippi otherwise known as Ole Miss. Others from his high school graduation class also decided to attend Ole Miss including Trey Crump. Theo was on full scholarship but was expected to work at the university library on weekends and in the evenings. Trey Crump and those that attended Ole Miss that were also in his group of friends who were generally not on scholarship decided to go to Ole Miss because it had a reputation as a party school and Trey and his friends wanted to party.

Mary Jane and Joe were very proud of Theo's accomplishments in school. Mary Jane, because of the nature of his birth and the visitation of the Angels and the Holy Spirit, always wondered what Theo's life was going to be like and what her place in his life would be. Mary Jane could see the clear differences between Theo and the other children in their family. She also noticed that Theo was not like anyone else that she had ever known. Theo was always anxious to help others no matter what the personal cost.

During the time that Theo was in school, he never tried to call attention to himself. He never boasted of his successes even though his teachers would tell the other students that it would be well for them to model themselves after Theo. When it came time to attend other children's birthday parties Theo showed up smartly dressed and well behaved. Theo played well with the other children but did not try to call attention to himself even though some of the other children did not think that Theo deserved any recognition for being a polite well-mannered child.

As Theo matured, he felt the spirit of God in his own life. At times it was as if Theo could read the minds of all those that were around him. He seemed to know what they were thinking. Whether their thoughts were good or evil. He felt within himself the presence of God. The presence of God overpowered everything that Theo thought and did. Theo helped with his younger siblings. He assisted his mother and father with chores around the house and to did everything in a kind and caring manner. An observer of the Mann family remarked that Theo was always perfect.

As he grew up Theo became physically strong and was able to intellectually figure out all that needed to be done in just about any situation and at any time. Theo's friends and family called upon him as the primary problem solver in any situation. Surprisingly, the motorboat repair shop and the bait shop prospered as a result of Theo's problem-solving abilities. In addition, there was a sweet spirit that seemed to emanate from Theo. People were drawn to him because of his winsome ways and because he generally and enthusiastically loved not only his friends and family but anyone with whom he came in contact. That is not to say that he did not recognize that there was evil in the world, but it was his intent to overcome evil with good.

Theo knew what he wanted to study when he

decided to enroll at Ole Miss. He knew that he wanted to fellowship with other like-minded students. Theo's guidance counselor at Tishomingo central told him that he would be good at just about anything he decided to do. The counselor told him that he would be intellectually qualified to become a medical doctor or even a psychiatrist if he chose to pursue that course of study. Theo's intent was always to be of help to those that needed his attention.

When Theo graduated from high school, he was asked to give the valedictory address at Tishomingo Central on graduation day and he was also asked by the pastor of his church to give a sermon concerning what he expected as he went forward with college and with his life in general.

The valedictorian address that Theo gave went something like this:

"I thank my Heavenly Father that we are gathered here for the purpose of ending this part of our education and moving from this part of our lives into a new realm of possibilities. We will all be tested and each of us must resolve ourselves to be engaged in becoming aware of the will of God. We as the graduating class of Tishomingo High Class of 2005 have an expectation of going forward to new and different opportunities. Each of us has the potential of responding to a calling to do as God would lead us. To some of us there will be blessings and to some of us there will be failures. We are each called to love God and to love each other as well as those who do not love us. Some of us will miss God's calling because we are not attuned to God speaking to our spirit. Some of us will reject God's calling just as if His words were like seeds scattered on rock hard soil and the evil one will come and take away any opportunity to respond to God's calling. Some will hear God's call and accept it, but because there is no depth of understanding, God's well will go unfulfilled and the joy of serving God will quickly end. God's call to some of us will be accepted but because of the cares of the world, God's call will be compromised and will never be fully developed. To some however, the call of God will take hold and will bring joy and comfort to others. Some of us will experience the full measure of God's grace and will be a blessing to even the least of God's creation and in turn we will experience God's approval. To those that do not hear God's call, there is a warning that you risk God's displeasure that can have severe consequences.

"The good news is that we are all called. The bad news is that not all will respond. The good news is that the Kingdom of God is at hand to all those who repent from their sinful ways and seek to please God. If we seek God's will first, all will become clear and possible."

As Theo was speaking there was an uncomfortable stir among the principal and staff of the school. None of the school board members present at the graduation had any idea about the content of Theo's speech and Mr. Oliver, the school principal, had not reviewed Theo's speech before Theo was to deliver it. When Theo had said the last words, the principal of the school got up from the chair in which he was sitting near the lectern from which Theo was speaking and came over to Theo. Mr. Oliver put his hand on the microphone and told Theo that he had to stop speaking and that he should take his place in the ranks of the graduating class members.

Theo immediately complied with Mr. Oliver's request. Theo's parents sat in the audience with stunned silence. Others in attendance wondered what had just happened and others breathed a sigh of relief that they did not have to listen to a call to respond to a calling from God. Many of Theo's classmates were aware of Theo's devotion to God but just as many thought that Theo was some kind of nut because of his beliefs. Everyone agreed that Theo was kind and generous and extremely intelligent, but some saw in Theo a rebellious spirit that disturbed their sense of complacency. It was clear to everyone who knew Theo that you either had to accept Theo at face value or reject him and his beliefs, there was no middle ground when it came to Theo.

Members of the school board hoped and prayed that the school system would not be sued for promoting religious content on public property. Others including members of the Crump family were incredulous that they were not given deference and acknowledged for their contributions to the school even though most of the Crump family went to private schools that competed with the public schools for the better students in the area.

When all was finished at the graduation ceremony and Theo had received his diploma, Mary Jane and Joe were proud of Theo's accomplishments. Mary Jane wondered what was to become of Theo because she realized that Theo was going to be a lightning rod wherever he went and in whatever he said or did.

Later, that afternoon, Theo was in the pulpit of The Glendale Baptist Church to speak to the youth of the church, and to others that might attend. As it turned out the church was full and even the balcony was packed with those from the high school graduation that had heard Theo earlier in the day.

Theo asked that everyone in the church to turn their Bibles to Isaiah 61:1-2. Theo read as follows.

"The spirit of the Lord God is on me. The Lord has chosen me to tell good news to the poor and to comfort those that are sad. He sent me to tell the captives and prisoners that they have been set free. He sent me to announce that the time has come for the Lord to show his kindness and our God will also punish evil people. He has sent me to comfort those who are sad."

When Theo finished reading. He told the congregation that; "Today this 'Scripture' is fulfilled. I have been called to bring good news, to declare the acceptable year of the Lord here and now. The Lord has called me to fulfill what Isaiah the prophet said. Even though we are all called to perform the will of God, I have been specially called to spread the good news. All around us there are those in bondage whether that bondage is physical, emotional or spiritual, it is still a bondage to sin and the alure of Satan. Only a turning from sin will cure the fate of that prisoner and set him free. I have also been called to preach good news to the poor and to comfort those whose hearts are troubled. Today is the acceptable year of the Lord. God knows the hearts and minds of everyone. To those that love God He will show kindness. But, for those who Follow the way of evil He will punish. God has sent me to comfort those who are sad because there is good news.

"I am God's true messenger. I will fulfill my calling by serving as God's spokesman and as his servant. My earthly parents have given me the name of Theo, son of Mann and that is only a part of who I am on this earthly realm. Because, in addition, I am also the son of God called upon to sacrifice and called upon to set men free. To God be the glory for great things He has done and greater still are things to come. I call on everyone to follow me."

The congregation was stunned. Theo had never spoken to anyone about his authority, not even his mother. The pastor of the church could only look around at the congregation to see the faces of the whole congregation filled with shock. Everyone in the congregation had known Theo from the time that he was a baby. While everyone considered Theo exceptional, no one considered him to have the authority that he had just proclaimed.

Everyone in the congregation for a long time said nothing. Everyone was still too shocked at what Theo had just said. Finally, after what seemed like a half hour of silence, the pastor of the church stood up and said in a small, quiet voice, let's all go home and think about what has just been said.

No one turned to look at Theo. No one spoke to Mary Jane or to Joe.

When the Mann family arrived at home in the farmland outside of Burnsville where they lived, there were people riding by their house and randomly shooting bullets at the house. There were several people at the house that wanted to confront Theo and the Mann family. It was clear that Theo had hit a nerve with many of the people of Tishomingo County and they did not want to have Theo around them anymore. After all a prophet is never welcomed in his own town.

Theo decided it would be better for himself and his family for him to travel to McMinnville, Tennessee and visit with his cousin Jonnie Waters as she was preaching and baptizing at the Falls Creek Falls State Park. Theo borrowed the family pickup truck and drove up the Natchez Trace Parkway to Shelbyville, Tennessee. He drove from Shelbyville to Falls Creek Falls on the back roads to avoid traffic and to see the local scenery in that very rural and beautiful part of Tennessee. It also gave Theo time to pray as he drove along and to prepare for his meeting with his cousin. Theo prayed that God's will would be accomplished, and that God's kingdom would be manifest. Theo prayed that God would supply his daily needs and that he would be a person that would be as forgiving as God was to the world. He prayed that when temptation arrived in his life that he would be able to overcome temptation, and that he would be protected from evil and the devil. Theo prayed that God's purpose and power through His Holy Spirit would be used to accomplish an identification of the nature of God.

By the time that Theo caught up with Jonnie he was deep into his conversation with God and a radiance shown from his face. When Theo had parked the pickup truck and saw Jonnie, she was speaking to a group of disciples, and was preparing to baptize some recent converts. Jonnie saw Theo and said to the congregation, "Behold the lamb of God who takes away the sin of the world."

Everyone stopped and looked intently at Theo as Theo wadded into the pool of water that was by the stream around which the congregation had gathered. Jonnie said, "it is you who should be baptizing me." But Theo replied, "It is right that you should baptize me in the presence of these and the presence of God." Jonnie then said," I baptize you with water, but you Theo will baptize many with the Holy Spirit."

When Theo came up from the water the Spirit of God visibly descended on Theo in the form of a dove, and the voice of God could be heard saying, "This is my beloved son in whom I am well pleased."

The group of people all around the pool of water looked on in amazement. They murmured one to another, "Who is this that Jonnie just baptized." A few of those in the congregation even decided to seek Theo out to see where he was staying and to try to understand why Jonnie had said that this is the lamb that takes away the sin of the world, and why the voice of God was heard when Theo was baptized. One of the men who decided to follow Theo was named Phillip and another was Andrew.

Phillip and Andrew were following Theo when unexpectedly Theo turned to them and said, "What are you seeking?"

Philip replied, "We want to know why Jonnie spoke about you the way she did, and we want to know what is the meaning of the voice that we heard from above when you came out of the water?"

Theo replied, "I don't have any place to stay for the night. But I would be happy to share a place with you two If you want to get to know me better."

Phillip said, "My brother Peter has a place In McMinnville where we can stay the night if you want to crash with us."

Theo said, "I know the place where you are staying, and I will meet you there in a couple of hours."

Phillip had a puzzled look on his face, and he

said., "How did you know where we stay? Are you some sort of psychic or something? Can you read our minds and see our thoughts? Who are you and what do you have to do with us?"

Theo replied, "You guys are going to see a whole lot more than that in the very near future." With that pronouncement Theo got into his pickup truck. and drove away.

Later that evening Theo showed up at the place where Phillip had said that they were staying in McMinnville. Theo answered all their questions. It turned out that Peter had many more questions than the rest of them and at the end of the evening Theo told them that he had several things to accomplish before he went off to college. Theo told them that it would be a certainty that they would meet again and that he would call them when it was the proper time for Theo to start his ministry.

Phillip, Andrew and Peter had lengthy discussions amongst themselves after Theo left. They each had a strange feeling concerning Theo, and each of them felt amazingly attached to Theo and to each other, even though they had only known Theo for a few hours. They did not know why they felt that way in their spirits, but they certainly felt in their own beings that they had met and had spent the night with one of the most amazing individuals they had ever met or hoped to meet. Each of them longed to have a much more lasting relation with Theo and could not wait for him to return.

Chapter 12

Theo goes camping.

Theo felt led by the Holy Spirit to go into the wilderness and to seek the council of God concerning the course of his life. Also, because things had not settled down in Burnsville, Theo decided that he needed to spend some time away from his family so that whatever had occurred as a result of his valedictorian speech and the sermon that he gave at church would simmer down. The Mann family was still getting threats especially from members of the church and also from others who had heard about what Theo had said when he had spoken to the congregation at the Glendale Baptist Church. On several occasions, Mary Jane and Joe had to clean the house and their cars because rotten eggs had been thrown at them as they traveled and while they were sleeping at their house.

Theo and Joe had gone camping on several occasions and Theo knew how to handle himself even in the mountainous areas of East Tennessee. It was still three months before college was to start and Theo decided that he needed to clear his head and to spend time with God, his Heavenly Father, before he went to Ole Miss.

Theo drove eastward on Interstate 40. He went through Knoxville then turned South towards Sevierville and Gatlinburg. After Gatlinburg, Theo drove into the Smoky Mountain National Park and looked for a place where he could safely put the truck down and hike into the mountains. The mountains were ablaze with pink, red, peach, lavender, white, orange and yellow Flame Azaleas strewn along the trails. Theo found the Little Bottoms Trail that led to Gregory Bald, and he could see the magnificence of God's creation. The perfume of the white and pink blooms was strong and pleasant. Plenty of colorful eastern tiger swallow tail and orange spangled fritillary butterflies doing their jobs as the chief pollinators of those amazingly beautiful flowering plants were at work.

Theo found a good place to park the truck, he took up his backpack and hiked a very secluded trail. Theo found a place that had a bubbling clear spring and decided to pitch his tent. Interestingly, Theo did not bring any food with him because he had decided that it would be right to fast as he sought a clear word from his Heavenly Father.

Sometimes the right thing to do is to get by yourself and seek to communicate with and specially to listen for the clear word from God. Theo's relationship with God was very intimate. He had often found himself speaking directly to the Lord as if God was standing next to him and was listening to every word that he said. In fact, that was the case. God did listen and not only did God listen, but God also spoke to Theo.

The words of God are not always audible but there is always a clear message to those who diligently seek to hear God's voice. It is most important to listen with spiritual understanding because God is Spirit and communicates on a spiritual level. God revealed to Theo that he would be tempted by Satan because after all, Theo was a human being and temptations come with the territory. If Theo was to fulfil God's plan for his life and for all mankind, Theo would need to always be prepared to meet Satan's challenges every minute of every day. With that in mind Theo often prayed for Godly wisdom and spiritual awareness of the ways of the evil one. Theo prayed. Theo asked for God's help in dealing with temptation, and he prayed that God would give him the ability to overcome those that would challenge him.

Theo did not have to wait long for the temptations to start. Satan was active from the beginning of Theo's entrance into the wilderness. However, because Theo was led by the spirit to the isolation that he sought, the Holy Spirit accompanied him. As he was tempted Theo was full of the spirit and was in communication with God. Even while Satan confronted Theo with temptation after temptation God's spirit continued to minister to Theo's every need.

Theo stayed in constant prayer for almost 40 days while he was at his mountain retreat in the wilderness of East Tennessee. Theo was able to drink out of the spring next to which he camped but by the end of his 40 days of seeking God's plan for his life Theo was famished and needed to eat.

Satan physically confronted Theo and said, "If you are really the son of God convert these stones that are here on the ground into bread." Theo because of the presence of the spirit was able to reply to Satan and said, "Man shall not live by bread alone."

Satan's temptation concerning the bread was to confront Theo with the physical needs of his physical body. The question presented by Satan was not whether Theo was truly human, but whether Theo was also a spiritual being. The spiritual nature of Theo's life came into direct conflict with Satan's suggestion that Theo was not the son of God after all. Theo's spiritual relationship to God was apparent in Theo's response to Satan. Round one went to Theo.

Satan then, in an instance, took Theo to a place where all the nations of the world and all the worldly treasures that the world possessed could be seen. Satan said, "Everything in the world has been given to me and I am able to transfer it to you, if you will acknowledge me and worshipped me."

Theo led by the Holy Spirit quoted Holy Scripture again and said, "Worship the Lord your God and serve Him only." The first commandment states, "I am the Lord your God you shall have no other God's before me."

Theo confirmed that materiality and Godliness are not compatible. Round two went to Theo as well.

Satan then took Theo to the top of the tallest church steeple in the world and said, "If you are the Son of God throw yourself down from here because scripture says, 'He will command his angels concerning you to guard you carefully and will not let you be hurt.'"

Satan said this to try to cause Theo to be tempted by sowing doubt as to Theo's relation with God.

Theo again led by the Holy Spirit recognized that Satan was taking scripture out of context and was leaving out significant parts of the verse he was quoting.

Theo's response was, "It is said, 'Do not put the Lord your God to the test.'"
Satan recognized that the third round was also

won by Theo and departed from his temptations for the time being, leaving Theo in the beauty of nature and ready for lunch.

Things had finally settled down back in Burnsville when Theo returned to prepare for college.

Chapter 13

DJ Crump's offer of employment.

Within a few days of arriving back in Burnsville after his time of being in the wilderness, Theo was visited by Buddy Crump. Buddy told Theo that Buddy's father wanted to see Theo and to discuss with him a proposition that Buddy described as an offer that Theo could not refuse. Theo expressed his regrets, but Buddy was insistent that Theo travel to the Tishomingo Bingo Parlor and have a sit-down meeting with DJ Crump.

On a ridiculously hot and sticky summers day Theo traveled on Hwy 72 from Burnsville towards Iuka to have the meeting with Mr. Crump who was now in his 70s. Theo's grandmother, Maggie Sullivan, who was in her early 60s had gone back to work at the bingo parlor though she managed to keep her distance from DJ Crump. By then DJ had his eyes on younger women who worked at the bingo parlor and who were more susceptible to DJ's advances.

Because Theo's grandmother was aware of the meeting and had warned Theo about what might happen when he came to visit DJ Crump, Theo felt as if he was able to meet any challenge that DJ Crump might offer. Additionally, Theo had been given the gift of discernment by the Holy Spirit and was full of spiritual wisdom granted by his Heavenly Father.

DJ Crump had his hands in all sorts of businesses in the northeast corner of Mississippi and in the adjoining counties in Tennessee. The businesses ranged from running car dealerships, interest in apartment buildings, the Tishomingo Bingo Parlor and other gambling interests especially in Hardin County Tennessee. DJ Crump also was heavenly involved in politics and most local elected politicians received financial assistance that DJ Crump was able to provide in order to get elected and maintain their elected status. As a result of his financial interest in the politicians DJ Crump was always able to get special favors from the politicians in order to keep his businesses under the radar of local law enforcement. The Crump family was also involved in the illegal drug business.

As soon as Theo reached the bingo parlor, he was greeted by young girl who he recognized from high school and ushered into an elaborately decorated reception area on the 2nd floor of the building. In a relatively brief time, a rather young and attractive secretary offered Theo a cup of coffee or a soft drink and told Theo that Mr. Crump would be with him very shortly. Theo noticed that the reception area was decorated with pictures of the Crump family including Trey Crump who Theo had met on several occasions during his time at Tishomingo Central High School.

After about a 15 minute wait the secretary told Theo that Mr. Crump would see him and that he should go on into Mr. Crump's office. Theo opened the door and went into a rather dark and foreboding room. The blinds on the windows were closed and there were only dim lights on in the office. Mr. Crump sat behind a large desk in an oversized chair. In front of the desk were two wooden chairs with straight backs. Towards the door through which Theo had entered there was a large, overstuffed couch with ornamental pillows. There were a few pictures on the walls mainly of seascapes that Theo found unusual for that office. There was a telephone on the desk but no computer. The desk had papers strewn about in no apparent order. DJ Crump was dressed in a leisure suit with a pair of orthopedic shoes that indicated that he had trouble walking.

DJ Crump sat behind his desk with his back turned to Theo. Crump said, "Have a seat Theo." and then there was a long silence.

Theo sat there in the darkened room for what seemed like an eternity until Mr. Crump spoke again. "Mr. Mann, I have asked you here because for the last few years I have decided to recruit the top students from your high school and from other high schools in this area. I want you to come to work in my organization because I want someone familiar with people of your age to become involved with the businesses that me and my family operate."

Theo asked, "What are the businesses that your family operates Mr. Crump?"

"We have many different businesses; I help to run this bingo parlor for one. We also have apartment buildings, and we have other business interests in Hardin County Tennessee." DJ Crump replied.

"I am aware of your business practices Mr. Crump. I am not interested in becoming involved with your organization because I do not believe that you are an honest man and I believe that your business practices are not in the best interest of the people that get involved with you. You have taken advantage of the poor and the helpless for too long." Theo said with a very stern expression on his face.

"Just a minute Sonny. How dare you to come

into my office and speak to me in those terms. I am one of the most influential men in this area of the country and I'm not used to having somebody like you talk to me like that." Mr. Crump replied with a snarl.

Crump obviously was more used to having people that always agreed with him and said yes to his propositions because everyone acknowledged that DJ Crump was rich and powerful. DJ Crump was not in a mood to take no for an answer from anyone, especially a young graduate from a local high school. By the time that Theo was asked to come to DJ Crump's office, Mr. Crump was generally able to hire the top students from around the area and to groom them for positions in his somewhat illicit operations. This was done much like the recruiting of young men into other rackets.

Theo said, "I have other plans for my life than working for a crook like you. I am going to college this fall and I plan on starting my ministry as soon as I get the go ahead from God."

"What has God to do with this situation or anything else for that matter?" was DJ Crump's reply. Obviously, DJ had never taken into consideration that there was even room for the idea that God had plans for people's lives.

"God has everything to do with my life. He directs me in the ways I should go and opens the way for me for every situation in which I find myself. If God wanted me to work for you, he would make that clear to me and I would immediately know that I was doing what God wanted me to do. To the contrary the spirit of God is directing me away from you and away from your business practices. At some point in time, I believe I will be called upon to confront you and your family. Until that time however it will be better if you have nothing to do with me and I have nothing to do with you." As soon as Theo had said those words, he got up from the chair in which he was sitting and left the Tishomingo Bingo Parlor. In his heart, Theo knew that there would be another day in which there would be a confrontation between the Crumps and the son of Mann.

Theo drove back to Burnsville. He felt the presence of his Heavenly Father and knew that he had said exactly the right things to DJ Crump. Theo knew in his soul that there would be another fight between the Crumps who were influenced by the forces of evil and the godly spirit that radiated from Theo. Theo instinctively knew that he would be called upon to stand up for the oppressed and to give good news to the poor. Theo realized that he had to take his time in order to prepare for his ministry because much would be required of him in the years to come.

Theo was content to work in the boat motor repair shop with his grandfather and Joe while he was waiting for freshman orientation to start in Oxford. Theo loved to spend time with his mother and his siblings as he prepared for his studies at Ole Miss to begin. Theo was not asked to speak at the church again, but he did attend church services regularly and was grateful to worship with his friends and family. The people of the church gave him a wide berth, but nothing was said, and peace was restored in the congregation.

Chapter 14

College-Freshman Orientation.

Near the end of August of 2005 Theo accompanied by his parents set out for Oxford, Mississippi. Joe had packed the family's pickup truck with Theo's clothes and the few belongings that Theo wanted to take with him when he checked into the dormitory to start his college career. Among his prized possessions was his Bible and a few other books that Theo considered to be helpful

The Mann family received letters from the housing office at Ole Miss that told them what to expect when Theo checked into the dormitory for freshman orientation. The letter informed Theo that all incoming freshmen would have a roommate and that they would live in a dormitory on campus that housed both male and female students. The letter contained a list of conditions and rules and regulations that each of the incoming freshmen had to meet. Some of the regulations seemed to be rather obvious such as no one could bring their motorcycle into their dorm room, everyone had to be appropriately dressed when they were in the common areas of the dormitory and there was a non-alcoholic beverage provision that stated that no one could be drinking or drunk while they were on campus.

The rules and regulations that the incoming freshman were to adhere to seemed to be more of suggestions than absolute requirements. Ole Miss had a reputation for being a party school and on any given night especially during the football season fraternity parties on campus were more bacchanalian than the rules implied. It was not unusual on any given weekend night for the fraternities along fraternity row to be lit up with party lights, loud music, party kegs, open bars, and pretty girls in very low-cut dresses.

Theo growing up in Burnsville, Tishomingo County, Mississippi, had not been around those kinds of social gatherings. Even though Theo was well familiar with what went on at the bingo parlor he had not been exposed to the social atmosphere that was prevalent on a college campus like Ole Miss. Entering the freshman class at a major university would be a unique experience, even though Theo was a different kind of a person than your average first year student from a rural farm community where people rarely adventured far from their closed community.

Mary Jane and Joe while not overly apprehensive about how Theo would adapt to his new surroundings, could not help but wonder with someone like Theo, what might be expected from his college experience. Mary Jane especially wondered whether Theo would be accepted by the other students and especially by a college roommate that had no idea about Theo's birth and his relationship with the almighty. As time got closer for freshman orientation, Mary Jane's apprehension grew just as any mother's apprehension would when her first child ventured away from home for the first time. Additionally, the fact that Theo was exceptional in all ways both gave her confidence and apprehension. Confidence that Theo was well above handling any problems that might exist in dealing with his studies, the professors at the college, and like-minded students. She was apprehensive however, because she knew that in the hearts of many there would be a natural dislike of someone as good and talented as Theo. Both Mary Jane and Joe had seen the reaction to Theo after he had made his valedictorian speech and had spoken in church. They knew that there was a spirit of evil that would confront Theo and they had never seen him in a situation where he had to deal with that form of evil.

Finally, the day came when everything was ready for the trip from Burnsville to Oxford. Joe, Theo, and Mary Jane put Theo's stuff in the back of the pickup truck, and they all piled into the Ford 150 and started their trip. It is about an hour and 30-minute drive from Burnsville to Oxford. The trip took them westward through many small towns and finally to the city of Oxford which is the home of the University of Mississippi also known as Ole Miss. The instructions that they received concerning moving into the dorm room were fairly simple. What was unanticipated was that Theo's roommate happen to be Trey Crump.

Everyone moving into the freshman dormitory at Ole Miss were to show up between the hours of 1:00 o'clock and 4:00 o'clock on Sunday August 16. It just so happened that at precisely 1:30 the Mann family and the Crump family met at the dorm room assigned to Theo and Trey. The reaction between the two families was quite the opposite of each other. Theo was calm and eager and held out his hand in an offer of acceptance, while Trey on the other hand looked at Theo as his rival and someone that he needed to treat with disdain.

It seemed that there had been some misgiving between the Mann family and the Crump family for many years. Trey was accompanied by his father Buddy Crump and his grandfather DJ Crump as they brought Trey's stuff to his dorm room. There had been a few encounters between these families dating back to the time DJ had tried to seduce Maggie Sullivan at the bingo parlor and the time Buddy and Joe had a confrontation regarding Mary Jane while Mary Jane was working at the Subway sandwich shop at the Valero gas station in Burnsville.

While Buddy Crump vaguely remembered the confrontation that he had had with Joe Mann and also recognized Mary Jane he did not have a real sense of who Theo was or what was to be expected from someone he considered to be of a lower social status than his son. It was only because of the regulations imposed by the Housing Authority at Ole Miss that Trey Crump was obligated to be the roommate of someone like Theo Mann. Theo immediately understood Trey Crump's mindset and also realized what Buddy Crump and DJ Crump were all about. Theo did not trust himself to disclose his feelings regarding his roommate and because he knew all men and needed no more to bear witness of man; for he knew what was in man.

After all the settling in at the freshman dormitory had taken place, the Crump delegation left in order to have a meal at the best restaurant in that area. Theo and the Mann family hugged and kissed and said their goodbyes with the promise that Theo would keep in close touch with his mom and with that, Theo was left alone. Of course, there was the constant noise of the other freshman students moving into the dormitory. There were happy expressions in some groups and tears shed by parents seeing their child leaving for the first time. All this Theo took in, knowing the thoughts and emotions that were in constant flux all around him.

Later that evening as a part of the freshman orientation all the freshman students were required to attend a social gathering at the University Center. There was a rock and roll band, refreshments, and young boys and girls gathered together many for the first time and some for the first time away from their small hometowns scattered throughout Mississippi. The young girls were all dressed in the new clothes that they had brought with them for the start of the new school year. The boys generally wore the clothes that had just been purchased for them by their parents, but there was a very eclectic styles ranging from Bermuda shorts and T shirts with flip flops to khaki pants with button down Oxford shirts and Wenjun penny loafers. Because it was Ole Miss many of the freshmen students were dressed in conservative looking clothes because that was how students at Ole Miss saw themselves. The flip flop and Bermuda short crowd were generally from out of state and from larger cities like New Orleans and Memphis while the more conservative dressers tended to come from places like Tupelo and Jackson and even from Biloxi. Theo was conservatively dressed signifying his small-town upbringing.

It was a warm summers evening and despite the fact that the air conditioners were running at full blast, it was still hot and steamy in the University Center where the freshman orientation mixer was going on. It was extremely hard to talk to anyone over the noise of the crowd and the loud music that was playing. If anyone wanted to talk to anyone, especially if a young man wanted to talk to a young lady, they had to agree to go out on the patio in order to hold any kind of conversation. Theo did not know anyone in particular because most of his friends had decided not to go to college or went to smaller community colleges. Theo did recognize that Trey Crump was at the party, and he seemed to be the center of much attention especially from the young ladies that were in attendance. Trey was dressed in khaki pants with a white shirt and a blue blazer. He was socially adept at meeting people and had a familiarity with how to socialize with the young ladies that were in attendance.

Theo was content to take in all of his new surroundings. He seemed to know what was going on in the minds of all the people that were around him. He eventually met a young lady who appeared to be as out of place as Theo and she agreed to get a cup of punch and retire to the patio in order to have a conversation. Theo started out by saying, "My name is Theo Mann and I'm from Burnsville which is in the extreme northeast corner of Mississippi. To whom do I have the pleasure of this company."

"My name is Janet Gilmore. I'm from Nashville, Tennessee." was her reply.

"I have an aunt and uncle that live in Murfreesboro. Do you know anything about Murfreesboro?" Theo asked.

"I also have some relatives that live in Murfreesboro but I'm not really that familiar with that town." was Janet Gilmore's reply.

"Do you know what you want to study?" Theo continued to ask.

Janet Gilmore was wearing a noticeably short skirt with a top that revealed her midriff which seemed to be the costume of the day for young ladies at Ole Miss. She wore glasses that covered a good portion of her face. She had a sweet smile and seemed to be adept at meeting people and at least carrying on a conversation.

"I don't know what I really want to study right now but I'm extremely interested in meeting new people and starting a new portion of my life. I went to a Catholic girl's school and have been somewhat sheltered from meeting new people. I have three sisters and two brothers, and my parents have kept an awfully close eye on my activities while I was in high school." Janet said as she looked closely at Theo and tried to figure out who he was and why she was talking to him.

As Theo studied Janet's face, that seemed to increase the insecurity in her demeanor. Theo at once became aware that Janet suffered from anxiety and that the anxiety was more than just being at college and away from home for the first time in her life. "Is there something that I can help you with, Janet." Theo said in a quiet and unassuming voice.

"Why do you ask me that? And who are you? I don't know you from anyone, we are strangers, and we just came outside to get a breath of fresh air and to drink this punch." Janet retorted.

"You seem to have a good deal of anxiety, way beyond just the normal anxiety that all of us have on the first day of freshman orientation." Theo observed. "All I want to do is be of help to you and to make you feel at ease. I know that you're suffering from anxiety due to an infection that you received from a young man that you hardly know."

Janet cast her eyes downwards and she didn't know what to say for a few moments. "How do you know these things, and why should I trust you?"

"It is my intent to be of help to all that I come in contact with, and I perceive that you need my help." Theo said.

"No one knows that I have herpes. I met this guy who took me to the prom at my high school. It happened at a party after the prom we all had a little bit too much to drink and it was the first time I had ever been with a boy. I really don't know how it happened, but I do know that I have this sore, and it just won't go away and I'm afraid. I haven't even gone to the doctor because I'm afraid of what my parents might do to me if they knew. They probably would not have allowed me to come to college and I'm afraid." Janet blurted out.

Theo looked intently into Janet's face and said, "Don't be afraid, I will not hurt you and I will not tell anybody about what you just told me." Theo reached out his hand and took Janet's into his. Theo smiled and said, "Don't tell anybody what has just happened to you, please keep everything between us just between us.

Janet immediately felt as if an overwhelming calmness flooded over her entire being, she was no longer afraid. She instinctively knew that her body had been healed and that the sore that had appeared on her body had been healed and would not return. When she turned around to look at Theo, he was gone and had evidently blended into the crowd at the University Center. Janet went back into the freshman mixer with the hope of finding Theo, but he was gone.

Later that evening Theo returned to his dorm room and found that Trey was in the room with some of his friends from the prep school that they had attended. The boys were passing around a bottle of Jack Daniels and were boasting about the girls that they had seduced. One of the preppy guys blurted out that he had put a baby into one of the girls he had met, and she didn't even know who he was. Each of the boys bragged that they undoubtedly would have great fun in college and get the pants off as many girls as was possible.

Theo knew that he did not fit into their discussion and excused himself and found others in the lobby of the dormitory that were in the same situation as he found himself that evening. The meeting between Trey and his preppy friends went on for most of the evening and well into the early morning hours. It was not until 4:30 in the morning that Theo was able to return to his room and get some sleep.

The next day there were other orientation activities for the freshmen at Ole Miss. There was an aptitude test that needed to be taken. Student IDs had to be produced. Classes needed to be registered for. All the while there was a crush of students all hurrying around on the campus trying to make friends and trying to act as if they knew what they were doing.

Unexpectedly, Theo happened to bump into Janet Gilmore as he was registering for first-year English. Janet looked gratefully at Theo as their eyes met for a brief moment. Janet could see the compassion and feelings in Theo's eyes and face. Beyond that they did not speak or further acknowledge each other's presence. Instinctively, Janet knew that while Theo was a compassionate and sincere person, she could also sense that there was a sorrow that he at some time would have to endure.

All around the campus there were posters and banners put up by the fraternities and sororities that had advertised their chapters on campus. The fraternities and sororities would be engaged in the annual process of recruiting first-year students to their fraternity or sorority. There would be elaborate parties that were announced throughout the campus. That process was called the Rush season. Each of these social gatherings would expose both male and female students to why each particular fraternity or sorority was the best and most prestigious organization that a student could join.

The rush season also allowed each of the fraternities and sororities to evaluate the first-year students that the sorority or fraternity might want in their organization. Fraternities and sororities came with their own living accommodations, meal plans, and everything that would make those joining their fraternity or sorority comfortable in their new surroundings. But to join a fraternity or sorority was expensive. The cost was well above the amount that Theo wanted to spend for his time at Ole Miss.

The selection process engaged in by the different sororities placed a premium on a girl's ability to get along with others and her looks. The better the girl looked the more likely it was that she would be offered membership by a sorority. It was also important if another member of the family of a particular girl had been a previous member of the sorority. Those girls were designated as having a legacy interest in the sorority and were given a preference in the selection process, but the better the girl looked the better the chance that she would be selected.

From the fraternity's point of view, a legacy was also important, but the male student was evaluated not only by his looks but also by his personality and to a certain extent by his athletic ability. The fraternities engaged in different sports on an intramural basis and therefore some emphasis was placed upon a freshman's athletic abilities in the selection process.

During rush week on the Ole Miss campus, the fraternities and sororities interviewed potential members, held various forms of parties, and when the weekend came, each fraternity house held a big blowout party that began shortly after the Ole Miss football team had played its first home game of the football season.

The general student population of Ole Miss is predominately white. Seventy eight percent of the student population is white while only fourteen percent is black. The general population of Mississippi is thirty seven percent black. On the other hand, the football team is made up of predominantly black players and the same is true of the basketball team.

Prior to football games at Ole Miss there is always a large social gathering in a part of the campus referred to as the Grove. The fraternity and sorority houses as well as alumni groups and even just plain old fans of Ole Miss football gather for elaborate tailgating parties to get prepared for the game. Tents and bar-b-que pits are set up in the Grove and there are plenty of refreshments to get the participants in the right frame of mind to support the Rebels, the mascot of the Ole Miss athletic teams. The Ole Miss Rebel was traditionally a caricature of Colonel Reb, and a male cheerleader dressed up as Colonel Reb patrolled the sidelines of the football stadium during the games. Colonel Reb also strolled through the Grove before football games.

The Saturday after freshman orientation began, Theo decided that he would walk through the Grove before the football game between Ole Miss and Memphis State. He saw many things that he had not seen before. The people were dressed very differently from what he expected. Both the students, alumni, and sports fans were dressed in what could be considered as business attire with the women dressed in sundresses with matching accessories and the men wore khaki pants with button down oxford shirts. The women had bright colored sandals and the men had penny loafers or saddle shoes on their sockless feet.

As Theo walked along, he realized that he was pretty much an outsider to the normal football crowd that was gathered in the Grove. He saw plenty of enthusiasm for Ole Miss football and people having lots to eat and adult beverages to drink. Theo wondered to himself why people wanted to dull their senses before going into a stadium and rooting for their favorite team. He wondered about the amount of money that was being spent just in getting prepared to watch a football game, and he wondered what commitments this group of football enthusiasts had to anything other than their favorite team and the sport of football.

Eventually, Theo came across the Crump family who had set up a tent and were being served bar-b-que by what appeared to be their butler. DJ Crump immediately recognized Theo and invited him over to their tent. The Crump family was all there. DJs wife appeared to be much younger than DJ. Buddy Crump was there, and he was accompanied by a young attractive lady. Trey Crump was also there, and he had several of his friends and there were also several young ladies with that group.

"Well, if it isn't our old friend Theo Mann. How's it going young man?" DJ asked. Before Theo could reply, Trey looked over at Theo and said, "You shouldn't even be here, this is not a place for someone like you. Me and my family are so much better than people like you. You don't deserve to be among people like us."

"Trey you're probably right, but we can be polite to somebody like this even if he is not in our class." DJ said from the easy chair in which he was sitting. "Offer young Theo a drink, Buddy."

Buddy Crump looked up at Theo and a rage started to boil up in his demeanor. "I wouldn't offer this kid a drink if he was standing here and on fire." Buddy Crump snorted. The young ladies that were in the Crump tent all held their breaths because they knew that trouble was going to start because of the way that Buddy or speaking to Theo.

Theo began to walk away with his back turned to Buddy. That seemed to anger Buddy all the more. Buddy's face was bright red in his hands were clenched in a fist. Even though Theo's back was turned to Buddy, he could sense that Buddy was hot on his heels. Buddy raised his hand as if he was ready to strike but for some reason he could not. Buddy tried even harder but still he had no strength in his arm to do anything that would cause malice. Finally, Theo faced Buddy. The rage in Buddy's face and body was apparent to all those sitting in the Crump tent. Theo was calm and he said, "I mean no one any harm. I want to just be a regular student. I want no trouble with any of you."

Buddy could do nothing. It was almost as if he was frozen in place. The rage seemed to dissipate as Theo spoke. After a few moments, Theo walked away, and Buddy returned to the Crump tent, but he could not explain what had just happened. Neither DJ nor Trey had ever seen anything like what had just happen after Buddy had gotten to the point of rage. Each of the people in the tent were well aware of the fact that when Buddy went after someone, like he had with Theo, there was no stopping him until blood was let. However, nobody said anything they just stared at Buddy in amazement.

After a few days, the freshman orientation ended. The fraternity rush season continued, and an offer was made to Trey Crump to join the Sigma Alpha Epsilon fraternity. Within a few days Trey moved from the dorm room that he shared with Theo and peace was restored. Theo studied effectively and was an honor student for all the time he spent at Ole Miss.

Chapter 15

The Message of Jonnie Waters and the Opposition to it.

In 2008 a great recession had hit the American and worldwide economies. There was a panic that settled in among the financial community that brought uncertainty and despair. People faced the loss of their homes and the loss of jobs as a result of poor economic policies by large financial organizations. The first response from the government was to allow the capital markets to correct themselves. If mortgage companies and banks went under it was their problem because in a free-market system, corrections happened and that was just the price of living in a capitalist economy in the United States.

As the recession raged on, the government and especially the American Federal Reserve realized that the country was in trouble if something was not done to ease the situation. In November 2008, the first African American President was elected and President-elect Obama even before his inauguration began to work on getting the country back on its collective feet. By the spring of 2009, the recession was still in full swing but there was an optimism that the country could recover from the bad economic policies that had gotten America and the world into recession.

Jonnie Waters looked out over the streams that ran by the cave in which she was currently living. It was early Spring and daffodils and other Spring plants were starting to appear in the central Tennessee area where Jonnie made her camp. She lived in a limestone cave with a group of disciples including both men and women old and young. In that part of Tennessee there were many limestone outcroppings and occasional caves. Jonnie and her disciples all dressed and very rustic clothing. Most of the group wore army fatigues of the camouflage type. The women dressed in fatigue pants and sweatshirts. They all wore rubber soled shoes of various makes and models. The group subsisted on survival foods that they were able to scavenge from the woods and meadows that were abundant in that area of Tennessee. Many among the group knew how to find mushrooms that would not make them sick and to make those mushrooms into delicious soups and other types of meals that were shared with the whole group.

Jonnie and her group of disciples lived communally, sharing everything that they possessed among the group. This style of living caused quite a stir among the local politicians and even some of the state authorities. Jonnie and her group were often visited by state police, the department of family and children services, the local sanitary department and others who had a keen interest in the lifestyle and ministry of Jonnie and her group of disciples. On each occasion the group was able to satisfy the government agencies that all was in accordance with local regulations, and they were allowed to continue to live in their commune,

The group was also visited by members of the local churches and by religious leaders from prominent denominations that wanted to question Jonnie about her beliefs and the impact that she was making with people who gathered to hear her preaching. The group was constantly adding new converts because of the lifestyle and because of the teachings that Jonnie preached on a frequent and regular basis.

Jonnie's message was simple, direct and powerful. "Repent, the Kingdom of God is close, love God with all your heart, mind, spirit and strength, and love your neighbor as you love yourself," Jonnie proclaimed. The power of her preaching was not just in the words that she was saying but in the lifestyle in which her community was engaging. Her rustic way of life, the power of her voice, and the urgency with which she spoke brought immediate acceptance by those who came to the wilderness to hear and see Jonnie Waters preach. The fact that people were coming to hear Jonnie was not very troubling to the local churches but the fact that the church collection plates were not as full as usual did cause concerns.

There were meetings of the pastors of the churches in McMinnville to discuss the growing attendance of converts to the Jonnie Waters preaching services. As far away as Nashville, religious leaders began to question by what authority Jonnie proclaimed her message. After all, Jonnie had not attended any denominational seminary and she had no theological degrees. No one had ever heard of Jonnie Waters until a rather large group of pilgrims started to show up at Jonnie Waters' wilderness retreat. Perhaps it was the economic conditions caused by the recession or it was merely the desire to be with a messenger from God that drove people into the wilderness. Jonnie believed it was the hand of God that caused her ministry to blossom just as the spring brought renewed life after the long cold winter.

A panel of Southern Baptist leaders paid a visit to hear Jonnie preach. They were sent to meet with Jonnie and report back to the convention as to what they learned. A private meeting was arraigned with Jonnie. Because her father Zack was still associated with the Southern Baptist Sunday School Board, Jonnie agreed that she would meet with the Southern Baptist delegation. The group of Southern Baptist traveled to the wilderness area where Jonnie and her disciples lived.

The spokesman that the group selected was Dr. Richard Jefferson a pastor from a large conservative church in Mobile, Alabama. Jefferson and the convention held with the conviction that only men could be ordained as pastors or could be allowed to preach. Jefferson earned a D. Min from Southwest Theological Seminary in Fort Worth, Texas. Pastor Jefferson preferred to be address as Dr. Jefferson by everyone including his wife.

Dr. Jefferson was also known to offer his congregation his opinion on who they should vote for during any election, and that was especially true of Presidential elections. Jefferson acknowledged that his political preference was conservative and that his own beliefs motivated his desire to have his congregation follow his lead in political matters. Dr. Jefferson often spoke of his belief that socialism was an especially loathsome practice and he expressed his displeasure with the communal living situation as practiced by Jonnie and her followers. Dr. Jefferson believed that if capitalism was good enough for the church in bible times it was good enough for now and should not be tampered with. Dr. Jefferson also believed that abortion was an abomination and that it should be fully outlawed though out the United States with no exceptions for rape or incest. To him life began at conception was as much a political conviction as well as a religious axiom.

While Dr. Jefferson had grown up on a farm in rural Mississippi, he had become acclimated to city life and was uncomfortable trapsing into the wilderness to hear Jonnie Waters preach. He was especially appalled by the fact that even some known leaders of the Southern Baptist had been convicted by Jonnie Waters' message of repentance. He was also sickened by the fact that a woman was preaching, even if it was her own congregation, and men were listening and responding to a woman's message. Dr. Jefferson was convinced in his heart that God would not honor a message preached by a woman and that it had to be satanic. Dr. Jefferson believed that Jonnie Waters was possessed by Satan, and it was his job to expose this sinful situation.

Dr. Jefferson refused to listen to recordings of Jonnie Waters message and preaching but relied on reports that he had received from another Southern Baptist pastor that took exception to Jonnie's message because it included references to a belief that men and women had equal obligations to usher in the Kingdom of God. The report given to Dr. Jefferson also referred to a belief by Jonnie Waters that material possessions could and should be held in common by those that believed in God. Jonnie preached that those individuals who were materialistic had refused to put God first and thus broke the first of the ten commandment that required that, "You shall have no other Gods before me."

On Monday April 12, 2009, Dr. Jefferson and a group of leaders from the Southern Baptist Convention traveled by passenger-van from Nashville to McMinnville and then to the wilderness area occupied by Jonnie Waters and her disciples. Dr. Jefferson was dressed as he always dressed. He wore a dark blue suit with a red tie tied in a Windsor knot so that the lower end of his tie was about four inches below his black shinny belt. He always wore a heavily starched white shirt that had a button-down collar. Dr. Jefferson's shoes were highly polished black wingtips that Mrs. Jefferson made sure that they met her husband's explicit demand.

The meeting between Dr. Jefferson and Jonnie started like this, "I am Dr. Richard Jefferson, president of the Southern Baptist convention and pastor of the First Baptist Church of Mobile, Alabama. Are you Jonnie Waters?"

"Yes, I am Jonnie Waters. I know who you are, and I know why you have traveled out here to see me."

Then without any further effort to ease into the conversation Dr. Jefferson asked, "By what authority do you presume to preach and baptize the people that follow your beliefs?" Dr. Jefferson rolled his green eyes up and peered over his nose.

"I have been called by God to deliver His message of redemption through repentance. As a sign of a changed life, we offer baptism by emersion in these flowing streams of water. We baptize with water but there is one coming after me who will baptize with the Holy Spirit. I am only a messenger crying out in the wilderness just as the prophet Isaiah foretold in ancient times. I am here preaching to alert the world about the coming savior." Jonnie replied to Dr. Jefferson who was amazed at the power of her voice and words that Jonnie spoke.

"We are here to understand what is going on and report back to the Convention about what we consider to be the acts of the devil. We know that a woman is not authorized to preach as you do, nor are women allowed to baptize. You have committed a grave sin and it should be you seeking forgiveness of your trespasses. You have cast an evil spell on your followers, and we will seek to cause this socialist operation of yours to be shut down. We, the Southern Baptist, hold great political power around here and we will get our way in this." Dr. Jefferson said in a self-righteous tone with his eyes still rolled back and his chin pointed up.

"We believe that God has sent His only begotten son into the world and that all who believe on him will have everlasting life. His son is among us today and he is the light of the world. He will be the savior of the world. I am but a messenger and I am unworthy to undo the laces of his boots. But I also have a calling from God from my birth. My father is a Southern Baptist and he and my mother have raised me to fulfill the calling that God has placed on me. You should also remember that 'God created men and women in his own image, in their own image created they them.'" Jonnie spoke as she looked intently into Dr. Jefferson's eyes and deeper into his soul.

"What you say cannot be true! Your lies will be revealed! The Southern Baptist will not allow your blasphemy to go unpunished. I will personally see to it that your little communist group is shut down and that our lawyers will find something in the criminal law to charge you with. You will be sorry that you met me Ms. Waters." Dr. Jefferson said with his face turning as red a tomato. Even the veins stood out on his neck and his fists were clinched as he spoke.

Jonnie did not reply to that tirade but merely turned her back and started to walk back into the cave where she and the group of her followers called home, at least for the time being.

"Don't you turn your back to me. God is not with you. You and your group are possessed by demons. We will see who is called by God." Jefferson yelled at Jonnie's back. The other men that were with Dr. Jefferson had to hold him back because he was so enraged that they feared he might do Jonnie physical harm. The others had to remind Jefferson that the people that were there were Jonnie's disciples and that they believed that Jonnie was truly a prophet sent by God to minister to godly people.

A few months later Jonnie was arrested and charged with contributing to the delinquency of minors even though the children living with their parents in the wilderness near Jonnie and her group were well cared for and there were no allegations of physical or emotional abuse. In fact, the children were unhappy when Jonnie was taken into custody because Jonnie cared for the children and often led them on hikes in the woods and watched over them as if they were her own.

Chapter 16

Theo graduates from college and begins his ministry.

Theo graduated from Ole Miss in May 2009. During Theo's sophomore year Joe Mann passed away from natural causes. Theo was summoned to Burnsville when Joe was very sick but did nothing to stop Joe's terminal illness. Theo could have intervened, but Joe was warned in a dream to let his sickness end in death. Joe related his dream to Theo and asked that he not interfere with this natural process. Theo prayed and realized that he was not ready to begin his ministry and call attention to his ability to exhibit the power of God that healing his earthly father would bring. Instead, Theo comforted his mother and his siblings. He was not asked to speak at Joe's funeral because people at the Glennville Baptist Church still remembered the sermon that Theo started to preach when he graduated from high school.

When Theo graduated from college, he was offered the opportunity to go to work at the Kimberly-Clark plant near Corinth, Mississippi. Theo was an excellent student and was well liked by fellow students and his professors. Theo kept mainly to himself and was constantly in prayer with his Heavenly Father. When Theo was baptized by his cousin Jonnie after he graduated from high school, and the Holy Spirit descended from heaven on him, Theo felt the full presence of the Spirit of God. Theo realized that the Spirit of God would direct every part of his life because the relationship between God and Theo was so close that Theo anticipated the will of God as the will of God was manifested in Theo. It was not in God's perfect will that Theo work for Kimberly-Clark. It was in God's perfect will for Theo to select men and women who would follow him and carry on his ministry when his time on earth was completed.

Soon after Theo's graduation he went to Pickwick Lake and searched for his old friends Andrew and Simon. Andrew and Simon had been hired as game wardens by the Tennessee Wildlife Resources Agency. Both Simon and Andrew constantly patrolled the TVA lakes to make sure that those who fished those lakes had proper licenses. Theo had driven to Pickwick dam because he knew that Andrew would be around there that day.

Theo was standing alone by the shore of the lake inside the confines of the Pickwick State Park. When Andrew saw Theo, his heart skipped a beat because he had often thought of the time that Theo had spent the night talking to Phillip, Simon and himself in McMinnville a few years back after they saw Theo being baptized by Jonnie. Even though Theo was standing alone on the beach Andrew was compelled by some unknown force to turn aside from his duties as a game warden to come to where Theo was standing.

Theo shouted to Andrew, "You will now be a fisher of men, follow me."

Andrew heard Theo's call and did exactly what Theo directed him to do. Andrew did not hesitate. He came to Theo and Theo got in the game warden boat that Andrew was operating. Theo said, "Where is Simon?"

Andrew said, "We are going to get Simon now he is not far from here and wants to join us."

Theo did not say another word until they got close to Simon.

Simon saw the game warden boat that Andrew was operating and then almost immediately recognized the passenger that Andrew had in the boat. Even though it had been a few years since Simon had last seen Theo, he was very happy that Theo was in the boat with Andrew. As soon as Andrew positioned the boat close enough to the boat that Simon was in, Simon jumped from his boat to the boat that Theo was in and greeted Theo with a full body hug. Simon was strong and his arms encircled Theo as if to squeeze the life out of Theo, but Theo was unfazed by Simon's enthusiasm.

"Simon you are as strong as an ox and as steady as a rock. From this day forward I am going to call you Peter." Theo then went on to explain that he was starting his ministry and that he wanted to have both Andrew and Peter in his group of followers that he could rely on to minister to the crowds that would be coming to hear Theo preach and especially who would want to be near Theo when he gave signs of the presence of the Heavenly Father.

"Peter you are an extrovert and often speak before you fully know what is happening, but you are also a natural leader of men and women, and you will be instrumental in my ministry. Each of these that I choose will have a prominent place and will perform the work that needs to be accomplished while I am still with you. Do either of you know where I can get in contact with Phillip?"

Andrew was quick to respond, "Yes' Phillip lives in Savannah, Tennessee, not many miles from here, and we can go see him tonight when he gets off from work."

Theo, Andrew and Peter spent the remainder of the day talking about what had gone on in their lives since they had last meet almost four years ago. Peter talked about how he and others had remained in the group with Jonnie Waters until she was arrested and what had gone on with her ministry once the Southern Baptist tried to insist that it was ungodly for women to preach or lead a congregation in the worship of God.

That evening they traveled in Peter's car north to Savannah, Tennessee and went to Phillip's apartment to see Phillip. Phillip greeted Theo and the others with a firm and hardy handshake. Theo said, "Phillip I am here to compel you to join our ministry. You must resign from your job and be ready to follow me in the service of God. Once you start down this path there will be no turning back."

"Ever since we met in McMinnville a few years back I haven't gotten you out of my mind. When you talked about your Fathers kingdom our hearts melted and we wanted to know more. We have been searching for something to fill our hearts with the wonder you gave us that spring night. I will follow you wherever you lead." was Phillips emphatic reply.

"I am calling each of you and you will be amazed at all that we will accomplish. Each of you will see signs from heaven. That does not mean however that you will not have to sacrifice many things too. My way is not an easy one!"

Neither of the three friends quite understood what Theo had in mind or even understood fully what Theo meant by the term sacrifice to which he had cautioned them. All they knew was that for some reason a young man named Theo the son of Joe and Mary Jane Mann had met them, and they were compelled to follow him to the end of their collective journeys.

Chapter 17

The First Public Sign Performed by Theo.

Theo and his three disciples stayed around Pickwick Lake for a few days. Theo told each of them of God's kingdom and the need to minister to a lost and dying world. Theo spoke in vivid stories about what being a follower would mean to each of these men who seemed to absorb each and every word that Theo spoke. On the third day they met James and his brother John. James and John came from a family that was well known in that area of Tennessee, Mississippi and Alabama. They were musicians and played backup for those that recorded at the Fame Music studio in Muscle Sholes, Alabama.

Phillip found his brother Bart and told him of his devotion to Theo. Bart met Theo and he also decided to commit to being a follower in the way that Theo proposed. Additionally, the group became acquainted with a man named Thomas who seemed to question every act that took place and every idea that anyone in the group offered even the ideas and statements of Theo himself. Later that day Theo met another James who Theo called Jimmy A. because his last name was Alphaeus. The group of the followers of Theo reached out and also found another Simon to become a member of the group and by the end of the day they found two guys who were named Jud. Theo called one of them Jud I because his last name was Iscariot and the other Jud, they all called Juddy so that each Jud was distinguished from the other. From a physical and intellectual prospective the Jud's were almost the exact opposite of each other.

Finally, Theo met a man that worked at the Tishomingo Bingo Parlor whose name was Matthew and who insisted on being called Matthew rather than Matt or Matty. Matthew was a friend of Theo's grandmother, Maggie Sullivan. Maggie told Theo that Matthew had gotten into trouble at the bingo parlor because DJ Crump had accused Matthew of taking money from the receipt of cash sales. DJ did that in order to throw off the state auditors who had to keep close watch on the bingo parlors receipts so that the bingo operation remained in compliance with Mississippi regulations. Actually, DJ had taken the money and was accusing Matthew to cover up DJ's illegal activities. Matthew was being investigated by the Mississippi Attorney General's office when he came to Theo's group of followers.

In addition to all the activity at the bingo parlor Matthew was a college graduate with a major in English and was reported to be an accurate observer of the events that happened around the group and a good writer.

After the selection of the group of close followers Theo was called by a friend from Burnsville and invited to a wedding that was being held at the large shelter in the Pickwick State Park. Theo's mother and siblings were going to be at the wedding, so Theo asked if he could bring his friends and they were invited too. There was going to be a large party and many people were going to attend. James and John had also been asked to supply musical entertainment.

The wedding took place, and a party was going on when the sherbet and ginger ale punch that was being served began to run low. Mary Jane saw Theo and his group and knew that Theo could handle the problem, so she went to Theo and whispered in his ear, "Theo you know that the punch is running low, could you and your friends do something to make sure the party keeps going because everyone was having such a wonderful time."

"Mother, what would you have me to do? You are always concerned about others, but what does that have to do with me?" Theo answered.

"Theo, you and your friends have had their fill of the punch. Those guys that you brought to the party must have been really thirsty, and you know our host's mother did not plan for so many to show up." Mary Jane told Theo.

Theo looked around and saw several large empty punch bowls under one of the picnic tables under the shelter where the wedding party was taking place. Theo found the ladies that had been serving the punch and told them to fill the empty punch bowls with water from the lake that was just a few yards away. At first the servers were reluctant to do as Theo asked them to do. After all, they knew of Theo and his family and were at the Glennville Baptist Church when Theo spoke after graduation and still remembered how shocking his speech had been. However, because of his insistence and because a feeling of calm came over them, they did as Theo asked.

After the bowls had been filled, Theo told one of the servers to take a cup of the water now turned into punch to the bride's mother. When the bride's mother tasted the contents of the cup she exclaimed to the server, "Where did you get this. This is the best punch that I have ever tasted. Whoever made this punch needs to give me the receipt and we can sell a million gallons of this stuff."

Theo had told the server ladies not to say how they had gotten the punch, but they all knew that Theo had worked a miracle. After the wedding, the server ladies spread the news that Theo was special and that he and his group should be listened to at any event to which they were invited. This was the first sign that Theo preformed after he started his ministry and crowds began to follow Theo whenever he appeared in public

A few days later Peter got word that his mother was extremely sick and that he needed to come home at once. Peter told Theo about his mother's illness and Theo went with Peter to his mother's house in Tuscumbia, Alabama. Tuscumbia is the birthplace of Helen Keller and the scene of the book <u>The Miracle Worker</u>. Peter's mother had an exceedingly high fever and could not get out of bed. While she was no spring chicken, Peter's mother was in her mid-fifties and still had plenty of life left in her. She was known for her generosity and was always open to having guest stay in her home.

Peter was naturally worried about his mother. Theo went with Peter into his mother's room. Without being asked, Theo took Peter's mothers' hand and gently lifted her to her feet. She knew immediately that her fever was gone and that she felt like her old self. Peter's mother proceeded to her kitchen and whipped up a meal for her son, Theo and the group of friends that had showed up at her house because Theo was known to be there.

Before long, a crowd gathered. Many of the people who came to visit were also sick with all kinds of ailments. Theo patiently placed his hands on each one that needed his attention. Each time Theo healed someone another sick person presented him or herself so that Peter's mother's house remained crowded until after midnight. Finally, Peter insisted that everyone should go home and get some sleep. Peter told everyone to come back in the morning and Theo would still be there.

As soon as everyone left Theo got into his old pickup truck that he had driven to Peter's mother's house and drove to a solitary place along the Natchez Trace close to where the Trace crosses Highway 72 in order to have time in prayer. Theo had never experienced the strain on his body and spirit that had just occurred while he was placing his hands on so many sick and tormented folks. In his spirit Theo knew he needed time alone with his Heavenly Father to recharge his spiritual batteries. Theo realized that there were many more people that needed his attention and Theo set his mind and spirit to be of help to as many people that came to him in need of his help. While medical science was a great boon to those that needed attention, even modern medicine could not bring about a complete healing to the soul that had to occur for someone to be truly complete.

At the crack of dawn Peter realized that Theo had left the building and Peter and the other followers had no clue where Theo had gone. They all wondered if the strain had been too much for Theo and they wondered if Theo's ministry had already come to an end. As they were talking among themselves suddenly Theo showed up and told his guys that it was time to move on to another town and to get ready for the next part of his mission to a lost and dying world. His followers did not know exactly what Theo meant but how could they refuse a man that had just physically healed a few hundred people and was able to turn lake water into the best punch they had ever tasted.

Chapter 18

Theo deals with a church that has Commercial rather than Spiritual interest and meets Nick O'Deamus.

Theo continued to train his group of followers and others that seemed to show up every time Theo poked his head out of his room. Theo proclaimed that those that were truly blessed were "poor in spirit." He explained that being poor in spirit meant that a person was totally dependent on God for everything that was essential to anyone's true self. Theo said, "Totally happy are those that are completely dependent on God because they will be included in God's kingdom."

Matthew asked if Theo would sit down with the 12 close associates that Theo had personally chosen and teach them about what a truly godly life would require. Theo promised he would give a comprehensive sermon as soon as he completed a pressing matter that was going to take him to Nashville and would probably cause some problems within the established church.

Theo, Peter, James and John traveled to Nashville on Saturday May 15, 2009, and found a place to stay near Hendersonville, Tennessee. The next morning the group got up and drove to the broadcasting studio of the Lakeview Spiritual Assembly at a mansion that once belonged to a rock-n-roll singer. There was a large group of people waiting to enter the studio that had a 2000 seat assembly hall in order to take part in the church services conducted by the Reverend Bobby Chandler.

As the group of friends and their teacher entered the narthex of the assembly hall they were overwhelmed by the sheer number of tables in which t-shirts, prayer clothes, audio tapes, books written by Rev. Chandler, and all sorts of merchandise were being offered to the people who attended the services.

Theo became angry with the spectacle and went into action. He overturned the tables on which the merchandise was being displayed. Theo then went to the cash register and threw the money and receipts into the air. Theo shouted, "This is supposed to be a house of prayer, but you have turned it into a den of commercial enterprises. You serve money rather than God!"

Reverend Chandler heard the noise caused by the overturning of the display tables and the shouts of Theo and those who had their businesses disrupted. Chandler and men that he called his "Armor Bearers," rushed into the area of the church where all this was going on and tried to stop Theo from his rampage, but Theo could not be stopped. Even the efforts of Chandler and his men could not stop Theo as he continued his rampage of turning over the tables and emptying the cash registers. Reverend Chandler had his "armor bearers" with him at all times because some of the men of his congregation had accused the Reverend of having affairs with their wives and Chandler thought that he needed protection. The armor bearers carried automatic weapons.

After what seemed to be 20 or 30 minutes of complete chaos Theo stopped and left the building along with Peter, James, and John. Several people in the crowd got all the commotion on their cell phone cameras and a lady who saw all the action called the news office of WSB Channel 2 and reported what had taken place. The TV station dispatched a reporter to the scene of the disruption of the sales activities.

The reporter arrived and began to interview some of the people who had witnessed the commotion. The news reporter, Ed O'Neil, had been a weekend reporter for WSB news for more than a decade but had never reported anything like the events that occurred that Sunday at the Lakeview Spiritual Assembly. O'Neil interviewed several people who had witnessed Theo turning the sales booths over.

O'Neil interviewed Connie Smith who was in charge of selling Reverend Chandler's video tapes. O'Neil asked," Connie, when the man who turned over your table came in what were you doing and what did you see?"

"I was at that table right over there. You know the Reverend wants us in place right when the doors open on Sunday morning because he does not want to miss any sales that he might get. Reverend Chandler thinks every dollar counts and Reverend needs his money to further his ministry. All of a sudden, I hear all kinds of commotion and tables and tapes and books are flying everywhere. I just backed up and got out of the way. That man had his face set, and you could tell he meant business. I never seen anyone like him. Not only did he look fierce, but he also had a look of absolute authority too. It was his look of authority that I can't get out of my mind. Not only that but I think he did the right thing, too." Connie Smith told the news reporter.

Ed O'Neil was taken aback by Connie Smith's account of the authority that Theo exhibited as he turned over the tables. "Can you explain what you mean by his look of authority?" O'Neil asked.

Connie Smith replied," I don't know how to explain what I felt any better than that. All I know was that man, I'd really like to know who he is, was doing the right thing and you could sense that he knew he was doing the right thing as soon as you could see his face and look in his eyes even if it was just for a second."

Ed O'Neil asked all those standing around if they had any idea of who the man that turned over the table might be. No one had any idea about his identity, but someone said that two of the men with him played in a band and he had seen them play backup at a record studio down on Music Row in Nashville. Based on surveillance cameras that Reverend Chandler had installed to keep an eye on the sales of his stuff, there was a picture of Theo as he was turning over the tables and warning the people about the violation of the house of prayer.

Ed O'Neil's report was broadcast on the Channel 2 eleven o'clock news that evening and it was seen by several church leaders including Dr. Jefferson who wondered in his mind who had the authority to prevent the sale of church related merchandise even if it was being produced by a pastor with whom Dr. Jefferson would not associate.

Another viewer who saw the news cast that evening was Zack Waters, and he immediately recognized his relative, Theo Mann. Even though it was late in the evening Zack made some calls and found out where Theo was staying. Zack then called his friend Nick O'Deamus. Nick O'Deamus was a pastor of a rather large church in Nashville. He had heard from family members in Alabama that there was a man who could heal people with just the touch of his hand. The family member identified the healer as Theo Mann and said that if Pastor O'Deamus ever got the opportunity to meet Theo Mann he should drop everything he was doing and meet this man who was obviously sent from God.

Pastor O'Deamus got in his car and drove to where Theo and his friends were staying and knocked on the door. Theo answered the door. Peter, James and John were asleep, but Theo was still awake, and he had been praying about the next steps that he needed to take to fulfill God's plan of ministry.

Pastor O'Deamus started the conversation, "Thank you for seeing me so late at night, but I know that you are a teacher sent from God because no one can do the healing and other signs that you do, unless God is with him."

Theo looked into Nick O'Deamus' face and soul and said, "Unless anyone is reborn, he or she cannot see the kingdom of God."

Pastor O'Deamus aware that Theo could see deep into his mind said, "How can anyone be born again after they are of age? Can anyone enter a second time into his mother's womb and be born a second time?"

Theo loved Pastor O'Deamus as he loved all that came to him and were truly seeking to follow the ways of God. Theo said in a loving and caring way, "Unless a person is born of water and the Holy Spirit, he cannot enter the kingdom of God. I am not talking of a physical rebirth. Don't be stunned that I have said that 'You must be reborn.' There are many things in the physical sphere that occur and even scientist cannot explain how they get started. The same is true about spiritual matters, the workings of the Holy Spirit are mysterious to many but to those who choose to live in God's kingdom they undergo a spiritual awaking."

Nick O'Deamus said, "I do not understand."

Theo went on, "You are the Pastor of a large church and you have been educated at a prestigious seminary. I am speaking of what I know and what I have experienced but you do not understand. You seem not to want to understand these spiritual truths. If I tell you earthly things and you do not understand, how can I tell you about a man's spirit and his spiritual needs, so you get what I am saying? Think of it this way. I have come from the Heavenly Father as you have stated when we started this conversation. Believe in the Son of Man. Just as Moses had to lift up a burnished serpent in the wilderness to heal those that had experienced snake bite, I too will be lifted up in order to bring spiritual life to those who see me with spiritual eyes. Whoever believes in me will have eternal life. This is how the love of God will be expressed to all humanity."

The night was almost spent. Theo and his visitor talked of many other matters and the pastor found a profound respect for the young itinerate minister. Nick O'Deamus knew that Theo was sent from God and that he was sent because God so loved the world that he sent his son into the world so that mankind could be saved. Nick O'Deamus was convinced that by believing in Theo and his teachings that the world would be saved. Theo did not judge the world but loved people and wanted to being everyone into the kingdom of God.

They parted just before sunrise. Nick O'Deamus knew in his heart that it was not just a new day but also a new world.

Chapter 19

Theo Meets a Woman Drawing Water.

Theo and his group of followers decided to head back to the area around Burnsville and prepare for their next mission adventure. Additionally, some of the pastors in both Nashville and the area around Tishomingo County were actively looking for Theo in order to confront him about whether his signs were authentic and authorized by the church. Reverend Chandler was looking for Theo to compensate his church because he had lost revenue from Theo's disruption of Chandler's sales. Theo insisted that the group live in the ways of righteousness and heal any that suffered physically, emotionally and spiritually. On more than one occasion complete strangers would seek Theo out because they were possessed by evil spirits, whether the evil spirit took the form of drug abuse or just a mean streak in their spirit. Theo would cast out the evil and bring mercy to the victim even if the victim brought the evil on him or herself.

The men and women that followed Theo, including Mary Jane, could see and feel the grace and mercy that seemed to endlessly flow from Theo. Theo was patient, tireless, and invariably knew what was in the hearts and minds of those around him. Theo was always quick to encourage those who need encouragement, stern with those who need discipline, and loving to everyone.

Theo decided that the group should go to Mc-Minnville and set up their headquarters at the location that Jonnie Waters had occupied before she was arrested. The group traveled by caravan by way of the Natchez Trace Parkway. As they were traveling the old truck that Theo drove experienced mechanical problems and Theo pulled off the parkway at a scenic area that had a marker indicating that there was a natural clear water spring located at that pull off. Theo stopped the truck and some of the others pulled off with him to see why he was stopping.

After a brief discussion one of the men knew exactly what was wrong with Theo's truck and said he would go into a nearby town to get the necessary part. Theo decided to wait alone with his truck until the men he was with got back. They were also going to get some snacks and have a cookout at the scenic spot on the Natchez Trace.

After the other guys left, a Hispanic woman pulled into the scenic area and proceeded to get out of her car and walk quickly past Theo as he sat on a bench that was provided by the park service. She was carrying a 5-gallon water container and was headed towards the natural spring.

Theo spoke up, "Would you mind dipping me out some of that spring water?"

The lady was shocked that Theo was speaking to her. "Non comphrendo, Senior." She replied with a Spanish accent.

Theo spoke to her in Spanish and repeated his request. The lady was mildly impressed that Theo spoke to her in Spanish, so she continued again in Spanish to see if this guy sitting there was for real or was a pretender. "Why do you dare to talk to me, you are obviously not a Latino because you are not brown like me."

"If you knew the gift of God and who it was asking you for a drink you would ask me for a drink of spiritual water that would well up inside so you would never be thirsty again." Theo said in flawless Spanish and with a perfect accent.

"Sir, it looks like you don't have any means of drawing water from the spring. How do you think you could give me a drink and where do you get spiritual water?" The lady with the 5-gallon jug replied.

Theo replied, "Everyone who drinks of the water from this spring will be thirsty again, but anyone who drinks of the water that I provide will never be thirsty again. The water that I will give will become a spring of living water welling up to eternal life."

"Sir, give me this living water so that I will not be thirsty again and I will not have to come to this spring to draw water again." She spoke.

Theo then said to her, "Go call your husband to come here."

She answered," I am not married."

Theo replied, "You have said correctly that you are not married. The man that you are living with is not your husband, but you have been married five times before."

"I think I am talking to a Prophet." The ladies countenance went from someone who was indifferent to this man's requests to that of someone who had met a close friend who had her best interest in mind. She continued, "My people have been using this spring because it is the only source of clean water that we have access to. We are a poor group and must live by our wits. You on the other hand seem to be able to go anywhere you want and you are accepted.”

Theo still speaking flawless Spanish said, “God does not look at people as being from one race or another. God cares for all people equally. God is spirit and those who will come into his kingdom will come in spirit and truth.”

“Sir, I have heard that the savior of the world will come, and he will tell us all things, do you know when that will be?” She said in a very reverent tone.

“I who is speaking to you is he.” Theo said with the authority that someone who has the assurance of who he is and where he has come from.

Just then, John and the others returned with the part that was needed to get Theo’s truck running again. They were very surprised to hear Theo speaking fluent Spanish to the lady at the spring. They started to set up the grill for the cookout they talked about and asked Theo if he was starving. Theo replied, “I have other food that satisfies my hunger.”

The lady that Theo was talking to took off. She went to the place where her group was camping and said to the whole group, “I have met a man that was able to see into my soul and he told me everything that I have ever done. Could this be the savior of the world?” Before she knew what further to say they all got in their cars and drove over to the spring to see who had confronted their sister.

When they arrived at the spring on the Natchez Trace, they found Theo’s group having a cookout and they were invited to dinner. Theo spoke to the group from which the lady that he had talked to before had come, in Spanish much to the surprise of the group of disciples that were following Theo. Before long, the Spanish speaking group were at ease and were joining in with Theo's group even if most of the two groups spoke different languages. The fellowship between the two groups was sweet. The Spanish speaking group said, "We now have come to believe that Theo is the savior of the world, not because of what our sister has said but because we can tell for ourselves who he is."

Theo and his group stayed with their new Hispanic friends for two more days before they resumed their journey to where Jonnie had been baptizing.

One Sunday morning Theo got up and went to Sunday School at a local church in very rural Tennessee. The class that Theo visited was a group of older men most of whom had been attending the same class for decades because their wife's insisted that their husbands go to church with them.

Theo was greeted as he entered the building by an older woman who said her name was Aida and she was from Decatur, but she said it in a way that Aida rhymed with "Decada." Aida took Theo to a small classroom and told the man in charge that they had a visitor and that his name was Theo Mann, and he was from Mississippi. The leader, R.L. Williams, held out his left-hand for Theo to shake because his right hand was deformed and withered. He said to Theo, "Excuse my left-hand but it's what I got."

Theo took his hand into his and smiled while looking deep into R.L. Williams' face. Theo knew the hearts, minds and ways of men. Theo knew that R.L. had endured the hurt of other men's taunts and rebuffs from the time he went to elementary school. Looking around the small classroom he could see that the other men in the class held R.L. in contempt because of his physical deformity.

The lesson started with R.L. talking about how worried he was about the fact that a black man was President of the United States. He repeatedly said that he just didn't know if the country would survive what was going on in Washington DC. After a period of lamenting by each of the class members about the political landscape, R.L. asked about the class member's families and then asked if there were any specific prayer request.

Finally, R.L. said that the class had been studying the Bible story of the Hebrew's Exodus from Egypt. That week the passage told the story of how Moses had gotten into a fight with an Egyptian slave driver. When Moses saw the cruel treatment that the Egyptian was meeting out to the Hebrew slaves Moses killed the slave driver and had to get outta Dodge. No one had any comment about the Bible lesson and the lesson quickly devolved into a general discussion of whether the Tennessee legislature would make abortion illegal in Tennessee in the next legislative session. Each of the men seemed to believe that the Republican controlled House and Senate would vote along with other Southern states to outlaw abortion because the Bible made it a sin. Additionally, some of the men spoke up about stores being allowed to do business on Sundays. There was one man who wanted to discuss the immigration crisis on the border between the U. S. and Mexico. He believed that the Mexicans were going to take all the low-income jobs from white Americans.

As the class ended R.L. said he hoped Theo would join them again if he ever came back to Decatur on a Sunday. Theo looked around the room and said, "Is it lawful for someone to heal on Sunday?" There was no response, but Theo knew each man's thoughts. None of the men had a clue of what was about to happen.

Theo said to R.L., "Stretch out your right hand."

R.L. did as Theo commanded and miraculously R.L.'s right hand was no longer withered and deformed.

No one could have seen that miracle coming and each man gasped as the healing of R.L.'s hand began to register in each man's mind. Each man in that class had pitied R.L. and had made fun of him behind his back since they were in elementary school. It was now decades later and a complete stranger that none of them had ever seen before walks into their Sunday School class and preforms a genuine miracle. There were blank stares on each man's face. Finally, one of the men got up and went and found the preacher who followed the man back to the classroom.

"Who are you mister?" Pastor Frank Reynolds asked Theo.

"Who are you expecting to find?" was Theo's reply.

"We are a God-fearing group of believers here at the Decatur Church. We don't want strangers poking around in our business and I'm not sure you fit in with our congregation. Perhaps it would be better if you moved on from here and left us be. We get along just fine here and don't need anybody upsetting the apple cart. You get my drift young man?"

By then R.L. was just understanding the full impact of the healing of his right hand. He was able to pick up the water bottle that he had not been able to hold with his previously withered hand. He was able to feel the coolness of the water as he poured some of the water on the previously useless hand that had been the butt of many jokes from his old classmates. R.L. looked on in wonderment at Theo's face and saw nothing but grace and mercy coming from Theo into his life.

R.L. with all the respect and humbleness he could muster took Theo's right hand into his own completely functional right hand and said, "I thank God that I have meet you this morning. You are a blessing to me. I will sing your praises always and will never forget your kindness to me. The world is better today because of you!"

Theo looked around once more and knew that there were some in that room that would like to kill him because they hated him even if they did not know exactly why. Theo knew the hearts and minds of men and he knew that there was evil in the world that would cause people to hate the goodness of God.

Chapter 20

A Mountain Top Sermon.

Theo looked for a place to speak to his disciples and the large group of followers that accompanied him to the place that Jonnie had formerly used as her headquarters before she was arrested on trumped up charges. Matthew had asked for Theo to instruct the group concerning how a truly committed and godly life could be lived. Theo found a place on a ridge that had a natural bowl from which he could speak to his followers, and they could hear and understand his message. Theo sat down and began to teach.

"Extremely happy is the person who is totally dependent on God, because such a person will find himself in the presence of God.

"Extremely happy will be the person who is incredibly sad because of his sins and repents, because he will be forgiven.

"Extremely happy will be the person who will allow himself to follow God's commandments, because he will reap the benefits that God gives.

"Extremely happy is the person who desires to follow Godliness as if it were his only choice, because that person will take on the very nature of God.

"Extremely happy is the person who is as forgiving as God, because he will be forgiven with the same measure as he forgives.

"Extremely happy is the person whose motives are in tune with God's will in their life, because that person will see God's purpose fulfilled.

"Extremely happy will be the person who brings about peace when all around there is no peace, because that person will be acting as God's child.

"Extremely happy will be the person who is rejected and persecuted by the ungodly, because theirs is the kingdom of heaven.

"You will be insulted, persecuted, falsely accused, and people will say all kinds of evil against you because of your belief in me. Rejoice and be extremely glad when that happens because you will be greatly rewarded in heaven, because that is the way they treated and persecuted those who were godly before you.

"Always remember that you are a group of influencers that add a special seasoning of flavor and saltiness to the world. But be careful not to lose the special nature of your godly influence. If you lose your ability to be a godly influencer you will not be of any use to God's kingdom and you will lose your status as an influencer.

"Always remember that because you follow me that you have the light of the word in you because God has sent light into the world, and it came to shed light into a dark and sinful place. Do not hide the light that is in you. Do not let your light be extinguished but make your light visible to all who see you; like a light house guiding ships at sea to a safe harbor and thus showing the good works that are in you.

"It is the purpose of my ministry to fulfill the law given by God to mankind from the earliest of times. I have come not to abolish the true law of God but to make the true law of the love for man by God, known so that it will never be extinguished by the evil that is in the world. God has given His commandments and they shall be followed until God's purposes in everything in this world are carried out. If anyone sets aside the commandments of God or teaches his children to disregard God' commandments that person will be considered as the least in God's kingdom. On the other hand, whoever keeps God's commandments and teaches others of God's love, he will be called great in the kingdom of heaven. Let your desire to do what is right exceed those who claim that they are doing God's will. There are many who are just showing off and there are many who would put conditions on God's mercy. If you act like those you will certainly not pass through the pearly gates.

"You know that it is against the law to murder someone because you can go to jail and even worse. But you should go even further and do not let your anger get the best of you, because you will be subject to God's judgment. If you say to your brother or sister, you do not deserve to live because you are angry at them, or even call them a 'dumb ass' you will be in danger of the fire of hell.

"If you are seeking a relationship with the heavenly Father and realize that you have an unresolved problem between you and someone that you have a relationship with, go and resolve your enmity between you and your friend before you try to have a closer relationship with God. Reconcile with everyone and show forgiveness to all who offend you.

"Settle all disputes between you and your neighbors as quickly and as amicably as you can. Do it before someone takes you to court. Remember only the lawyers will make money from your disputes unless you work the problems out between you and your neighbor.

"Committing adultery is never the right thing to do. That is one of the ten commandments. But I am telling you that anyone who looks at another in such a way that in your mind you would seek to seduce that person you have already committed adultery and that is offensive to God.

"If you cannot help looking at someone without causing yourself to have lustful thoughts you would be better off to be blind than to go around chasing after sexual pleasures. Being blind would be better than ending up in hell because you cannot control your sexual appetites. The same is true of another part of you. If you cannot keep your hands off of a pretty girl cut your hand off or keep yourself away from those situations that cause those problems. It is better to become a hermit than to go to hell because you groped someone.

"The law allows men and women to get divorces. But be careful if you do, because you wind up committing adultery if you divorce just because someone you desire more comes along.

"Swearing that you will do something that is unlikely to be done is just like lying. Do not give the impression that you will do something that you know or even probably will not do. That is a fraudulent act, and it is not acceptable to God.

"You should not repay evil with evil. Even if

someone takes advantage of you do not try to get back at him. If someone wants to wrongfully sue you and even claims that you owe something that you do not owe do not fight back in such a way that you bring dishonor to God and yourself.

"Love even those you consider to be your enemies. Pray for your enemies and those who persecuted you so that you will be known as godly people. After all, your heavenly Father causes the sun to rise on both good and evil people and He causes the rain to fall on both good and evil people. How can you look into the hearts of the righteous and the unrighteous? If you only love those who love you, are you not doing exactly what the ungodly do? Be perfect even as your heavenly Father is perfect."

That last statement had many of Theo's followers confused. "How could anyone be perfect?" they asked themselves. Some of the inner twelve even scratched their heads. Also, many of the things that Theo was saying went against what they had been taught.

Theo offered the crowd a bathroom break and after a half hour he started to preach again. No one got up and left but they were not prepared for what Theo had to say next.

"Be careful of being someone who likes to enjoy the praise of those you seek to impress, because by doing that you will receive no reward from your heavenly Father.

"When you give your offering at church do not call attention to yourself by acting 'holier than thou,' and don't make a big deal out of it when you give to the homeless man on the corner. Just give the money without calling attention to yourself or the poor man you should be helping. If you make a spectacle of yourself, you have already gotten the reward you were looking for. Instead, don't let your left hand know what your right hand is doing and God who knows everything will reward you.

"You should pray all the time, but not like the hypocrite's do. Don't make long winded prayers in which you call attention to yourself. When you pray, pray in a quite secluded place because your heavenly Father who hears in secret will know that your prayers are sincere.

"When you pray say something like this.

"Dear loving heavenly Father, you are holy and separate from us, but you want to hear from us.

"Your will, will be done in all things whether here on earth or in the domain of heaven.

"You know our daily needs and we realize that you are the source of having those needs met.

"Please forgive me of my sin and sinfulness when I am willing to forgive anyone who steps on my toes either literally or figuratively.

"Please do not let me fall into a temptation that will overwhelm me.

"Evil is all around me, please deliver me from the evil and the evil one.

"By being a forgiving person, you are acting in a godly manner and by forgiving someone you should expect that God will act in the same way to you. On the other hand, if you don't forgive others don't expect your Heavenly Father to show you mercy.

"There are many health benefits to periodic fasting. There is also prayerful abstinence. When you fast don't call attention to yourself by acting as if you are doing it in a painful manner. Fast in secret and pray in secret so that it is only between God and you.

"We all like to be rewarded for what we do, but don't go around fishing for money and earthly glory. Instead, lay-up treasures for yourself in heaven. Earthly rewards can be easily taken from you. You know that there are always some out there who will take your stuff by theft or deceit. Heavenly treasures, such as doing good to others that are in need or speaking up for those in trouble will earn treasures in heaven and the most skilled thief would not dare go there to take your heavenly treasure.

"You have heard it said, 'what you see is what you get.' Be careful about what you set your eyes on. You can look at things that will poison your spirit. Guard what you see because your eyes are the entry way to your mind. If you continually look at porn or dwell on violence, you will become unable to see what is really beautiful and you will not appreciate the beauty that faithfulness and calmness will provide to you. Your relationships will take on a dark countenance. You will lose sight of what is really important, and you will suffer the loss of your soul. Don't get caught up in conspiracy theories, they will drive you nuts.

"Money is an exceedingly difficult master. Be careful not to become materialistic. Materialism will eat your lunch and become your god if you let it. If you want to be godly, serve God. The choice is yours, but it is axiomatic you can't serve both God and money they are mutually exclusive objects of adoration. If you love money you will wind up hating God, but if you love God, money is only a tool to be of service to others.

"Anxiety and worry are extremely dangerous emotions that have spiritual overtones. Think of anxiety this way. Consider nature. Birds don't worry about where their next meal will come from. Birds neither gather up food or build barns. Yet God takes care of all verities of birds. Who of you can add a moment more to your life span by worrying that you are about to die for lack of clothes or food or drink. God cares about you. Don't you think that God who knows the number of hairs on your head or even the lack thereof, Peter, also knows what you need and is willing to supply what you need. Consider the beautiful wildflowers. No one can dress as well as the wildflowers when they are in bloom, even if they are here today and gone tomorrow. Your Heavenly Father knows that clothing is a necessity, and He will supply your needs. Therefore, do not be anxious for material things. Unbelievers worry about all those things because they do not have the wherewithal to rely on God. Seek first the kingdom of God and all these things will be added to you.'

"Therefore, do not be anxious about tomorrow. Tomorrow is just another day, and it will be there tomorrow. Take care of the problems you have today because that is enough for today.

As more time had passed since the group had had its first bathroom break, Theo told the people to get up and walk around for a few minutes and that he would resume the lesson he was giving to them after a short break. After the second session the people seemed more anxious to hear what Theo was going to say next. After a few minutes everyone got back into their place and we're waiting when Theo got back to the place from where he had been speaking. He resumed his message.

"Do not presume that you are better than anyone because when you judge people, they tend to judge you right back with the same judgement by which you are judging them. If you are always looking for faults in someone else, you may be missing an even bigger fault that you have. If you are looking for faults, then you must resolve your own faults before you can even think about dealing with someone else's faults.

"Be careful with whom you associate. You don't want to give away your good qualities by associating with people who will drag you down. If you follow the wrong crowd, you may suffer guilt by association.

"We are to be people who are constantly and prayerfully asking for the grace of God, we are to seek to do God's will continually, and to find a place of service by knocking on heaven's door. If you ask for God's grace, he will surely give it because his grace is never ending. If you seek God's will, he will lead you in the right direction. If you continue to knock, God will always answer those who diligently want to have an intimate relationship with Him. Think of it this way, if your child asks you for something to eat, don't you go and get them a snack? You even try to give your children things that are healthy for them rather than junk food. Your heavenly Father is much more in tune to your needs than you are to your children's needs. Therefore, you should live and treat everyone exactly as you want to be treated.

"Be careful of the path that you follow when seeking God and His righteousness. There are many ways that seem easy to follow in order to become a child of God. Invariably the effortless ways lead to destruction. It is better to seek the difficult path that requires the utmost devotion that leads to God. Those who walk the difficult way, that true path, are few.

"I cannot warn you enough about those who will try to deceive you. Those false preachers will make you believe that they have a corner on the truth but in reality, they are just trying to get over on you. Look at their works. Are they all about money? Does the preacher really care about his congregation, or does he play favorites with the in crowd? If he does such things, you will know he is not with me. If that preacher is not with me then he is against me and he will not see eternal life.

"Not everyone who professes to be a man of God, I'm not only talking about false preachers, but I'm also talking about any man who says that he is doing God's will, shall entered the Kingdom of heaven. When the final trumpet sounds and time shall be no more, there will be some who will say Lord, Lord, didn't we preach in your name, and we even used your name in doing many services for those in our congregations. But I will have to say to them I do not know you, depart from me because what you have done is evil.

"If you are hearing these words and you take them to heart, and do as I am teaching, you will be like a person who has a house built on a firm foundation. When trials and temptations come you can rely on the teachings that I have given you and even when the trials seem to be desperate you will be able

to endure until the end. On the other hand, if you ig-
nore my teachings, you will be just like a person who
builds his house in a floodplain. When the floods
come, that is when trouble is at your door, you will
not be able to keep it all together and you will be destroyed."

Theo stood up and everyone knew that he was
finished speaking, but the people who heard him
speak were astonished at his teachings because he
taught them as if he had complete authority to say
what he said and he was not like other teachers.

Within a day Theo told his disciples that they
needed to go back to the area around Pickwick Dam
in North Mississippi. When they packed up and
started to leave a great crowd of people also packed
their tents and followed Theo and his band of men.

Chapter 21

Theo tells stories that have practical meanings.

It was really amazing that so many people were excited to see and hear Theo preach and teach about the kingdom of God. Theo got a permit to hold an outdoor event at the Pickwick State Park in Tennessee and with little or no advance notice the whole park was filled by people wanting to see and touch Theo. Theo healed many that day and he also dealt with evil spirits that tormented the souls of many.

Theo told stories to the crowd. One of the stories went like this:

"A farmer decided to grow a field of corn in the old way of farming. He plowed his field and scattered the corn kernels in the field. As he scattered the corn kernels, some of the kernels fell on the road that ran by the field, some of the kernels fell on rocky ground, some of the kernels fell among the briars, but some of the kernels fell on the plowed ground that was good for growing a good crop of corn. After the farmer scattered the kernels, the birds quickly got to the corn that fell on the road and took the kernels away. The kernels that fell on the rocky ground sprang up quickly but because they had no depth of soil the new plants burned up in the hot sun and withered away. As for the kernels that were scattered among the briars and weeds the corn grew but it was choaked out by the other plants. The kernels that fell on the good ground, however, they were well cared for and brought forth an incredibly good crop. Those that are able to hear this story with spiritual ears let him understand and do likewise."

Theo preached on and told other stories to the crowd. When he was finished speaking, some of his disciples came to Theo and asked, "What is the meaning of the story about the farmer and his corn field?"

Theo responded, "I am telling stories that have spiritual implications in such a way that only those with spiritual ears will get the meaning. Spiritual ears will come from God. But for your sakes here is the meaning to this story about the farmer and his corn crop. The kernels of corn represent the word of God that is available to be heard by anyone who is called to become believers. The kernels that fall on the street represent people who hear the word of God but are hardened of heart and cannot accept the word. The birds represent Satan. They quickly come and take away any hope of acceptance of the word. The kernels that fall on rocky ground represent people who hear the word, but who have no depth of spirit and they soon burn out and give up their faith when trouble knocks at their door. The kernels that fall among the briars represent those who are influenced by money and materialism. Their chance of following God and becoming a part of God's kingdom is stifled by material rather than spiritual desires. The kernels that fall on the plowed ground represent people who want and desire a spiritual relationship with the heavenly Father. Those people will produce a good crop of good works that will benefit God and mankind."

After Theo had another session of healing and casting out unclean spirits, he asked his guys to get a boat for them to go across the lake so that Theo could rest. As soon as Theo got in the boat, he laid down and fell fast asleep. As they were traveling across the lake a ferocious storm came up out of the west as happens in that area of the country. The winds were so strong that the guys were afraid that the boat would capsize. They feared for their lives. Theo was still asleep, and they had to shake him to awaken him. They cried out, "Don't you see we are all going to drown, do something!"

Theo calmly got to his feet even though the boat was pitching back and forth and said to the men and to the storm itself, "Calm down, be at peace." Immediately the wind became a slight breeze and the water in the lake became as smooth as glass. Theo's disciples looked at each other in astonishment because they had never seen anything like that. They wondered at how even the natural forces of a storm would obey the words of Theo. There was also an unexplained calmness in their own spirits that surpassed their ability to understand.

Chapter 22

Multiple evil spirits overpower Trey Crump.

After crossing Pickwick Lake, the group of men arrived on the north shore near Savannah, Tennessee. They docked the pontoon boat that they rented from the state park authority at a public facility and started up the steep bank of the lake. Suddenly, Trey Crump appeared out of nowhere. He ran up to Theo, who had briefly been his roommate at Ole Miss, and screamed, "Theo, son of God, what do you have to do with us?"

Trey had fallen on tough times. While he was still attending Ole Miss, he had started smoking methamphetamine and had such a habit that his grandfather, DJ Crump had disinherited him and even Buddy Crump would not allow him in his house. Trey had become homeless. Trey wore nothing but tattered shorts and went around barefoot most of the time. When Trey come into town, he usually caused trouble. He yelled and screamed at everyone and even the police could not control him. Because he was DJ Crump's grandson no one tried to arrest him or even suggest that he stay out of town. The good citizens of Savannah were content to let Trey Crump live in the woods near the public boat ramp where Theo and his men docked that afternoon.

Theo looked intently into Trey's face and said, "You said 'us,' how many are there?"

"We are a large group that have taken up residence here, we know that you are the savior of the world and have come from God. Do not destroy us but allow us to leave this man and enter into that heard of cows that are grazing near to here."

Theo then commanded with a loud voice, "You evil spirits that have taken up residence in Trey Crump come out of him and never enter him again. In the name of the Holy Father come out." The evil spirits rushed out of Trey and entered the cattle that were grazing near the lake. The cattle then rushed down the slope of the lake bank into the lake and they all drowned.

Trey convulsed violently and fell to the ground at Theo's feet, and then became completely still as if he were dead. Theo stooped down and took Trey's arm and lifted him up to his feet. Trey put his arms around Theo's neck and pulled him close. The disciples did not know if they needed to separate Trey from Theo but soon realized that Trey was only showing his gratitude. Trey was in his right mind for the first time in two years. Theo told his guys to find Trey some clothes and they sat and talked for an hour. The farmer whose cattle the drug addiction spirits had entered quickly got in his pickup and went for the sheriff.

Within an hour the sheriff, two deputies, the farmer and a group of concerned citizens arrived at the public boat dock and were amazed to find Trey Crump in his right mind, fully dressed, and calmly talking to Theo as if they had been long time friends. The sheriff looked over the situation and told Theo and his group that they needed to get back on their boat and go back to where they had come from. The farmer demanded that he receive compensation for the cattle that he lost. Trey told Theo that he wanted to go with him and become one of Theo's disciples.

Theo loved Trey but said, "You need to go back to your family and tell them what God has done for you and to lead them to repent of the evil that they do. That would be the best thing for you and me too."

Trey stayed in Savannah and he and Theo agreed that they would keep in touch and remain friends.

When Theo and his group got back across the lake a big crowd of people were waiting to see Theo and to see what he would do next. A local pastor, Jerry West pushed his way through the crowd and grabbed Theo and pulled him aside. Jerry West said, "My little daughter is so sick, and the doctors don't know what to do for her. I believe that you and only you can save her." Theo agreed that he would go to pastor West's house and deal with the young girl.

As the group of people were going to the parking lot to get in their cars and trucks, a woman intentionally came up from behind Theo and bumped into him. Theo felt a measure of grace leave his spirit and stopped the procession. "Who has bumped into me?" Theo asked.

Phillip spoke up and said, "There is a whole bunch of people around you all the time. It was probably an innocent mistake for someone to get that close to you."

Theo still insisted that whoever had bumped into him come forward. Reluctantly, an older woman came forward and she said, "It was me. I have had feminine problems since I was a teenager. The doctors are confounded by the medical condition that I have. To resolve this issue, I have tried one thing and then another for many years and have spent all of my money trying to get well. I have gone to every specialist to be treated but nothing has worked to eliminate the problem. I have seen you in action and believe that it is within your power to heal me and just now when I bumped into you on purpose, I felt the power of your spirit within me and healing me like nothing I have ever felt before. I know that I am whole again and that I am blessed by you."

While the woman was still speaking pastor West's associate pastor drove up and said to pastor West that his little girl had died. Jerry West almost fainted and had to be held up by one of Theo's disciples. Theo said, "The little girl will be OK. Let's get on over there, now."

When Theo and the group got to pastor West's home, Mrs. West was crying and some of the church members were trying to comfort her. Theo asked that only he, the girl's parents and the disciples that were with him, go into the room where the little girl was laying. Some of the church members scoffed at Theo and said that he could do nothing for the girl. Theo went into the room and closed the door. Theo took the little girl by the hand and lifted her from the bed. She was alive. Theo told her mother to get her something to eat. When the child walked out of the room you could have heard a pin drop. Two of the ladies from the church fainted and had to be caught before they hit the floor. Theo told the church people to keep what they had just seen to themselves. However, it was impossible for what had happened to not be spread around the whole town and all of north Mississippi.

Theo and the group of followers traveled back to Tuscumbia, Alabama where Peter was from and visited with Peter's mother. While they were there an enormously large crowd of folks came to the place where Theo was because there were many people in need of Theo's gift of healing and his ability to deal with the evil that infects some. Theo, although he could become physically tired and even worn out acted with complete understanding and patience with everyone who sought his help. Theo's fame had spread all around north Alabama, middle Tennessee and north Mississippi. Many people came to Peter's mother's house to get close to Theo and have their needs met.

The press of the crowd was so great that a man who was paralyzed needed the help of several big men to push through the crowd. There were so many people in front of Peter's mother's house that the paralyzed man's friends carried him on a blanket around to the back yard and broke open the back door to get the man before Theo.

Interestingly, there was also a delegation of Clergymen from several denominations in the crowd at Peter's mother's house as well. These members of the clergy were tasked with keeping an eye on Theo and reporting back to the leaders in their respective denominations.

When the paralyzed man was laid in front of Theo, Theo said, "Your sins are forgiven now get up and walk."

The paralyzed man began to get up, but Theo said, "Just a minute Brother. Keep still for a minute or two more please. There are some here who doubt my authority to forgive sins."

Theo knew the minds of the Clergymen that were there to judge him, and Theo wanted to call their doubting minds out. The Clergymen said nothing out loud, but it was not hard to read the expressions on their faces. They collectively showed disgust with what Theo was doing and saying. The Clergymen without exception thought in their mind, "Who does this man think he is? Only God can forgive sins. Is this human being putting himself on the same level with God? Someone needs to teach this faker a lesson."

Theo continued, "Is it better for you Clergymen, if I say to this man who needs my help, 'you are healed' or to say, 'your sins are forgiven.' The results as far as this paralyzed man is concerned, are the same. In any event he is no longer paralyzed and can walk out of here, but as for you, members of the clergy, you need to go back to your churches and report by what authority that I am doing these acts of healing. You are asking, 'is he doing everything on his own or is he doing these acts on behalf of God?'"

No one moved. All eyes were on Theo. It was perfectly quiet. Theo then said, "Brother get up and take your blanket with you. We need all the space we have here." With that being said, the formerly paralyzed men got up, shouted his thanks to God and left.

Those that were there were amazed. They had never seen anything like what had just happened. The people other than the Clergymen praised God and sang hymns of praise to the glory of God. The Clergymen all got together after the meeting broke up and decided that Theo had to go. They started to discuss a plot to have Theo arrested for practicing medicine without a license, some even discussed taking out a contract on Theo's life.

Chapter 23

Theo returns to Burnsville and gets a chilly reception.

After finishing his work in Tuscumbia, Alabama, Theo told his group that he needed to go back to Burnsville in order to see about his mother. Mary Jane often wondered what would become of Theo if the rumors about how he was received by the church leaders and local politicians were true. Despite Theo's healing of Trey Crump, Trey's family still had scores to settle with the Mann family. DJ Crump still maintained his office and criminal syndicate hub at the Tishomingo Bingo Parlor. The criminal element could be seen coming and going seeking an audience with DJ.

Theo arrived at home and spent a quite few days with his mother and siblings. On Sunday the family all went to the Glennville Baptist church and the pastor recognized the fact that Theo and family were all in attendance. Theo was asked to give the closing prayer following the service and a few people came up to him because of health problems that could not be solved by the local doctors. Theo obliged the few that asked but there were many more that would not have anything to do with Theo because of their unbelief. Theo said to his mother, "Even someone filled without measure by the Holy Spirit is unable to reach those who will not believe."

Some of the people who knew Theo as a child even questioned whether Theo was sincerely doing the great works that had been reported about him.

Some said it was all fake news. Even though the reports were made by those that had been healed or who had been rescued from addiction to drugs and alcohol by Theo.

After that Sunday in Burnsville, Theo returned to McMinnville to be with his group of close associates. The next order of business was to prepare Theo's disciples for the evangelism crusade that was going to send missionaries to towns in the greater Middle Tennessee area.

Theo met with his 12 disciples and imparted the ability to heal the sick and to remove the evil spirits that were inflicting such pain and misery especially among young adults in that region of the country. Drug abuse was at high levels. The use of methamphetamines was at epidemic proportions in the smaller towns in the region.

Theo instructed the 12 that they should take nothing with them because he did not want anyone to get the impression that his men were going to take up residence where they went. When they got to a small community, they were to find a room in someone's home and stay there while they performed the services that they were sent to perform.

If the disciple was accepted by the community all was well and good but if the disciple was rejected and not allowed to do the good works they were sent to do, they should leave and not even let dust settle on their shoes.

So, the twelve set out and went from McMinnville to Winchester, Lascassas, Belbuckle, Wartrace, Shelbyville, Lynchburg, LaVern, and Antioch. The group spoke at local churches and in the town squares on Saturdays. They placed their hands on the sick and cured drug users of their addictions. The twelve were generally accepted, except they were despised by the drug dealers and the DJ Crump crime syndicate that saw a sharp decrease in sales.

After a few weeks the twelve returned to McMinnville and gave their reports to Theo. When Theo heard of all the good work that had been done in the towns in which his men had success, he thanked God and he and his guys basked in the glow of what they had accomplished.

Large groups of people from all around the region came to hear Theo and to be cured of what ailed them. One time a throng of about 5000 men plus their wives and children followed Theo and his men to an especially isolated area near Carthage, Tennessee. The service that Theo was conducting went past the time when the local stores and fast-food stands had closed.

Theo had compassion for the people and told his men that they needed to find a way to feed the crowd. Juddy spoke up and said, "What? All the supermarkets are closed, and we couldn't feed this many if we loaded up a whole truck load of food. It would take 12,000 big macs and fries to make a dent in feeding this many folks, and what will they drink?"

Theo looked around and asked, "What resources do we have as far as food is concerned?"

Phillip found a lad who had packed a lunch and brought him to Theo.

"Theo this is Andre. Andre is a smart fellow,

and he packed a lunch for himself. He has two stacks of saltine crackers and a tin of sardines, but what is that when we have so many mouths to feed?" Phillip said with a little sarcasm in his voice.

Theo then said to the amazement of his guys, "Have everybody find a good place to sit, arrange the people into groups of fifty and bring me the sardines and saltines."

Theo took the job of feeding the people that were there that day into his loving hands. He then took the saltines and sardines into his hands, lifted his eyes to heaven and thanked the Heavenly Father for what was available to feed the multitude. Theo then told the disciples to start distributing the crackers and sardines to the people as Theo handed it to them.

Surprisingly, no one grumbled about the picnic or the food that they were receiving. Also, as surprising as the fact that everyone enjoyed sardines and saltines, was the fact that everyone ate their fill and there were even leftovers. The disciples took up twelve baskets full of sardines and crackers that were uneaten. Without a doubt the people were impressed. They somehow began to believe that Theo could do anything that he chose to do.

Some of the people thought that Theo would make a good governor and began to pull the disciples aside to try to convince them to approach Theo with that suggestion. Theo knew what they were up to and sent the people away. Theo told his guys to get a boat at the Cordell Hull Lake marina and go to Carthage and he would meet them there.

Theo had had a busy day and needed to be alone. He withdrew into a secluded hill side and prayed. Theo often spent many hours in prayer. He needed the close communion with his Heavenly Father to keep his earthly life balanced and progressing in the direction that was necessary to fulfill God's ultimate plan.

At midnight Theo decided to catch up with his guys. He walked down the hillside and got to the lake and kept on walking right across the top of the lake.

The twelve rented a pontoon boat and started out at a slow pace toward Carthage. They were all really drowsy, so they assigned James to keep a lookout to make sure they did not run aground or hit something. James was looking for logs and stuff in the water when he spotted Theo walking toward the boat right across the top of the lake. James rubbed his eyes. He stood up and looked more carefully. It was Theo all right, but how was he just walking on the water. James shook his brother John and they both saw what James saw but had a hard time believing it. Finally, the whole group saw it and Peter called out to Theo, "I want to come to you."

"Come on." Theo called back.

Peter climbed out of the boat and began to also walk across the top of the water. He was good as long as he kept his eyes on Theo. Peter took about a dozen steps but then realized that he had never walked on water before. Peter froze, looked down at the water and sank. Peter also realized that he was not able to swim back to the boat because he was fully clothed, and his shoes and pants were weighing him down. When Peter thought he would drown he felt the hand of Theo on his shoulder. Theo didn't say a word but lifted Peter up and carried him to the boat all the while keeping both him and Peter on top of the water.

Theo put Peter in the boat and climbed in too. Within a blink of an eye the boat and its passengers were at the public dock in Carthage and everyone, but Theo, was wanting pancakes. The guys had evidently forgotten to pack anything to eat. Theo looked at them and wondered if they had learned even a little form the feeding of the five thousand that had occurred just hours before.

Chapter 24

Transfiguration.

The group of disciples and Theo sat down at a table at the public boat dock near Carthage, Tennessee and Theo asked the group, "You guys have talked to the larger group of folks that have come to be ministered to in our crusades. You have heard what they have had to say about me and who that they say that I am. Who do the people think that I am and what are they saying about me?"

The group took a few minutes to come up with a response to Theo's question but they each knew that the question that Theo posed was rather profound. It seemed that they all spoke at once. There was no real consensus among the average person that attended Theo's rallies. They all wanted to receive a healing or relief from the torment of the evil that surrounded them. People agreed that Theo was special. Some said that he was like the ancient prophets. Some said that he was a wizard. Some said that he was Jonnie raised from the dead or even Elijah coming back from heaven.

Then Theo asked, "Who do you say that I am?"

As usual it was Peter who jumped in first. "You are the savior of the world sent by God."

Theo looked at each man intently and could tell that each of them understood the implications of what Peter had just announced. Theo then said, "Keep this to yourselves until after the events that will soon occur make it clear why Peter's statement is the correct one. You all know that there are many people that are seeking to destroy me. In fact, those that want to kill me will succeed in getting people aroused against me. I will submit to a cruel death at the insistence of so-called religious men, and they will be aided by evil men who are in the religious leader's pockets."

Theo said this to prepare his men for the type of death that Theo would allow himself to endure. Theo's guys did not understand what Theo was talking about because the knowledge of the true purpose of Theo's earthly mission had not been revealed to them and they did not understand the depth of love that Theo had for all mankind. The 12 disciples only knew that each one had an expectation that Theo's earthly mission would eventually lead to an earthly reward for each of Theo's inner circle. They were unprepared for what was going to happen and their part in the worldwide mission of God.

A few days later when the group was back in Tishomingo County, Theo asked Peter, James, and John to take a hike with him. Theo always wanted to climb Woodall Mountain which is the highest point in Tishomingo County and all of Mississippi. It was a beautiful autumn day. The leaves had started to turn to their fall colors. Maples bright red, oaks golden, dogwood's bright yellow, and the pine trees were starting to shed some but not all of their needles. The four men were enjoying the cooler weather but as they approached the summit on Woodall Mountain Theo's three guys started to get drowsy and asked Theo if he would not mind if they took a little rest on the mountain top. Before long Peter, James and John were snoring.

When Peter woke up sometime later, he saw Theo speaking to two other men. Theo and each man were dressed in dazzling and bedazzled white clothes. Eventually, John and James cleared the cobwebs from their brains and recognized that Theo's company was composed of Moses and Elijah. How they knew it was those two men is a mystery but then as usual Peter not knowing what else to do blurted out to Theo, "It's good that you invited us along with you to this mountain top. We can build a shelter here for you and your guest and we can stay up here for as long as you want." Peter said that because he was afraid and didn't know what was going to happen and that was just his personally to speak first and ask questions later.

While Peter was still speaking a low cloud came drifting over the mountain top and it covered everything including the ability to see Theo and his guests. A powerful voice emanated from the cloud like rolling thunder. The words that Theo's guys heard were, "This is my son, whom I have chosen, listen to him and follow his instructions."

As soon as the last syllable of the voice from the cloud was heard Theo was standing alone with his three guys in the clothes that Theo had on when he first got there. Peter, James and John were dumbfounded and could only stand in awe of what had just happened. They did not move one muscle until Theo said, "We need to get back to the rest of the guys."

When they all started down the path that had led them to the top of Woodall Mountain, Theo said, "I know that you want to share what you have just seen and heard with the others. Keep it under your hats until you see me glorified." What Theo meant by him being glorified was also a mystery to Peter, James and John at the time but later they came to understand what Theo meant. Besides they had just heard a voice from a cloud say that they were to do exactly what Theo told them to do. Each of them in their minds said that they were going to do what Theo said to do for as long as they lived.

Meanwhile back in Burnsville, the other disciples of Theo had encountered a man who brought his teenaged son to them because he had a condition that perplexed the neurosurgeons and other doctors all around Corinth and even as far away as Boonville and Tupelo. The boy whose name was Charles was being treated for epilepsy and was prescribed with Diazepam in both tablets and in nasal spray form to relieve Charles of his frequent focal seizures. Charles' father George and his mother Gail were worried about Charles because the medicines that he took often did not prevent Charles from having a seizure.

The other disciples tried their best to bring Charles' seizures under control, but they were unsuccessful. Some of the neurosurgeons and many of the local pastors and the delegation of Clergymen who were constantly following Theo and his guys wherever they went in order to catch any one of them doing something for which they could criticize them, scoffed at Theo's disciples. The Clergymen especially wanted to catch Theo in some act or saying something for which they could point out as being against the law or even against church tradition.

When Theo, James, John and Peter arrived at the place where all the commotion was going on, Charles' father, George came running up to Theo and said, "Teacher, I beg you to do something for my boy. He is possessed. The evil that is in him causes him to have violent seizures. The seizures cause him to foam at the mouth and it throws him to the floor. I once had to pull him out of the river because it threw him in and almost drowned him. I asked your disciples to cure him, but they couldn't help him."

Theo was anguished by what he saw. The Clergymen gloating, the neurosurgeons waiting to catch Theo practicing medicine and the local pastors standing around doing nothing, was just too much. Theo said," You all are such a group of unfortunate people who would rather criticize me and my guys who are here trying to help the sick and possessed. How long shall I be with you, and you do not lift a finger to relive the burdens of the lost. Why do I put up with you."

Theo turned to George and asked, "Do you believe that I can heal your son?'

George replied, "I believe, help my unbelief."

Theo said, "Bring the boy to me."

When the father was nearing Theo with Charles, Charles had a violent seizure. The neurosurgeon's backed away and got out of sight so that they would not have any responsibility if something happened to the boy. The Clergymen turned their backs and ran, and the local pastors decided it was time to form a committee and also left. Theo grabbed Charles and immediately he was as still as if he were dead. Then he came back to himself and was completely healed. Everyone who stayed to see what had happened was amazed.

After all the events of that day Theo and his men sat together at the house of Mary Jane in Burnsville. One of the disciples that had tried unsuccessfully to cure Charles of the seizures asked Theo, "Why were we unable to help Charlie?"

Theo looked around at each of his men and said, "The evil that was in Charles was especially strong and only with fervent prayer can evil such as that be cast out."

Theo then again told the twelve about what was going to happen to him in the not-too-distant future. He told them of how the son of man would be delivered into the hands of those such as the Clergymen and the others that were following them around and that he would be killed. The disciples did not understand what Theo was talking about because it was hidden from them. They were also afraid to ask.

The next day Theo and the guys were off to Pickwick Lake. When they got there somehow a group was already forming. A man came up to Theo and said, "I will follow you to the ends of the earth."

Theo replied, "Birds have nests and foxes have dens but me and my people have nowhere to lay our heads."

Another man came running to Theo and said, "I want to be in your group, but my father is old and will die one of these days and I need to stay with him until he dies."

Theo said, "Let the dead bury themselves. If you want to be in my group, proclaim the kingdom of God."

Then another came to Theo and said, "I have a family and they need me now but when I can safely say goodbye to my responsibilities, I will follow you."

Theo's response was, "No one sets a course and then deviates form it if they are really committed to it. Anyone who looks back after commitment is not fit for the kingdom of God."

Chapter 25

Theo sends out 72 to the villages of Middle Tennessee.

After Theo and his men had spent some time in northeast Mississippi, they returned to the Nashville megaplex, and Theo appointed 72 followers to go into the towns of Middle Tennessee to prepare for his planned Middle Tennessee crusade. Theo instructed his associated to go into the towns in pairs of two. He said, "When you go into a town, if you are accepted in the town, find a citizen of that town that will let you crash with them for a day and a night. Take nothing with you but announce who you are and that you represent the Theo Mann evangelical team, and you will be available to do the same signs as Theo Mann.

"If they accept you well and good. Heal the sick and confront evil. Eat what is provided and tell all the people who will listen that 'The kingdom of God has come near.'

"If you are not accepted in any town, leave as quickly as possible and that town will be dealt with later, but woe be to that town."

The 72 did as Theo had instructed and returned with joy in their hearts because the people in the towns were cooperative and accepted the invitations of the team.

Theo was also full of joy when he announced that he was going to hold a crusade in Centennial

Park in Nashville starting on Wednesday September 8 and ending on Friday September10, 2010. The planned crusade would co-inside with the Jewish celebration of Rosh Hashana also known as the Jewish New year. The focus of the crusade was going to be "Repent for the Kingdom of God is at Hand." Theo would be available to heal the sick and minister to and feed the hungry, to clothe the naked, to preach good news to the outcast, visit the hospitalized and those in jail and encourage the poor. Everything was made ready. Permits were obtained. Tents were set up as first aid stations. Country music stars would provide songs and entertain the large crowds that were expected. Even the local TV stations had exclusive reports about the upcoming event.

The day of the crusade arrived, and a very large crowd gathered near the replica of the Parthenon in Centennial Park close to the baseball fields used by the local high schools. As Theo stepped up to the microphone one of the Clergymen that always were close at hand yelled a question to Theo. "Theo, what must I do to inherit eternal life?' he asked.

"You are a student of religious law, what does it say?' Theo answered the clergyman's question with a question.

The clergyman being self-righteous yelled back, "Love God with all your heart and with all your soul and with all your strength. And love your neighbor as yourself."

"You know your Bible because that is exactly what the Bible says." Theo replied.

"But who is your neighbor?" The man yelled back because he thought that the question might give him the ability to engage Theo in debate even more.

Theo began a story. "A regular man from around these parts had business in Tullahoma and packed up his car and drove to a gas station over on Murfreesboro Road. When he stopped to get gas, a band of thieves high jacked his car and took the traveler with them. They drove to a side street. Beat the traveler senseless, took everything he had including his wallet and clothes. The bandits left the traveler half dead lying on the side of residential street in a pool of his own blood.

"After a while an Elder from a local church who lived in that neighborhood was out walking his dog and saw the half dead man lying there. The dog even went up to him and sniffed him over. The Elder was in a hurry to get home and moved on. Soon thereafter a Deacon who lived in the neighborhood came by and did not want to get involved because after all he didn't know the man lying there and the police might think he had something to do with it. He said to himself 'It ain't my problem.'

"Finally, a black man who worked on lawns around that mainly white area of town saw the injured man lying there and had compassion on him. The black man knew he could be accused of the crime that had obviously taken place, but he risked being arrested and standing trial for something he didn't do. The lawn care man picked up the stranger, put him in his truck and took him over to Vanderbilt Hospital. He carried the half dead man into the emergency room and did everything he could to help this complete stranger.

"The next day the black lawn care man went back to the hospital to check on the man that he had brought in and even visited the victim of the beating until he was well enough to get back on his feet. The black lawn care man even offered to give the man he had brought to the hospital, some money to help him out."

Theo them looked at the clergyman and asked, "Who do you say was the neighbor of the man who was robbed and left for dead?"

The clergyman who had been raised in a privileged white family then spoke more softly because he had a dislike for black people and he said, "I suppose you want me to say the one who showed compassion. But that is not how life really is. There is a burden with privilege. It is the white man's burden to keep this country from being overrun with non-white people. White people have an obligation to not be replaced."

"It is everyone's duty to show mercy. Without mercy we are all unforgiven and we will die. The road to eternal life must be full of mercy." Theo said as the clergyman faded into the audience.

The crusade continued to draw large crowds for the entire few days that Theo and his disciples dealt with the needs of the people who came to participate. One night a familiar face showed up and got close to Theo. Theo recognized Janet Gilmore from his days at Ole Miss and they started up a conversation about old times. Finally, Janet invited Theo and a few others to her apartment for dinner. Theo quickly accepted Janet's invitation.

Janet and her sister lived in the West End

section of Nashville, not too far from the location of the crusade. Janet's sister, Renee, lived together in the same complex on Blair Boulevard as their older brother Laz. When Theo arrived at Janet's apartment, he was introduced to her older sister Renee and her brother. Renee was busy in the kitchen and that allowed Theo to get acquainted with Laz who Theo immediately liked. When dinner was served, they all sat around a small glass top table the chairs were wrought iron with wicker backs and seats. Janet and Renee had a cat that they had named Coral because the cat had off white fur and a pink nose that Janet said reminded her of the color of the coral reef she had seen when she once traveled to St. Thomas.

Theo was very happy to be entertained by Janet and her sister and brother. It gave him a welcomed respite from crowds of people who constantly needed Theo's attention. The group of friends talked about their families and friends. Theo talked about the crusade and all the lost people that brought their sicknesses and worries to him. Theo spoke of the closeness of God and of God's love for mankind. He then pronounced that even in death that they would remain friends after the resurrection. They all loved the time they spent together that night and vowed that they would always remain friends and watch each other's backs. When Theo stood up to go back to the hotel room in which he was staying, Theo prayed for Janet and her family and for the people who would be saved at the Crusade.

The next day as the Crusade was winding down a man who could not hear or speak was brought up from the audience as Theo was teaching about the kingdom of God. The man that brought the hearing and speech impaired man to Theo announced that

the man he had brought to Theo had been speechless for his entire life and that the man's parents
were also speechless.

Theo motioned for the two men to come up to
the stage from which Theo was preaching. Theo then
compelled the evil spirit to come out of the man. The
previously deaf man began to speak. The people in
the audience were amazed, but the man who had
brought the man to the stage said, "Theo preforms
miracles because he is possessed by the Devil."

When the man said that Theo was controlled
by the Devil, there were some in the crowd that
seemed to agree with the somewhat ungrateful guy
who had the hutzpah to bring an obviously suffering
man to Theo and then try to turn the crowd against
Theo. Some in the audience even murmured for a
trick to be performed by Theo to prove that the man
was actually relieved of the evil that had plagued
him because they liked to be entertained rather than
equipped for the Kingdom of God. Unphased by the
attack, Theo knew what was in their minds and in
their hearts as well.

Theo started to preach.

"A kingdom divided against itself will be ruined
because it cannot stand against itself. If Satan is divided against himself how can his kingdom stand. I
say this because some of you are questioning whether I am driving out evil spirits on behalf of the Devil
or am driving out demons by the finger of God. If I
am acting on the authority of God, then the Kingdom
of God has come upon you.

"If the deaf man was prevented from hearing
and speaking because an evil spirit had embedded

itself in this man's spirit, then could or should the Devil who controls evil spirits drive his own evil out. No, that does not make a bit of sense, Evil does not drive out evil. It requires someone stronger than the Devil to overcome evil. You saw that the presence of evil has been overcome with in your own sight.

"If you are not for me then you are against me, and who ever does not accept that God is with me, has rejected God and in condemned.

"When an evil spirit is cast out from a man like the one standing here with me, it roams around in places seeking to find a soul that it can corrupt. If it cannot find a new place to inhabit it will return to the place that it had inhabited before. If the evil spirit finds that the former host is still receptive to evil, it will invite its friends and the state of the person who was freed of the evil will be worse than before. So, it is necessary to guard against evil always and not let the evil of the world take up a place in your life."

A lady in the audience shouted out, "Theo, you are an awesome man, your mother should be very proud of you."

Theo replied, "A truly happy person is someone who hears the word of God and obeys His commandments."

The crowds got larger and larger as the day progressed. As the sun was setting and the Crusade was ending. Theo said, "This is a wicked and perverse generation. You are always looking for a sign to convince you, but you will not receive any sign except that what you already know. History tells you that God has been at work from the beginning of time in the affairs of mankind. When it seemed that all was lost to the people of Israel, God intervened and instructed Jonah to preach repentance to the Ninevites. Even though Jonah was reluctant, the Ninevites repented, and Judea was spared from the wrath that would have destroyed them.

"You Clergymen are complicit with this wickedness. You claim to be experts in religion and the law. You place your own rules on people claiming that you speak with the authority of the church, but the church you claim to represent is not the church that God has built. God's church dwells in the life of each person that is called by God and accepts God's invitation to follow Him.

"You teachers of the church want riches for yourselves at the expense of the people. You teachers of the church are really politicians in disguise. You have a party line agenda. You claim to be speaking on behalf of God when you are really trying to keep political power.

"Why do you support a political party that allows weapon sellers to get away with murder. Hypocrites and thieves, you would allow a mad man to regain political power because he pays lip service to your political policy regarding a woman's right to control her own body when he could care less about anybody but himself. You claim to be prolife when only God can control life and the salvation of mankind. God creates life not the legislature of any particular government.

"Woe to you Clergymen because you have taken away the key to Godly wisdom and understanding. You yourselves have not repented and asked to hear with spiritual ears what God is saying to your own spirit. Shame on you."

When Theo had finished speaking, he left the building and went to dinner with his disciples. The Clergymen formed a committee with the intent of seeking ways to trap Theo into making mistakes in his teachings and ultimately bring an end to Theo's preaching and some even said an end to Theo.

The people wanted to continue to follow Theo wherever he went but because of the Clergymen's threats to his safety Theo and his disciples withdrew to a remote region of Mississippi. Theo trained his guys and prepared them for the continuation of his ministry even though his disciples did not realize that they would be on their own sooner rather than later.

Chapter 26

Theo continues to warn his followers.

After Theo and his guys set up camp on the Natchez Trace south of Tupelo in territory that had been once claimed by the Chickasaw Nation as their ancestral homeland, Theo taught as follows:

"Be very careful when you are confronted by right-wing extremist. Their beliefs are repugnant to God. When they say that white people are the only ones chosen by God and that the other races are trying to replace the white race in the United States do not be fooled by their reasoning. The evil in their hearts will be revealed. Some of those who claim to know, really do not know anything. Evil has been stirred up in their minds and they are infected with an evil intent. Their intent will be recognized by their actions, and many will be hurt.

"I tell you my friends, do not be afraid of those who may kill your body. Your spirit will live beyond a physical death. However, fear those who can cause your soul to dwell in hell. By convincing you that their message of hate is the correct way of living in this world, and you give up the love of God for all men without consideration of race you will lose your eternal soul to evil. Fear God who knows your heart and mind. God knows everything about you. He knows the number of hairs on your head and thus he knows your secret thoughts and desires. Don't be fooled by the promises of the worldly life, it will only deceive you into false beliefs and evil actions. You are precious to God and should seek His righteousness because that is the way to truth.

"You must acknowledge me before men. If you love me and acknowledge me, I, the Son of Man, will acknowledge you before God and His angels. If you disown me before men, I will disown you before God and His angels. If you speak against me, you can be forgiven but if you speak evil of the Holy Spirit, you will not be forgiven.

"Because of me you will be brought before the authorities to give account of your faith in me, do not be worried how to defend yourself or what you shall say. The Holy Spirit will give you what to say."

Someone in the crowd shouted at Theo, "Tell my brother to divide his inheritance with me."

Theo yelled back," Who made me a judge between you and your brother. Be careful, watch out regarding all kinds of greed.; life does not consist in an abundance of possessions."

He continued with a story.

"A farmer who owned a lot of land one year had a very good crop and made plenty of money. The farmer thought to himself, 'life is good, and I have more than enough money to live on for the rest of my life. I should tear down my old barns and build back bigger ones because I'm likely to have even a better crop next year. In the meantime, I'm going to sit back, eat, drink and enjoy my life.'

"But God said to him 'What a foolish approach to life. This very night your life will be taken from you, and then who will receive help from all that you have stored up for yourself.'

"This is how it will be with those who store up things for themselves and are not concerned with how he and his possessions will satisfy God's purposes."

Theo didn't even break for lunch but kept on instructing his disciples and those who were close enough to hear and see what was going on between Theo and his guys. "Make sure you are ready when the Lord calls on you to perform a service on his behalf."

Theo then gave an illustration of what he was talking about. "You never know when the owner of a business will call on his employees to do something so important that the future of the business will depend on the preparedness of the employees to keep the business going. Suppose the business owner is expecting an important customer to show up at the plant. The customer's order of the products of the company is so essential that if the company does not get the order from this most important customer the company would go bankrupt. When the customer arrives at the plant the CEO of the company will walk him through the factory. If the employees are sitting around playing cards the customer will look at the CEO, shake his head and find another supplier. The CEO will walk back into the factory and fire all the employees he saw playing cards. Those employees will have to go home and tell their children that they will get no dinner because their father or mother was fired because they were not vigilant and were caught goofing off.

"Always be ready because you do not know when the Son of Man will come again. Keep you lives prepared so that when God takes measure of you, you will not be found wanting."

Peter jumped up and asked, "Theo, are you speaking to us. Is your story for everyone or just for us guys."

Theo continued, "Who then is a faithful and prudent person that the CEO puts in charge of operations of the business? It is the good and prudent person whom the boss can put in charge because that person is trusted with the continuation of the operations so that all will receive the benefits that flow from a successful business. Even more so in God's Kingdom. The prudent and faithful follower of God will adhere to His commandments and will not say to himself, 'God is not here to watch over what we are doing. I can sluff off for a while and be rude to my fellow workers, get high and fool around.' Don't act so foolishly. God always knows what is going on. The backslider will receive his punishment and it could be severe.

"The worker who does not have experience in how to conduct God's work will not receive as much punishment as the one who knows what to do but goofs off anyway. The bottom line is that everyone needs to be watchful and live in such a way as brings honor and glory to God. The watchful person is the one who God will find faithful to the work God has given him until the end."

Then someone asked, "What must we do to do the works that God requires."

Theo immediately replied," You are looking for signs that will give you comfort in how you can act. That is exactly what trying to follow the law allowed you to get so far. But being legalistic does not work. Men are not able to abide by the law on a consistent basis. However, the works of God is this: Believe in the one that God has sent."

The crowd clamored, "Give us a sign, give us some miracle, feed us again just like Moses fed those in the wilderness, as it is written: He gave them bread from heaven to eat."

"I am telling you the truth if you will listen. Moses did not provide manna, but it was given by God who gives you the prefect bread. It is that bread that comes down from heaven; and it is that bread that gives everlasting life to the world." Theo replied.

"Mr. Mann," someone cried out, "Give us this bread, always."

Theo then declared, "I am the bread of life. Whoever comes to me will never be hungry, and whoever believes in me will never be thirsty. But you have seen me, and you still do not believe in me. All those who the Father has sent will come to me and I will not chase them away. I have come down from heaven, not to do my own will but the will of He who has sent me. The will of God is that I will not lose anyone who God has sent to believe in me, but to give them eternal life so that at the end I will raise them up to be with me."

Some Clergymen had infiltrated Theo's group of followers and they began to grumble under their breath, "Theo is claiming to be equal to God by saying that he came down from heaven and is the bread of life. Isn't this Joe and Mary Jane's kid, we know where he came from. Who does he think he is?"

Theo sensed what they were thinking and said," Stop grumbling, no one comes to me unless the Father sends them to me. I speak only of those things that I have been given to say by God. Truly I tell you that the ones who believe in me will have eternal life, a life full of Godliness and full of grace.

"I am the bread of life that has come down from heaven. Unless you eat of my flesh and drink of my blood you have no life in you. Whoever eats my flesh and drinks my blood will remain in me and I in them. You may not catch on to this now, but shortly you will understand. My flesh is real food, and my blood is real drink. Just as God the living Father has sent me, and I live because of the Father, so the one who feeds on me will live because of me. This (Theo pointed to himself) is the bread that has come down from heaven. Your ancestors ate manna, but they died, anyone who feeds on me will live forever."

After Theo said what he said many of his followers turned their backs on Theo and walked away. They said, "These are hard words to understand. Who can deal with what was just said?"

Theo knowing that there were many who did not have the capability of understanding spiritual matters about which he was speaking, said," Are you offended by what I said? What if I told you that I am going to ascend to where I was before I was born. The spirit gives life. The flesh counts for nothing. The words that I have spoken to you, they are full of the Spirit and life. This is why I told you from the beginning that no one can come to me unless the Father sends them to me."

Theo knew that Jud-I did not believe in him and that he would betray him if he got a chance to do it. That is why Theo said that God had to call people to him and if God did not call a person to Theo what Theo was saying would not register and would cause confusion in the minds of non-believers.

After the many followers turned their backs on Theo, he turned to his twelve guys and said, "You all are still with me, aren't you?"

Peter as usual was the first to speak up. "Where would we go. You have the words of eternal life. We have come to believe that you are the Holy One of God."

Theo then replied, "Have I not chosen each of you and yet one of you is a devil." he was speaking of Jud-I because even though he was one of the twelve, later he would go nark him out.

Chapter 27

Theo heals a man that had been crippled from birth.

Theo had been with his followers at a camp they had set up around Tupelo, Mississippi for several weeks. Theo had taught them many things to prepare them for what was eventually going to happen to Theo and how they would be responsible for carrying on the mission that God had sent Theo to start. The group needed a change of scenery, and they got up one morning and moved their whole group back up to Nashville where they had conducted the Middle Tennessee crusade a few months earlier. Theo made no announcement of the decision to change locations, but they all arrived near Franklin, Tennessee and found a suitable camp site to set up their headquarters.

A few of the disciples including John and Theo took a side trip to Nashville. They were walking down Music Row when they came across a man lying on the sidewalk begging for money. Theo engaged the man in conversation. When Theo started the conversation a group of gawkers started to gather around the obviously crippled man and Theo.

"Sir, how long have you been in this condition?" Theo asked.

"From my birth. I was born with a spinal cord problem that has prevented me from walking. I have received treatment and assistance from the government, but it just is not enough to pay my bills. I am brought to this spot everyday by some of my relatives and I lie here and beg." The man said in a hushed voice so that only Theo and John could hear the words he was saying.

Theo looked him in the eye and had compassion on him and said, "Do you want to be able to walk?"

"Yes, but medical science is not yet able to do anything for me." Was his reply.

Theo took him by his hand and lifted him to his feet. The man became overjoyed and leapt into the air as if he were Michael Jorden. He twirled around and kept that up for a few minutes. In the meantime, Theo disappeared into the crowd and was out of sight when the man stopped dancing.

Because Bellemead University was just up the street from where all this was going on, some Clergymen were alerted that Theo had made an appearance on Bellemead Avenue near the Sony music studio and they came running down to see what was going on. The Clergymen pulled the formerly crippled man aside and began to question him.

One of the Clergymen asked, "I have seen you lying on the street for many years. How is it that you are now able to dance around like I just have seen you doing?"

"Sir, I have been crippled from my birth. My parents live over on 16th street and can tell you of my birth defect. I was in the place that I am daily delivered to in order to beg. I was there when a man who I do not know came up to me and we talked for a moment. He asked me if I wanted to walk, and I said

'Yes.' He lifted me to my feet and now I can dance."

"Do you not know that Nashville has a city ordinance that prohibits people like you from begging on the streets? The man that helped you was also breaking the law. Do you know who he was? I need to call the Metro police and report you and the man that broke the law. You stay right here with me until I get this reported." The clergyman said emphatically.

By then what had happened to the previously crippled man had been reported to his parents and the came running over to see for themselves. They found their son sitting in the outer office of the dean of students at Bellemead University. The dean came out and confronted the crippled man's parents. "We think you and your son are con artists. We believe you all are just lazy people who don't want to work for a living, and you send this charlatan out to beg. We are reporting you to the police."

The mother of the formerly crippled man replied, "You don't know what you are talking about. Me and my husband work as night janitors right here on Music Row. We don't make a lot of money, but we do support ourselves and pay our taxes. Our son suffered a birth defect that has made him an invalid since birth. He is above 21 years you should talk to him and not us." She said that because she was afraid that the Dean of Student would make trouble for them as well.

By then the Metro police arrived at the Dean of Students office and tried to get to the bottom of what the police had been called for. The policeman asked a few questions. The dean wanted the formerly crippled man arrested and demanded that the police find the man who had started this whole affair by healing the formerly crippled man. The policeman realized that he had no reason to arrest anyone and told the Dean that he would get back to him later. The policeman got back in his patrol car and went back to his regular duties.

The formerly crippled man went back out on to Music Row and searched for Theo. Theo found the man he had healed, and the healed man hugged Theo thanked him over and over again. Theo said, "Do you believe in the Son of Man.?"

The healed man asked, "Who is he that I may worship him."

"He that is speaking to you is he." Theo replied.

The man fell on his knees and said, "I believe." and he worshiped Theo.

Later a clergyman found Theo walking the streets around Music Row and confronted Theo.

Theo said, "For judgment I have come into this world, so that the lame can walk and those who walk will be lame."

The Clergymen who had gathered around said, "What? Are we lame too."

"If you were physically lame, you would not be as spiritually lame as you are. But now that you claim to be spiritually fit, your guilt and your lame hearts are apparent." Theo told each of them.

The Clergymen were cast in the shade of their spiritual denial of the authority that Theo's presence demanded.

A group had gathered around, and Theo cried out, "Come to me all you who are tired, weak and weighed down by the cares of this world, and I will give you the rest you crave. Take my way of life as your own, learn my ways of living a life that is free of the sinful ways that so easily cause you to lose your ability to come to God and find his will for your life. My ways are gentle and humble in heart, and you will find rest for your souls. My burden is easy, and the way is right."

The disciples and Theo headed back to Franklin.

Chapter 28

Jonnie's men come to Theo to report back what they learned.

Theo and his guys were conducting an effort to bring healing to people who had been affected by drugs and alcohol in that part of Tennessee that was south and west of Nashville, including northeast Mississippi and northwest Alabama. Franklin, Tennessee was not far from Lynchburg the place where Jack Daniels whiskey is distilled and where the production of methamphetamine has become more prevalent. Many people were caught in the throes of addiction and drug abuse and Theo, and his guys were busy in casting out the evil and healing those that came in need of rescue from the evil of alcohol and drugs.

One day while the twelve guys and Theo were dealing with the people who came bring their children, wives and husbands to Theo for healing a delegation of Jonnie Waters disciples came to Theo. The disciples of Jonnie were sent by Jonnie while she was still alive in prison and before she was assassinated. Jonnie told her disciples to ask Theo if he was the Christ of God or should they look for someone else.

When Jonnie's disciples caught up with Theo they asked and Theo replied, "What have you seen when you see the work that I am doing? The sick are being healed, the deaf are getting the ability to hear, sight is being restored to the blind, people are being raised from the dead. Tell Jonnie what you have seen, and she will have her answer."

On the other hand, DJ Crump and his criminal enterprise were beginning to feel the loss of income that came from the loss of drug sales in his territories in Middle Tennessee and North Alabama and Mississippi. DJ called a meeting at the Tishomingo Bingo Parlor of his top lieutenants to plan their strategy to stop the efforts of Theo and his disciples even if it meant the murder of Theo.

DJ was seated at the head of a long table in the conference room of the bingo parlor. Seven other men sat around the table. Buddy Crump sat in a chair behind DJ and looked on with an expressionless face only nodding his head in agreement when DJ gave an order to the other men seated at the table. DJ started, "Why are you guys letting that Theo Mann guy disrupt what is our bread-and-butter business. There are several college campuses in your territories. We have supplied you with a good supply of products and these college kids are easy sales why are your dealers not moving the products that we provide?"

One of the lieutenants spoke up, "These damn Theo guys are causing us problems. They come into town and the next thing you know the regular customers don't want any more product from our dealers. We keep pushing product on the dealers, but they are losing sales. We have had to get tough on the dealers, but the cause is these damn Theo guys going around and causing the students and other customers to stop using our stuff."

Another lieutenant said," We need to do something to Theo and his guys. I sent a coupla hard hitters out after some of the guys that are interfering with our sales. They roughed up two of Theo's guys pretty hard, but it didn't stop them. The problem is that when we act, Theo is there to help them out and so far, we haven't been able to get to Theo himself. He is never where we think he is going to be. He is always one step ahead of us."

DJ looked over his group of lieutenants and knew that they were all experienced veterans of drug wars that kept others out of DJ's territories. They had taken care of business on many occasions before. They had busted skulls and lite fires when the circumstances required action and DJ knew that what they were saying was the truth regarding the sale of meth to college students and the regular customers in his territories. DJ told the guys seated around the table, "This is a job that me and Buddy will handle. Keep pushing sales in your territories and we will take care of Theo. We know where his mother lives."

After the sales meeting broke up DJ and Buddy huddled together in DJ's office.

"Buddy you are going to need to visit Mary Jane Mann to get at Theo. You may need to step on some toes or even bust some heads, but we need to stop Theo and we need to do it now before it gets out of hand. Take some men with you and don't come back until you get results." DJ ordered.

Buddy was more than happy to head over to Burnsville and pay a visit to Mary Jane Mann. He remembered how Joe Mann had shown him up way back before all the business with Theo got going. He also remembered how Theo had escaped the beating that he wanted to give him when they had tangled when Theo was just starting college and he remembered how his son Trey, was now alienated from his family because of the interference of Theo. Neither Buddy nor DJ gave any thought of how Theo had saved Trey from a life of drug addiction, they only thought about getting rid of Theo once and for all.

Buddy did as DJ said and took two men with him to the house where Mary Jane Mann lived near Burnsville. They drove up into the yard and blew the horn of the new Ram truck Buddy was driving, expecting anyone in the house to come out into the yard and see who was blowing the horn.

When the horn blew Stevie, the youngest child of Mary Jane and Joe Mann, came out the back door of the house and stood in the carport that also housed a myriad of boat motor parts neatly arranged so that they could be easily accessed. There were tools for working on the boat motors and a beat-up riding lawn mower sat near the carport. Stevie was wearing a pair of overalls without a shirt and a pair of running shoes that looked like they had seen better days. Stevie knew who Buddy Crump was and that he was not there to see Stevie. Stevie was 16 years old and going into his junior year at Tishomingo High School.

Buddy was the first to speak as he leaned out of the driver's side window of the Ram pickup, "Hay boy, your mama home. We need to see her."

"No, she ain't here right now, she went up to B & J's to get some ice. She should be back pretty soon." Stevie replied.

"You work on boat motors?" Buddy asked as he climbed down from the pickup and walked over to the carport. Buddy picked up a large wrench and held it close to Stevie's head.

Stevie flinched as Buddy Crump looked menacingly at Stevie. Buddy got so close to Stevie that Stevie could smell the tobacco residue on Buddy's breath. Buddy was about to let loose on Stevie's head when the sound of another car coming up the driveway distracted Buddy enough to let Stevie move away and escape the swing of the wrench from Buddy's hand.

Mary Jane saw what was about to happen and yelled towards the carport, "You leave my child alone. If you want to hurt someone you need to come after me, Buddy Crump."

"Well, well, well, look what we got here boys. Pretty little Mary Jane Sullivan. You know, you and me never got to go out when we was young and in our primes. But you know Mary Jane you are still as good looking as ever. You come over here I want to get a closer look at you." Buddy leered at Mary Jane.

Mary Jane, sensing the trouble that Buddy had brought with him, moved closer to Stevie and put her arm around her youngest son. Stevie to her surprise and to the surprise of everyone there said, "It's ok, Mom me and Buddy have some business that we were discussing when you drove up. Ain't that right Buddy?"

Buddy had no idea what Stevie was talking about or what he would say next, but he was willing to play along to see where it went.

Stevie continued, "Buddy has a new boat, and it has a minor problem with the motor that he has asked if I can fix."

Mary Jane looked at Stevie to see if she could determine if he was being honest or not after the words that Buddy said to her.

"Buddy was going to take me to see his boat. We will only be gone for about an hour." Stevie said in order to get Buddy away from the house so that they could talk for a few minutes without Mary Jane listening in.

Buddy picked up on the intent of Stevie to talk alone with him and confirmed that that was exactly why he had visited Mary Jane's house to begin with. Stevie before Mary Jane could protest climbed into Buddy's truck and they backed out of the driveway.

As soon as they got out of sight from Mary Jane's house Stevie said, "Buddy I know why you came over here. You want to get at Theo, don't you? Well guess what, I want to help you. That goody brother of mine is too good for his own self. He needs to be taken down a notch or two."

"So, you're not too happy with Theo either." Buddy replied.

"I want to help you get at Theo. He has made my life miserable trying to live up to his standards. All the teachers at high school talk about is how great Theo was. It makes me puke." Stevie said with disgust.

What Stevie did not know was that Buddy had two objectives. First, he wanted Theo dead and second, he wanted to get into Mary Jane's pants.

Buddy drove Stevie to the Tishomingo Bingo Parlor on Highway 72 and they went in looking to see DJ. They found the old gangster seated in his office with a young scantily clad woman sitting on his lap. As soon as Buddy and Stevie came in the office the young woman slowly got up and strolled to the door. DJ said nothing and Buddy seemed not even to notice. Stevie looked at the almost naked woman as she went into the adjoining room.

"Who is this kid that you have brought to see me." DJ growled as he straightened himself from the position he was in when the young woman left.

Buddy spoke, "This is Stevie Mann, Theo Mann's little brother and he wants to join up with us to get Theo under control. We can use a good man like Stevie, can't we Dad?" Buddy had a sinister smile on his deeply tanned face.

DJ cleared his throat and said, "We are always looking for men that can get things done."

"We need someone on the inside of Theo's family to let us keep track of where Theo might show up next and what he plans on doing. We think you may be the right man for the job, and we can make it worth it to you, if you decide to join us." Buddy said as he winked at DJ with his back turned to Stevie.

Stevie thought for a second or two and said, "Theo is my brother, and I don't want to hurt him physically, but I sure would like to bring him down a notch or two. Theo always has something going on and he rarely even has time to call, and we are always guessing when he might show up. When he does come home, he only stays for short periods, and he is gone again. Why are you guys interested in Theo, he certainly is not someone that has anything in common with you?"

Buddy spoke again, "Well Stevie, let's just say we want to know more about Theo so that we can anticipate how we can best avoid any conflict between Theo and our business interest."

Stevie was smart enough to understand that he may have gotten himself into a situation that he did not really want to be in because it could backfire on him.

"Stevie, we need your help, but if you don't feel comfortable helping us, we have other means of getting what we want. We know your mom can give us what we need, and Stevie believe you me Buddy would really like to visit with her in a very personal and close way. So, Stevie the choice is yours. You can give us what we want, or Buddy can go and fetch your mother to come down here and keep Buddy company in an intimate way." DJ said without taking his eyes off of Stevie's face.

"All I know about Theo is that he hangs out around McMinnville, Tennessee where he and his men live in some kind of camp and in caves. Theo has a way about him so that he seems to always know what people are thinking and he can respond even to your thoughts. Sometimes he even responds before your thought is completely formed in your mind. Theo is also not afraid of anything or anyone." Stevie said as he tried to get himself out of the situation that he was in.

"We are able to get into see someone, even if they don't want to see us or have us around them. All we need to know is when Theo is coming back to Burnsville so we can meet up with him for a little talk. Can you do that for us, Stevie?" Buddy asked.

Stevie agreed that he would keep in touch with Buddy Crump and let him know when Theo would come again to see their mother. Buddy had one of his men drive Stevie back to his home and Stevie departed.

When Stevie got home, Mary Jane wanted to know everything that went on between Stevie and Buddy. She insisted that she did not want Stevie to ever have any dealings with the Crump family and that he was to stay away from to Tishomingo Bingo Parlor as she believed it was an evil place inhabited by evil men.

Chapter 29

Theo confronts Buddy and DJ Crump.

Mary Jane had hardly gotten to the phone when it rang. It was Theo telling her that he would be home later that afternoon and that she should not tell anyone that he was coming. She started to tell Theo about the meeting that Stevie had with Buddy and DJ Crump when Theo said, "I am on my way to the bingo parlor, and when I leave there, I will come to see you and let you know what you and Stevie will need to do next."

Theo arrived at the Tishomingo Bingo Parlor right at noon on June 1, 2013. He was unannounced and walked past the guard that was always posted at the entrance when bingo was not being played in the building. Theo passed by the secretary sitting just outside of DJ Crump's office and entered the office. DJ and Buddy were unprepared for and surprised by Theo's visit as he entered the room. Theo did not sit down but he did speak in a voice that clearly expressed his authority and power over Buddy and DJ.

"We have been together before, and I have told you both what I know about you and your criminal enterprise. I know that I am cutting into your profits in the drug trafficking business, and I will continue to do that while my earthly ministry continues. You are powerless to stop what the Heavenly Father has determined to do. You will leave my mother and brothers and sisters alone. I will protect them with angels, and you will not be able to get near them.

"You are evil and perverse men, but you are also a part of God's creation. Satan has entered into your hearts, and you are controlled by evil and cause misery wherever you go and with whatever you touch. Unless you change your evil ways, repent and ask for forgiveness from God, you will be overcome by the evil one, and end up tormented with other evil men." All this was said as Theo walked around DJ's office and neither DJ nor Buddy was able to move or call for anyone to come and kill Theo.

Theo walked back to his pickup truck and headed for Burnsville to see Mary Jane and Stevie. He parked his truck near the carport and walked into the living room. Stevie was watching a movie on television and Mary Jane was busy in the kitchen. Theo sat down next to Stevie and put his arm around Stevie's neck. "You are my brother, and your life is important to me. There is good in you, and you should always be aware that evil can come close. You must be ready to rely on the Holy Spirit to lead you away from evil. I will not be able to come here anymore, and you will not be able to see me again so keep yourself in a way that seeks God first. If you seek the Kingdom of God first all the things that you will grow to love will be yours. You will pray and ask whatever you will as long as you keep me in your spirit and obey my words, and it will be given to you."

Theo stood up as Mary Jane came from the kitchen where she had prepared an early supper of fried catfish, hush puppies and coleslaw. Theo put his arms around his mother and held her close. They did not say anything, but Mary Jane knew that Theo's spirit was troubled. Theo was happy to share the meal with his family. He needed the time to prepare for the days ahead as he turned his face towards his final confrontation with the evil that was in the hearts and minds of men.

The family stayed together that night. On June 2, 2013, Theo left the home in which he had been raised and that had provided a haven form all the evil that did and would continue to be forced at Theo.

Theo headed east on Highway 72 and rode past the Tishomingo Bingo Parlor. It was a beautiful Thursday and Theo was happy to be alone and in prayer with his Heavenly Father. He knew that his time on earth was nearly completed. He prayed for the wisdom and strength that can only come from the closeness of God. The sight of the bingo parlor and the evil that he had felt there caused a slight case of nausea, but it soon passed as he felt the sun on his face and looked at the beauty of the creation that he had a hand in making. He saw that all was done well and believed that if men could find the beauty of creation as a path towards God that they could find common ground to deal with the problems of hatred and strife.

Theo turned off Highway 72 on to the Natchez Trace Parkway and headed north. He crossed over the Tennessee River and came close to Florence, Alabama. Theo exited the parkway and drove into Florence and found the campus of the University of North Alabama. The campus had a few students because it was the summer semester and the students that attended in the summer either had to make up for failed courses that they had taken during the fall and winter, or they had nothing better to do with their time and decided to go to college in the summer because it was easier. Theo looked around and saw a group of students sitting on the lawn near an ancient Magnolia tree that was in full bloom with fragrant white blossoms that smelled of citrus. The perfumed air was intoxicating, and the summer students were curious as Theo walked up to them and sat in the grass beside them.

One of the young men in the group of students said," I haven't seen you on campus before. Are you lost? Can we help you with anything?"

Theo immediately loved this group of students and said, "How are things going in the summer semester? What a beautiful day the Lord has made, we should rejoice and be glad."

The group just stared at Theo as if he was some nut case and neither of them responded to anything Theo said. Theo thought to himself, "have I been out of touch with college life for so long that I can't communicate with these young people?" Then he realized that the students that he was talking to may not realize that the world and everything in it comes from God. So, he decided to take a different approach in finding a means of meaningful communication. Actually, by the time Theo was thinking of a way to engage these summer school students a larger group started to gather. Someone in the crowd recognized Theo from the Middle Tennessee Crusade because Theo had healed someone he knew. Word spread quickly that Theo was a maker of miracles. A carnival atmosphere quickly developed, and a clergyman stepped up to say under his breath, "This man deals with students that are here because they could not pass during the regular school year."

Theo then raised his voice and told a story:

"Who of you thinks that graduation from college and getting a degree is so important that you are willing to spend your summer taking or even retaking a course that you need to graduate?

"Once there was a student that wanted to become a high school geography teacher and she had taken all the courses that she needed to take to get her teaching certification. The day for her graduation was soon approaching and she had applied for teaching positions with several school districts.

"She received a message from the Dean of Students that she needed to come to his office because there was a matter of great importance that had to be cleared up before she would be allowed to graduate.

"When she got to the Dean's office, she was ushered in, and the Dean presented her with a handful of campus parking tickets that the Dean said that she had accrued while she was a student at her college. She looked carefully at the tickets and realized that she had in fact been ticketed for illegally parking while she attended classes.

"Our graduating student looked the Dean in the eye and told him that she was sure that she had paid the tickets when she incurred them. The Dean said that the school records did not show that she had paid the tickets but if she could give him proof that the tickets were in fact paid all would be well and she could graduate and receive her teaching certification.

"She ran out of the Dean's office and went to her apartment and searched for lost proof that she had paid. She had started to pack up all of her stuff and could not remember exactly where she had put her important papers. She searched for the lost receipts and after opening several boxes she found her receipts for the payment of the parking tickets she had incurred.

"She quickly went back to the Dean's office and presented the receipts to the Dean. The Dean rejoiced with her that she could graduate on time. She called her friends together to celebrate with her that she had found the receipts that were lost and now she could graduate.

"I tell you that in the same way there will be more rejoicing in heaven over the one sinner who repents than over the self-righteous that do not feel the need to repent and go about criticizing those who need to go to summer school.

"Or suppose a woman had ten antique gold pieces and somehow one of them goes missing. Would she not search under her bed, behind the fridge and even in the washing machine until she found the piece of gold that she was going to show on "Antiques Road Show." When she finally finds it, she calls her friends over to her house and tells them that the gold that was lost has now been found, rejoice with me.

"In the same way, I tell you there is rejoicing in the presence of angels of God over one sinner who repents."

The stories only resonated with some of the students and with none of the Clergymen that had now gathered around Theo on the North Alabama campus. Theo decided that he should double down and tell another story because even though not all of the crowd was paying attention a significant number were listening and trying to understand what Theo meant by the term, "repent."

"A prosperous farmer had two sons. The youngest was full of himself and could not see himself living on a farm for the rest of his life. The older son was a steady Eddie and almost always could be found doing the chores that he had been assigned by the old man.

"The wild child said to himself, 'I have had enough of this,' and he told his father he was leaving and that he needed his share of the inheritance so he could be on his way.

"Reluctantly the father pulled out his check book and wrote the younger son a fat check that represented his share of the inheritance, gave it the young man, and off he went.

"The sophomoric son went straight to Los Vegas and started to party-hearty. He met fast women who didn't mind spending his money as fast as he would let them. He bet on the ponies and on football and by the time that the Super Bowl rolled around he found himself more than a little short on his room rent. The bookies were looking for him and he heard that they did not take no for an answer.

"The young man had to get out of town quickly, but he had spent it all and did not know what to do. Even his cell phone was broken, and he had not paid the bill in two months. He was in bad shape and was miserable. He hitchhiked over to Southern California and found work picking tomatoes with the Mexican laborers.

"Our young man hardly had anything to eat. He was dirty all the time and could not speak any Spanish even to ask for a handout. Finally, he came to his senses and said to himself, 'Even the hired workers that work for my daddy are better off than I am here in these fields picking tomatoes. My back hurts. My clothes are falling apart, and I have a headache. I will go home and say to my father, I have sinned against heaven and you. I am no longer worthy to be called your son, but I will become one of your hired hands if you will take me.' The young man started the long journey home.

"Our guy got a ride to about 3 miles from his father's house and began the final distance on foot. While he was still a long way off his father who was always expecting his younger sons return spied him and ran down the road until he got to him. The young man said just as he had rehearsed, 'Father, I have sinned against heaven and you, I am no longer worthy of being your son, let me be one of your hired hands.'

"The father threw his arms around the boy's neck and kissed him. He told his foreman to bring a new set of clothes and shoes. The father took a ring off his finger and put it on his son's finger. He told the foreman, 'Call all of our neighbors. We are going to have a bar-b-que to rank right up there with the best we have ever had. My son who was dead to us is alive.

"The older son heard all the commotion when he returned from his everyday duties and told the foreman to tell the father that he needed to talk to his father in private. When the father got to the older son, the son said, 'Father, WTF? Why are you having a party for that no-good son of yours. He is rotten, he has spent your money on loose women and pissed it away on bets on football games. I have been here day after day doing as you have asked, and you have never given me a party.'

"The father replied, 'My son you are always with me and everything I have is yours. But we must celebrate this brother of yours was dead to us but now he is alive. He has repented and asked for forgiveness. We must celebrate because he has returned to us and is alive, he was lost but now he is found.'"

Theo finished talking and many of the summer semester students stood around and wanted to ask questions. Theo stood there with the students and answered all the questions they cared to ask. Many of the students believed in him. Some repented and asked for baptism. Still many more were undecided, and some totally rejected Theo's message.

Chapter 30

The Clergymen meet to discuss what to do about Theo.

Theo went back to the area around McMinnville and retreated with his disciples to prepare them for his final days with them before he returned to his Heavenly Father. While he was meeting, he continued to heal people brought to him and to cast out the evil that had taken up residence in the spirits of mainly young folks plagued by drug use.

Because another form of evil took hold of the group of Clergymen that believed that Theo and his teachings were impacting the organized religion that they represented, they had a meeting in Nashville to discuss what steps they needed to take to bring Theo's ministry to an end. Meeting together were representatives from a wide verity of denominations. The group included representatives from hierarchical denominations, independent church groups, groups that used television as their method of ministry, and others who took issue with the crowds that were following Theo and were believing in his teachings. The evil that plagued these men and women was the belief that their churches were money making operations that could control not just the minds of those that claimed membership in their denominations but also the financial contributions to their church. Often the money collected by the church supported lavish lifestyles of the Clergymen who were the leaders of the church organizations.

Theo had made a point of telling his followers that no one could serve two masters. He said that "You cannot serve God and money." The churches represented by the Clergymen meeting in Nashville in the late winter of 2014, had given in to a compromise with the forces of evil that allowed them to accumulate great wealth while ignoring the poverty of the people that they continually ask to support their churches.

The meeting of Clergymen was Chaired by Dr. Jefferson and took place at the downtown Cambria Hotel that advertises that it is just minutes away from the honky-tonk music scene in downtown Nashville. Reverend Chandler attended along with two of his "armor bearers" and large group of church leaders from Middle Tennessee, North Alabama, and Northeast Mississippi.

Dr. Jefferson started by making a statement:

"In the name of all that is holy, the teachings and ministry of Theo Mann are a dangerous threat to the stability of our churches and threatens the collection of the financial resources we need to keep our churches functioning. I have gone out to Theo's crusades, and he preaches that men and woman have a freedom to accept the will of God. That is a most dangerous proposition. How are common people to know the will of God unless we, the church tells them what to believe. It is as if Theo wants everyone to believe that God gives them a choice to accept his commands and live a life of freedom from established church doctrines. The next thing you know Theo would allow women to make up their own minds about such things as abortion or when life is created, or even worse to allow them to preach in our churches.

"It is obvious that Theo's teachings are at odds with keeping order in this chaotic world. We offer our members security from the need to seek God's will and taking the time to follow his commandments. We, the church set up rules of behavior and belief that our members can follow and that brings about stability in the world.

"I have heard that Theo has refused to turn rocks into bread because he says that mankind should not live by bread alone. Most people are too weak to trust God for their ability to eat. The church gives its members direction to work hard, give to the church and they will have plenty. The world needs these values not some reliance on a God that cannot be seen.

"Theo refuses to perform miracles that would prove that he is the Christ, leaving people wondering if he is for real. Theo says that God should not be tempted because he has identified with people who must live by faith and not base their belief in the supernatural. We are keepers of the supernatural because we let people know that they too can be millionaires if they faithfully give to the church.

"The world order derives its power from the church. When Theo rejected the temptation of world power, that left a vacuum that religious leaders had to fill. We have taken the power that Theo and his sort has always rejected. People know what we stand for, and it is not freedom of choice but stability and the security of order.

"We must not let Theo and his ideas of freedom continue. Theo's gotta go."

Almost with one accord the group of Clergymen jumped to their feet and gave Dr. Jefferson a loud round of applause. The men and women were aroused and overwhelmingly approved of everything Dr. Jefferson had said. None of them had actually thought of how to parse their feeling about the threat that Theo's ministry posed to their churches. However, when they heard Dr. Jefferson's speech, they all agreed that the threat of Theo's message of freedom and the discipline that was required in following the true commands that God had given, threatened their churches. They as a group felt that they had good reason to do as Dr. Jefferson suggested and get rid of Theo Mann.

The group of Clergymen then did what they were very accustomed to do. They separated into committees to hold discussion of how to formulate a plan of action to bring Theo down. There was a committee that was to study the finances of the Theo Mann organization. There was a committee to study the teachings that Theo had given his followers and there was a committee to find out how to keep track of where at any moment Theo could be found. There was even a committee that studied a means of infiltrating Theo disciples and causing desertion in the ranks. The last committee appointed by the group was tasked with determining a way to cause the permanent elimination of Theo Mann. The groups split up and the committees were to report at a meeting that would take place on March 21, 2014.

On the first day of Spring 2014 the meeting of the Clergymen re-convened. Dr. Jefferson called the meeting to order and asked the committee chairs to give reports of any progress they had made on the recommendations of each specific topic their respective committee was tasked with. The committee on the study of Theo's finances reported that they were unable to determine that Theo actually had any known financial resources to support Theo's crusades or ministry outreach. However, they also reported that their committee was given a check in the amount of $10,000 from the Tishomingo Bingo Parlor to support their continued study of Theo's finances.

The reports from each of the committees were very similar to the extent that each committee had received a $10,000 grant from the Tishomingo Bingo Parlor to assist them in the study and elimination of the Theo Mann organization. That is except the Committee to permanently eliminate Theo himself and they received $20,000 from the bingo parlor.

The elimination committee reported that they had been contacted by Buddy Crump and informed that his organization was prepared to carry out any and all plans that the committee came up with to get rid of Theo Mann. Buddy offered to give the committee and the Clergymen group all the intelligence needed to put Theo away including any and all means to cause the elimination of Theo with extreme prejudice.

Dr. Jefferson thanked each of the committees for their fine work and clear and concise reports. He said that the Clergymen Group, LLC had been formed by a lawyer that was sympathetic to the Clergymen and who contributed to the group by offering his services for free. The lawyer was also a preacher and he said that he could represent any of the churches represented by the group. Dr. Jefferson also said that he had opened a bank account for the LLC and asked that each committee turnover the money that they had received to him so that the money could be deposited into the LLC's new account. Slowly the committees agreed to deposit the funds into the LLC's account.

Dr. Jefferson asked that the committee chair for the elimination committee meet privately with him when the meeting adjourned. After the group meeting broke up Dr. Jefferson met with Pastor Bobby Chandler the chairman of the committee to permanently eliminate Theo Mann. Jefferson looked Chandler over and noted that Chandler was the only group member that had brought two bodyguards with him to the meetings. Jefferson was somewhat impressed that Chandler's bodyguards carried automatic assault rifles with them to all the meetings. Jefferson asked, "Bobby how do you justify having men armed with AK-47 rifles with you at all times? Can you tell me where I can also get men with guns to escort me around. You never know when you are going to need someone to protect you from others carrying guns."

Chandler replied, "These guys are my armor barres, and you only need to ask, and I can set you up with any amount of firepower that you want."

"We can discuss that later. What I really wanted to talk about is how we can bring an end to Theo. Do you have any ideas about the solution to the Theo problem?" Jefferson posed the question to Chandler.

"After Theo came to my church and place of business and overturned the sales tables I decided that I needed to get back at that guy. I would have shot him down like a dog if there weren't so many people around. My armor bearers have orders to shoot to kill if they ever get the chance to get him in their sights."

Dr. Jefferson thought for a moment and rejected Chandler's method of eliminating Theo's threat to the religious order that had been established in that part of the country. Finally, Dr. Jefferson said, "Now Bobby we need to be much more subtle than that. What we need is to come up with a plan that turns the everyday people against Theo so that it looks like it is the actions of the mob that does Theo in. We need a plan to disgrace Theo Mann to his own followers so that they do the dirty work for us. We need to get some public statement form one of his close followers that Theo engages in morally corrupt practices. I was able to get rid of Jonnie by telling the local authorities that she engaged in child abuse. We need something that will make people think twice about Theo's message and his words of acceptance. We need a smear campaign that will get regular people with guns excited enough to lynch Theo."

"I got it. We need an influencer to say some shit against Theo and I think I know just the right person for the job. It may take a little cash to persuade my associate to do the job, but he can get it done just like you said." Bobby Chandler who now wanted to be referred to as Bishop Chandler assured Dr. Jefferson.

"Who do you have in mind, Bobby?" Dr. Jefferson asked.

"Plausible denial is what you need. You don't need to know her name right now but when she comes out and says what I get her to say you will know where its coming from." Bishop Chandler replied.

"Just get it done and don't let it get back to me." Dr. Jefferson snorted.

Chapter 31

Laz gets sick and dies.

Janet Gilmore sent a message to Theo while he was in the wilderness around McMinnville informing Theo that his friend Laz had gotten sick, and the doctors did not have a specific treatment for him. Laz was a 35-year-old man who was in fairly good health. So, it came as a surprise to Janet and her sister Renee, that their brother was sick enough that they should worry about him. Theo told his disciples that Laz, who they all knew, was sick. Thomas said, "Let's all go up to Nashville and we can visit and lay our hands on Laz and get him well."

Theo reminded his guys that there was now a contract out on his life and that it would be risky for all of them to travel together. Theo said, "Laz can wait on us for now, besides he has fallen asleep."

Thomas said, "It's good that he can get some rest. I always feel better if I can sleep off an illness."

Theo in a whisper said, "Laz is dead. But for your sakes we will stay here for another two days before we travel."

You could have heard a pin drop. They all knew that Theo loved Laz and his sisters and that he had the power to heal Laz of any illness that Laz may have had. They were all mystified as to why Theo would not rush up to Nashville to be with Laz and his sisters in their time of impending crisis.

Theo then said to his close friends, "Expect the worst when I go up to Nashville. There is a plot to make us look like the worst kind of criminals. They will have me arrested. There will be a mob that will grab me, beat me, curse me, spit in my face, and kill me. If you go with me, I cannot guarantee your safety. But for your sake I must go and suffer these cruelties so that the will of our Heavenly Father may be completed."

Thomas said, "If you are going to suffer and die, I am going with you." They all were encouraged by Thomas' declaration and embraced each other and vowed to see the matters through to the end.

The next day they drove to the West End of Nashville and called Renee on her cell phone to meet Theo near the funeral home where they had taken Laz to be prepared for burial. When Renee saw Theo, she ran up to him and said that if Theo had been there a day or two before, he could have saved Laz and the whole family from the sadness that they were all feeling at that moment.

Theo said, "Laz will live again."

Renee said, "I know that we will see Laz in heaven but it's not the same as having him here with us now."

As Theo and Renee were speaking Janet arrived at the funeral home with a large group of family and friends. The whole group of them were crying and carrying on because Laz was loved by everybody. Janet put her arms around Theo's neck and would not stop kissing Theo. Finally, Theo was moved to tears and told Janet to get a hold of herself. Theo said, "Take me to where Laz's body is."

Janet said, "We are not allowed. Laz had a sickness that the doctors say is highly contagious. They are afraid to handle his body. They have sealed his body in a hazmat suit and will not let any near his body. The infectious disease doctors from the CDC are on their way here to examine the body and then safely dispose of it."

Theo, without a word, went into the embalming room followed by a group of Janet's family. Theo stood just outside of the room where Laz's body was stored. Theo lifted up his head and prayed, "Father I am praying for the sake of these that are here. I know that you have given me the power to bring our brother up from the dead. I pray so that those who are here will believe that you have sent me and that you are able to do all things through your only son."

When he finished praying Theo shouted with a loud voice, "Laz, come out of there."

Everyone was stunned. Nobody said a word. All eyes were fixed on Theo and Theo's eyes were set on Janet and Renee. Slowly, the door to the embalming room began to open. Laz dressed in a bright orange hazmat suit came walking out as if he had never been sick a day in his life. Laz walked up to Theo and Theo hugged him and said, "Get him out of that gear. We shall all dine at Laz's house tonight."

Some of the Clergymen saw what had happened and quickly reported it to Dr. Jefferson and their committee chairmen. That night Dr. Jefferson called a special meeting of Clergymen Group, LLC at the Southern Baptist Sunday School Board offices in downtown Nashville. They were of different opinions about the report that was given to them about how Theo had raised Laz from the dead. Some said that it was fake news, and it could not be believed. Some reported that even the Clergymen who had seen what had transpired believed in Theo.

That evening on the 11 o'clock news on WSB-TV, reporter Ed O'Neil had a late breaking news report. O'Neil who had reported before about Theo Mann going on a rampage at a large church in Hendersonville was excited to report of a miraculous raising of Laz Gilmore at a funeral home in Nashville. An on the scene report stated that a man had entered the embalming room of the funeral home and shouted for the presumed dead man to get up and come to the door. Witnesses said that the dead man's family and friends saw all that had happened and that it was a genuine miracle. No one ventured how the minister Theo Mann could have performed the raising of the dead but that it had happened just as reporter O'Neil said.

The report went on to say that there were some skeptics in the crowd that had gathered in the aftermath of the miracle and said that the whole event was staged to get publicity for Theo Mann. No one could say how the events were to benefit Theo other than to say they just didn't believe that he could bring someone back from the dead. O'Neil was trying to get a statement from Theo and Laz Gilmore but was unable to get an interview with either of the men involved.

Dr. Jefferson said, "Now more than ever we need to be done with Theo Mann and that Laz friend of his. We all know that what happened in the West End today was a staged event. Its purpose was to make all of us look bad. Bishop Chandler and his associates are working on a plan to make Theo and his friends including that faker Laz hated by every good church member around here. I for one have confidence that Bishop Chandler can get the job done. We are going to get him and it's not going to be pretty."

When the meeting broke up Chandler and Jefferson got in Jefferson's car and went to Chandler's penthouse condo to unwind and discuss their next moves. They got off the elevator on the 36th floor. A glass wall across the room from the elevator overlooked the Cumberland River that was lite up by the barge traffic using the river to deliver building supplies to the growing Nashville population. The penthouse was lavishly decorated, and a very young and very pretty ebony lady met Chandler and Jefferson as they got off the express elevator. Chandler gave the young woman a squeeze and she wrapped her arms and legs around Chandler. Chandler was used to such a greeting but quickly pushed the lady away so as not to offend Dr. Jefferson." Would you care for something to drink?" Chandler asked.

Jefferson was actually more of a worldly person than he appeared to be when he was under the scrutiny of his wife and fellow Clergymen. The hard shell of his puritanical upbringing melted away when he saw the lifestyle that the penthouse and young adoring woman in Chandler's company expressed. "Do you have a very dry vodka martini that you can whip up, Bobby?" Dr. Jefferson, the current President of the Southern Baptist Convention, asked the man who wanted to be called Bishop Chandler.

After each man had had a few libations, they got down to business. "You said that know somebody that can get people riled up against Theo Mann and his ministry." Dr. Jefferson asked Bishop Chandler as they each continued to sip on the drinks that the pretty young lady supplied them.

"Yeah, I gotta woman that can get the job done. All men are controlled by the desire to have this woman and Theo is just a man isn't he." Chandler said with a lured smile.

Jefferson looked at the long black legs of the woman who was serving them drinks and had to agree that men are tempted by their lust and said, "You seem to have an answer for how we can corrupt Theo's morals, but how do we get Joe Q Public to get outraged when Theo is caught by your seductress?"

"Leave the details to me. Actually, the less you know the better off you will be when all of this gets out in the open. You can then deny that you know anything about it. It's going to take some money to get it done."

"How much do you think that you, or she will need?" Jefferson asked.

"The going price for her services is $150,000. But I think that we can persuade her to do the job if we give her the publishing rights to any story that we sell to the media. You know that I have some experience with writing and publishing books. It's all in the marketing and publicity and I got that covered." Chandler replied.

"Do you have a source of the money?" Dr. Jefferson asked.

"That's where you come in. You just deposit $60,000 into the LLC account you set up; we only need another $100,000 and I think you can easily convince our brothers in the Clergymen Group to come up with it. The only thing is that we need an oath of secrecy so that it doesn't fall back on us that we set Theo up." Chandler said in very low tones as if he thought that he might be being recorded.

"Keeping something like raising a hundred grand especially from a group of preachers while keeping the purpose of the money secret could be difficult, but it can be done if we accuse Theo before the money is collected." Dr. Jefferson mused.

"You got the right idea, man. We say out front that we have found out that Theo has some really bad skeletons in his background, and we want the help of our brothers to get to the bottom of it. We throw in our shady lady, and we got something going for sure. All we need is a little publicity and we are rolling." Chandler whispered while seated next to Dr. Jefferson.

"Leave the publicity to me, Bobby, I got it covered." Dr. Jefferson said as he got up from his seat and headed for the elevator. Evidently being with Chandler for that long was too much for Dr. Jefferson who preached racial equality but really did not believe that a man who came up from the ghetto around Jefferson Avenue in Nashville was his equal.

Chapter 32

The Clergymen bring a loose woman to Theo.

Theo was teaching a small group of students on the mall of what was formerly Peabody College but was now a part of Vanderbilt University. A group of Clergymen approached Theo with a woman dressed in tight jeans and a very low-cut blouse that barely covered her ample breasts.

One of the Clergymen pushed the woman up to Theo so that she was standing face to face with Theo. Theo could feel her breath on his face and feel the warmth of her body next to his. Any man who was as young as Theo would have been aroused by this young voluptuous woman almost standing in his pants. The clergyman snarled out, "This woman is here to see you. She does not mind meeting any sexual need that you might want her to perform, in fact and we have caught her in the very act of getting it on with someone you know. What do you think we should do about such women as this?"

Another clergy man who was somewhat older, said, "When I was being brought up in the church, we would not have tolerated her behavior and we would have made an example of her in front the whole church on a Sunday morning, but on the other hand, she sure is sweet and a little fling now and then will not hurt her.

Another self-righteous clergyman spoke up, "A woman caught in adultery like her, ought to be publicly flogged. How dare any one like her get away with such lack of morals."

Theo knew exactly what each of the Clergymen was thinking and also knew what each man had done in the past that would have caused an outrage if their past was brought to light. It was recently reported that Southern Baptist ministers had engaged in sexual misconduct on a scale that was as bad as the scandals that had rocked the Catholic Priesthood for decades. The woman in question had been sexually abused by so called men of faith. The woman was caught in the act with a man that had some political pull. The paramour was a married man who the other Clergymen kept away from the confrontation with Theo, because they did not want their friend to get any publicity as a result of bring a troubled woman to tempt Theo.

The Clergymen stood around and waited for Theo to do or say something. Instead, Theo bent down and took a small pebble and started to write on the sidewalk. He then stood up, looked at each of the Clergymen in the eye and said, "If any of you are without sin then you can do to this woman as you think is best for all sinners to see." Theo then bent down again and continued to write on the sidewalk.

One by one each of the Clergymen kicked the grass and hit the bricks. Each of them was convicted of his own sinful nature and each of them was overcome with a profound since of shame. Theo again stood up and he and the woman caught in adultery and with whom the Clergymen had tried to tempt Theo, were alone, but they were not standing as close together as when she was thrust upon him. Theo asked, "Where have your accusers gone? Is there no one here to accuse you?"

The woman looked tenderly into Theo's face and said, "There is no one."

"Then I do not accuse you either. Go but sin no more." Theo said as he also looked deeply into her face. "What is your name?" He asked.

"My name is Mary, and I am from Magdala, Arkansas. I would like to become one of your disciples." Said the woman who now had a name to go with her face.

Theo said, "Mary you will indeed become my loyal follower, but as of now the Clergymen are out to get me and cause a scandal. If you don't want to get caught up in a storm of controversy it would be better if you kept yourself at a distance from me."

Mary from Magdala did not say anything but her expression revealed that she was disappointed that Theo would not welcome her into his group of followers. She backed away from Theo but also knew that she would not be too far away if she could be of help to Theo. She wanted to bask in the light of his love for all who believed in him and were willing to listen to his commandments.

Theo continued to teach anyone who wanted to hear his words. He decided that it was better if he left Nashville for the time being. Theo decided to move his operation to Murfreesboro and to the campus of Middle Tennessee State University. Close to the MTSU campus was Stones River the location of an important Civil War battle won by the Union. The battle took place from December 31, 1862, through January 2, 1863. It was a rare winter battle that had a strategic impact on the war to end slavery in the United States. The freedom from slavery as a result of the civil war was not as nearly as impactful as the spiritual war that was and is being fought all around Theo and his believers. Evil had entered into the spirits of the Clergymen, the DJ Crump syndicate and all those who refused to believe that Theo was truly the son of God. Evil had also entered into even one of Theo's closest followers.

Chapter 33

More stories with moral meanings.

As was his custom Theo told stories to those who gathered wherever he went. One of his stories went as follows:

"There was a wealthy man who relied on managers to handle his money, pay his bills and collect form those that owed for the goods and services that that the entrepreneur produced. The chief manager was also a crook and thought that the boss would not notice his thievery because the boss had lots of other stuff to do. The cheating and stealing went on for some time until the boss called the crooked manager in one day and said, 'I hear that you are wasting my possessions. Give an account of your management of my money. By the way you are given two weeks' notice.'

"The crooked manager thought to himself, 'This is really bad. I'm not sure what to do. I'm too old to work at McDonald's and I'm too vain to beg. I don't qualify for a government grant, and I don't think I will win the lottery. 'He thought and thought some more and came up with a plan so that he would survive after the boss cut him loose. He said, 'I will deal with the boss's debtors. I will tell the one that owes a million dollars to settle with me for half of what he owes while I still have authority to settle his debt. To the next borrower who owed $500,000 I will say, settle with me for $400,000 and to another who owes $250,000 I will say settle with me for $200,000.'

"The boss commented on the shrewd crook's actions and said, 'The shrewd crooks of this world are more adapt at worldly pursuits than the people of light when it comes to dealing with their own. I tell you that you should use worldly wealth to gain friends for yourselves, so when it is gone you will be welcomed into eternal dwellings.

"Whoever can be trusted with little, can also be trusted with much, and whoever is dishonest with very little will also be dishonest with much. For if you have not been trustworthy with handling worldly wealth, who will trust you with true riches. If you are not trustworthy with someone else's property who will give you property of your own.

"No one can serve two masters. Either you will hate the one and love the other or you will be devoted to one and despise the other. You cannot serve both God and money."

The Clergymen, who loved money heard all of this and were sneering at Theo. He said to them, "You are the ones who justify yourselves in the eyes of others, but God knows your hearts. What people value highly is detestable in God's sight. "

Then, Theo told another story. "A rich man who dressed in the latest fashion and had all the latest electronic gadgets lived in very grand and opulent surroundings and every meal that was served to him was a banquet. At his gate was a man whose name was Lazarus. Poor old Laz was covered in sores as if he had contracted Monkey Pox. Day in and day out Laz just wanted to pick through the rich man's garbage to find something decent to eat.

"The beggars time came, and the poor beggar died, and angels carried him to heaven. Correspondingly, the rich man died and wound up in a bad place tormented in the flames of hell. The rich man looked up and from a great distance he spotted Laz in a safe and secure place that was in fact paradise. So, seeing that he was tormented in the flames he called out to the keeper of the heavenly gate and said, 'Sir, would you please tell Laz to dip his little finger in a glass of water and come here to touch the drip of water to my tongue because where I am I cannot tolerate the heat.'

"The keeper of the gate said, 'Son, during your lifetime you received good stuff and had plenty, but poor Laz had nothing and had to endure a bad situation. For Laz to come to you, it can't be done. There in a barrier between us and you that cannot be crossed.'

"Then the man cried out from hell, 'I beg you then to send Laz to my family to warn my five brothers so that they will not wind up here too.'

"They can read can't they. Let them read the Bible and listen to what it says.' Was the reply from heaven.

"The rich man in hell said, 'But sir, if someone comes back from the dead and warns them then surely it would make a difference.'

"The voice from heaven replied, 'If they are not convinced by the Bible and preachers who share the word of God faithfully, they will not be convinced even by someone coming back from the dead."

Theo called his disciples aside and said to them, "Things that cause people to stumble and sin will inevitably come into people's lives, but woe to anyone through whom they come. It would be better for that person who causes even the least of these to stumble, to be thrown into the river wearing cement boots. So, watch out for what you do and how it impacts others.

"If your brother or sister sins against you, rebuke them, and if they are genuinely sorry forgive them. Do that even if they mess up all day long, forgive them if they are genuinely sorry for messing up."

One of the disciples spoke up, "Increase our faith."

Theo replied, "If any of you had as much faith as that needed for even a mustard seed to grow from nothing into something large enough for birds to roost in its branches, you could say to a mulberry tree be up rooted and replanted in the ocean, and it would be done."

A clergyman shouted at Theo and said, "When is the Kingdom of God going to come into existence?"

Theo said," The coming of the Kingdom of God is not something that you can observe. People will not say 'Here it is' or 'There it is' because the Kingdom of God is already in the midst of you."

"Remember, The Son of Man must suffer many indignities, be rejected by those who are not called to believe and be killed. I have told you this before. Even then, some will say, 'Here he is, or there he is.' But when I shall return it will be suddenly and with the power to change everything.

"When the Kingdom comes it will be like a rich man taking a long journey. He had cash deposits that he wanted his agents to manage while he was gone.

He gave $500,000 to one of his agents to manage while he was gone, $300,000 to the next to manage, $200,000 to the next and lastly $100,000 to another

"The first agent invested the money wisely and increased the amount entrusted to him by 100%, the second guy did the same and he also had a 100% return on the principal's money. The same was true of the third agent. The fourth agent not so much. That guy took the money and converted it into cash and stuffed it into a pillowcase and kept it under his bed.

"When the boss returned, he asked for an accounting. The top agent gave his report first and showed how he had increased the Chief's money by 100%. The second and the third agents did the same. The Boss was very happy and told his agents, 'Well done good and faithful agents! You have been faithful over a few things; I will put you in charge of many things.'

"The last agent then gave his report and said, 'Boss, I know the kind of man that you are. You are a big-time operator and take advantage of what the markets will yield and make sure that you don't lose any money even if the banks are closed. I took the money, converted it to cash and hid it under my bed. Here it is in stacks.'

"The principal looked at the last agent and said, 'You are a wicked and lazy agent. You knew what kind of man that I am, and you know that I will not lose a single dollar. You could have at least kept the money in the bank where it would have earned interest, but no you didn't do anything to increase my fortune.'

"The boss told his other servants to take the cash form the last agent and give it to the agent who was managing the most money. The boss then said, 'Whoever has will be given more, and they will have an abundance. Whoever does not have, what they do have will be taken from them. Take this worthless guy away and put him out in the street where there will be weeping and hard times.

"When I return and the end of time is upon all men, I will gather all people before me, and they will be separated into two camps. On my right hand will be people who have followed me just like a flock of sheep follow their shepherd. On the left will be a large group that did their own thing just like goats that wander here and there and do not follow the direction of anyone in particular.

"To the one's on my right hand I will say, 'Well done good and faithful folks. When you saw that I was hungry you brought me food. When you saw that I was thirsty, you brought me something good to drink. When I was naked you clothed me. When I was sick, you brought medicine to me. When I was a stranger, you took me in, and when I was in jail you visited me and tried to help me.

"The Righteous folks on the right-hand side of the Master said, 'When did we see you hungry, thirsty, naked, sick, lonely, and in jail."

"The Master said, 'When you did that to the least of these brothers and sisters of mine you did it for me.'

"Then the Master will say to those on the left, depart from me, you are cursed and relegated to eternal torment prepared for the devil and his angels.

Because when I was hungry, you turned your backs. When I was thirsty you said find yourself something elsewhere. When I was naked you just stared and laughed. When I was sick you said let the government do something, and when I was in jail you said it serves him right.

"The ones on the left will say, "when did we see you hungry, thirsty, naked, lonely, sick on in jail.'

"The Lord will say, 'When you failed to take care of the needs of the least of my people you neglected me.

"Then they will go away to eternal punishment, while the righteous will go to eternal life."

Chapter 34

The plot to kill Theo thickens.

Easter was approaching and Theo said to his disciples, "It's almost time for Spring break and we need to go up to Nashville. The Clergymen are having a big gathering and they are expecting us to be there to celebrate the holiday. "

The Clergymen did in fact have a meeting in Nashville. They met at the newly elected President of the Southern Baptist Convention's home. The newly elected president's name was Caleb Jones and like Dr. Jefferson insisted on being referred to as Dr. Jones. He like his predecessor, fully bought into the plot to get rid of Theo with extreme prejudice. During the Clergymen meeting, Buddy Crump also showed up and was invited into the discussions of how to end Theo.

Bishop Bobby Chandler was invited to give a report on his progress in getting someone to morally corrupt Theo and his men. Chandler reported that he had enlisted the services of Mary from Magdala, Arkansas to get close to Theo. A group of Clergymen took Mary to confront Theo, but it did not work out as they had hoped. In fact, that plot had backfired, and Mary had become a follower of Theo's and also became one of his very vocal supporters. Chandler said that the turnaround of Mary from Magdala was as if the red-hot good time girl in her, had been replaced by a true love for Theo.

Bishop Chandler did relate that his efforts were still in progress, and he had been in touch with one of Theo's inside guys who he thought that he could turn against Theo. Chandler said it was a matter of getting the money right and the guy named Jud-I would betray Theo at the right time.

The clergyman group also discussed an advertising campaign that they would launch on TV, radio and on social media that would portray Theo as standing in the way of having a good time and making him look like he favored minorities over the good white people of America. The slogan that was discussed was, "Make America Great, Support American Made Products and You Too Will be Happy for the Rest of Your Life." The group of Clergymen with the support of the Crump syndicate set up a fund to buy media time at local TV stations and radio stations and opened a web site to promote their agenda.

The Clergymen group agreed that making Theo look like he stood in the way of good old American values and that he was a socialist would compromise him in the eyes of his followers and eventually cause Theo's ministry to collapse on itself. The group enlisted the aid of marketing specialist to design a media blitz that would get the desired result of making Theo look like a politically inept person who supported extreme values. They even went so far as to get Theo on video tape and edit it in such away so that it appeared that Theo was some kind of nut.

In the meantime, while Theo was still in the small towns around Nashville, he was staying at the home of Doug Kerr one of the meth dealers that he had cleansed from drug abuse and drug trafficking. While they were having dinner of ribs and baked beans, Mary of Magdala came in uninvited and took out an expensive bottle of perfume and anointed Theo so that he and the whole house was filled with the sweet smell of the perfume. Jud-I told Mary to stop wasting expensive perfume on Theo because Theo was not the kind of person that would waste money like that.

Theo looked sadly at Jud-I and said, "What she has done is a good thing. She has anointed me in anticipation of my death. And if you are making the argument that she could have sold the perfume and given the money to poor people, I say that you are being disingenuous.

"Poor people are always around, but you will not have me with you much longer."

By then Jud-I had already been in contact with Bishop Chandler and was mulling over the distinct possibility that the Clergymen would get to Theo and end Jud-I's dreams of wealth and political power. Jud-I reasoned that he should cash in on the plot to discredit Theo and become as important as Clergymen leaders. Besides that, Jud-I loved money just like the Clergymen. While Jud-I admired Theo and realized Theo was a special person he also resented the fact that Theo often admonished Jud-I for his laziness and lack of care in the treatment of the poor.

Chapter 35

Theo washes his disciple's feet.

Theo had planned to make his entrance into Metro Nashville, but prior to getting to Nashville, Theo was contacted by Ed O'Neil from Channel 2 news and was asked for an exclusive interview regarding his ministry and especially about the raising of Laz from the dead. Other topics of interest were other reported miracles that Theo and his guys had performed in and around the local viewing area. Initially, Theo refused, but after O'Neil told Theo about the media blitz that the Clergymen had initiated and that it was their intent to undermine any good that Theo had done to reduce the meth sales in Middle Tennessee, Theo agreed to the interview.

The interview was to take place in a live broadcast at the television station studio on Sunday, April 5, 2015, during the Jewish Passover celebration. Channel 2 news station had had great interest in the news stories that they had covered about Theo. When the report of the raising of Laz from the dead was aired the station was inundated with request to know more about Theo and some even volunteered to allow Theo to raise recently deceased friends and relatives from those buried close by. The promotion of the scheduled interview was promoted effectively, and they created an intense interest among their viewing audience.

Not to be out done, the Clergymen promoted a counter demonstration in the pulpits of their churches. The Clergymen organized a carpool service for church members in church buses to protest the

Theo interview from the parking lot of the Channel 2 television station. The media campaign controlled by the marketing company hired by the Clergymen had already been busy on their website contending that Theo was a socialist and anti-American.

When the day and time of the Channel 2 interview arrived, there were large crowds of people standing all around the TV station hoping to either cheer or boo the arrival of Theo. There were competing factions. The Clergyman faction was definitely anti-Theo while Theo's long-time followers were enthusiastically in support of Theo and his ministry. There was also a third group of people who were just curious to see Theo and to hear what Theo had to say about raising Laz from the dead. It was estimated that those viewing on TV numbered in the millions.

Theo was driven to the station by Peter in a new convertible fire engine red Ford Mustang that Theo told Peter to borrow from a friend who had offered the car to Theo a day or two before. Theo sent two of his disciples to the home of his friend and Theo told Peter that he would find the car in the driveway with the keys under the driver's seat mat. When Peter got to the house he was to say, "Theo has need of your car," if anyone questioned what he was doing.

When Theo arrived at the driveway to the offices of Channel 2, the crowd was so large and dense that Peter could only drive the car at the pace that a small donkey would travel in order to not run over the throng that had gathered. Theo's followers began to shout "Hooray, Hooray for he who comes in the name of the Lord." They kept up the Hosannas all the while that Theo moved toward to TV studio.

The group of Clergymen, that were there, pulled at Theo and told him to stop the enthusiasm of his followers because it was just not proper. Theo said, "If my followers were not vocal in their support of me the rocks and trees would shout in support." That shut up the opposition for the moment, but it would not stop them for long. Others shouted for Theo to show then a sign and others looked on as spectators at a football game cheering for the team that had possession of the football.

After struggling to get through the crowd, Theo finally stepped into the television studio and was immediately greeted by Ed O'Neil. Theo was taken to a dressing room and prepped by a makeup artist. The young lady looked Theo's face over and was overcome by intense feelings that extruded from the man seated before her. She felt a powerful urge to embrace Theo and to tell Theo everything that she had ever done. Before she could get anything out, Theo took her hand and told her that everything would be OK. All she needed to do was to straighten Theo's tie and make sure his hair was in place. She reacted with gratitude and realized that the man before her was no ordinary person. She finally said, "My name is Rebecca, and I will love you always." Theo gripped her hand and headed in the direction of the newsroom where the interview was to take place.

In the studio sat Ed O'Neil already miked up and ready to get started with the interview. Ed had several pages of questions prepared to ask the young teacher, preacher, healer, radical and miracle worker. The show producer got Theo seated across a small table from the reporter/interviewer and had the camera man check to make sure that the cameras were appropriately placed. Finally, there was a mic check to verify that Theo would be heard loud and clear over television. The producer examined his watch to determine that the broadcast was on time, and he counted down the seconds for the live broadcast program to start. Exactly on time the producer pointed his finger at Ed O'Neil and the interview started.

O' Neil started the program by saying, "Channel 2 news is proud to present a live interview this evening with a very controversial individual that has caused a wide spectrum of belief in and around the Middle Tennessee community and the Channel 2's viewing audience. We have with us tonight, Theo Mann who has never been interviewed, as far as anyone knows, by broadcast journalist. This interview is unscripted, and the views expressed by Mr. Mann are solely his own and do not represent the views or beliefs of this station or its owner. With that said, I am happy to be with you Mr. Mann and would like to know more about you and your beliefs.

"Would you mind telling us where you come from and how you got into your profession as a minister?" Ed O'Neil posed his first question.

"I have come from my Father. I do as my Father commands. The actions that I perform are at the direction of my Father and I and the Father are one." Theo stated as he looked intently into the TV camera operated by a cameraman experienced in focusing in on the facial expressions of the person in front of the camera.

O'Neil was not ready for that response and said, "Are you not the son of Joe and Mary Jane Mann from Burnsville, Mississippi. You are an honors graduate of the University of Mississippi, having a bachelor's degree in divinity. What do you mean by saying that you and the father are one?"

Theo replied, "You know neither me nor my Father. If you knew who I am you would know the Father also. Soon you will see me no more. Where I go you cannot follow, you will die in your sins."

O'Neil said, "Are you going to kill yourself is that what you mean by saying that we cannot follow you?"

"You are from below, I am from above; you are of this world, I am not of this world. I told you that you would die in your sins, you will die because you do not believe that I am he." Theo answered.

"Who are you really?" Ed O'Neil asked as the frustration with Theo's responses registered in his voice.

"I have told you from the beginning who I am and who sent me. I have much to say and much to judge; but he who sent me is true, and I declare to the world that I have heard from him." Theo was speaking of the Heavenly Father, but O'Neil did not understand.

So, Theo went on, "After I am put to death in the manner that the Clergymen and the crime syndicate have set out, then you will know that I am he, and do nothing on my own authority but speak only as the Father has put in my spirit. He who has sent me is with me; he has not left me alone and He will be with me till the end of my days with you."

As soon as Theo finished his last word, the program was interrupted by an unknown source. "This is my beloved son, listen to him." Were the words heard in the studio and across the TV air waves. Nobody moved for a few seconds until Ed O'Neil whispered into his microphone, "Who said that? What does it mean?" Then looking at Theo and trembling visibly, took off his microphone got up from his chair and walked off the set.

Theo was by himself with the cameras and the cameramen sill focused on Theo's face. Theo said, "I am the way the truth and the life, no one comes to the Father except through belief in me. I am going to prepare a place for all who will believe that I and the Father are one."

Theo calmly got up from his seat and exited the building. People in the crowed still outside the building had heard the voice from heaven and many believed that Theo was exactly who he claimed to be. Others said the sound was either a sonic boom or thunder, even though there was not a cloud in the sky. Still others were turned off by Theo and turned their backs on Theo and were inclined to believe that the Clergymen were right, and Theo was a danger to good order.

Theo went back to LaVern where he was staying. On Monday April 6, 2015, Theo got up and returned to Music Row in Nashville and continued to teach groups of people who recognized him from the TV interview that had occurred the night before. There was a multitude of folks that believed in Theo and Theo continued to touch them and heal them. Someone in the crowd said, "What is the destiny of those who believe that you are sent by God."

Theo began to teach them in these terms: "I am the true grape vine and God is the vine dresser. If you believe in me, you are like branches on the grape vine. For the vine to continue to produce fruit the vine and the branches must work together. Without the vine the branches do not exist. Without the branches the vine cannot produce fruit. When the vine dresser comes to tend to the grape vine, he cuts off the branches that are non-productive and throws them out. Later someone gathers up the dead and withered branches and burns them.

"As the vine dresser observes the vine and branches, he looks for branches that produce abundant fruit. He prunes the branches that could produce more fruit so that the harvest will be plentiful. The vine dresser is always observing and pruning so that all will be as productive as possible.

"Apart from me you can do nothing. Become a part of me, and I will become a part of you. Let my words sink in not just to your intellect but also to your spirit so that my words become a part of your very being. When you and I have such a close relationship, you can ask whatever you want from me, and I will give you whatever you ask.

"By this my Father is glorified, that you bear much fruit, and therefore prove that you are my true disciples. As the Father has loved me, I have also loved you; stay committed to the love that is between us. If you keep my commandments, you will stay committed to the love that I have for you, just as I remain committed to the love that the Father has for me. I have said these things that my joy may be in you, and that your joy may be full."

Theo kept up his appearances on Music Row on Monday, Tuesday and Wednesday. On Wednesday night Theo called his twelve original guys to meet him at a downtown hotel for a banquet.

That night Theo and the disciples rented a large room on an upper floor of a hotel in Nashville.

The group had not been together for a while, and they all were excited to get together again. They were waiting for Theo to arrive when a discussion broke out among them as to who would become the greatest of Theo's followers. When Theo came into the upper room, they were still in disagreement about their status and rank.

Theo had them all to sit down and he took off his coat and tie, he untucked his shirt tail and rolled up his sleeves. He had each of the guys take off their socks and shoes and to roll up their pants legs. Theo took a large tub of water that just happened to be near and put a towel around his neck. Theo then went from man to man and washed and dried their feet. As he went from man to man, he said to each of them, "Remember this day and how I have treated you and what I am doing for you. After I'm gone do to others as I have done for you."

When Theo got around to Peter; Peter said, "You know foot washing is a nasty job, you don't need to wash my feet. I get what you are doing, and I am OK with the program."

Theo continued with washing Peter's feet and said, "It is necessary that I do this for you too Peter, even you."

Peter said, "Then not just my feet but my head and the rest of me as well."

"It is sufficient that I wash your feet. You have been with me from the beginning, and you have heard my words and seen my actions. You will look back on this event and understand that I, your teacher, am willing to serve all of you and you will learn to do the same."

Then so that all could hear his exact words, he said, "If any of you would be great, then you must become the servant of all. In the Kingdom of God, the servant will be recognized as great and those who want to be recognized as great and powerful will be last. You are my closest friends. I don't call you followers or underlings anymore. You will be with me in heaven because I am going to the Father to prepare a place for you to join me. As mere followers and students you are not entitled to know all that the Father has set before me, but you are not just followers you are my friends and what I tell you is from the Father, and you will be with me always. I say all of you but one of you is a trader and will betray me to the authorities."

With that said, Theo tucked his shirt tail in and rolled down his sleeves and sat back down. Theo then picked up a loaf of French bread that was on the table and broke it into a piece for each man to eat. Theo said, "This bread represents my body. I am offering my body as a sacrifice for the sins of the world. When you come together in remembrance of this time take bread and pass it around as a symbol of the brokenness of my body and of my sacrifice. You must feast on my broken body if you want to have a part of me in your life."

Theo then took a bottle of wine that was being served with dinner, he opened the bottle and went from man to man and poured out a sip of the wine for each man including Jud-I. Theo said, "This wine represents my blood that well soon be poured out when I am murdered by those under the control of the evil one. My blood will usher in a new covenant between God and humanity. As often as you gather together, take a drink of wine and think of the sacrifice that I am offering on your behalf. Do likewise as often as you can."

After they had eaten Theo looked at Jud-I and said, "What you are about to do; do it quickly." Jud-I immediately got up from the table and went to the home of the Clergyman in charge of the plot to kill Theo.

Theo and his other disciples sat around, and the disciples were quiet and introspective. Finally, Peter spoke and said, "Theo, we have been with you for a while and I for one don't want to leave your side. I believe in you, and we know that you are heaven sent. I will follow you even into a machine gun nest."

Theo looked lovingly into Peter's face and said, "Before this night draws to a close you will deny that you know me three times."

Peter just shook his head in disbelief.

Theo then lifted his head towards heaven in prayer and said, "Father the time has come, glorify your son so that I may glorify you. You have given me power over the world to give eternal life to those you have called and who have accepted your call. Eternal life is that they know you and that they have accepted you into their lives because you are the only true God, and I am the one you have sent. I glorify you on earth; I have accomplished the work that you have given me to do; now glorify me in your presence with the glory that I had before you sent me into the world, even before the world was made.

"I have expressed who you are to the men that you have given me, they were yours and you have given them to me, and they have kept your word. They are completely aware that what I have was given to me by you. I have given them the words that were given to me by you; they know that I have come from you. I am praying for them, not for the world but for them that you have given me, for they are yours, and yours are mine and I am glorified in them. I am not in the world anymore, but they remain in the world, I am coming to be with you. Keep them and protect them by your holy will that they may be one with us even as you and I are one. While I was here on earth, I protected them by your strength. None of them were lost form our protection, but evil has entered into one of them. I am coming to you, and these things I speak in the world, that they may have my own joy fulfilled in them. I have given them your words, and the world has hated them because they are not of this world, even as I am not of this world. I am not praying that you should take them out of this world but that you should protect them from the evil one. Sanctify them with the truth, your word is the truth. As you sent me into the world, I now send them. For their sake I dedicate myself to you that they too may be dedicated in your truth.

"I do not pray only for these but also for those who will believe in me because of the testimony of the ones you have given me, so that they all may be one as you Father are in me and I in you, that they may also be in us, so that the world may believe that you have sent me. The glory that you have given me I give to them, that they may be one even as we are one, I in them, you in me, that they may be perfectly one, so that the world may know that you have sent me and that you have loved them as you have loved me. Father, I desire, that they whom you have given me will be with me where I am so that they may behold the glory that you have given me in your love before the foundation of the world. Father the world has not known you, but I have known you, and these know that you have sent me. I make your name known to them, and I will continue to make your name known, that the love with which you have loved me may be in them, and I in them."

Chapter 36

Theo's arrest.

When Theo finished praying each man left at the table and embraced one another. Theo said that it had gotten quite stuffy in the room, and he wanted some fresh air. The group followed Theo to Percy Warner Park and stopped at a familiar spot where Theo and the group had rested during the Middle Tennessee Crusade.

Theo got out of the car and took Peter, James and John with him and walked a couple of hundred yards down a lonely path. The others stayed in the location where the cars were parked. Theo told the three that he had taken on the walk to stay behind a little as Theo wanted to be alone to pray. Peter, James and John found a comfortable spot to lay down. Theo told them to keep alert because something important was about to happen.

Theo went about 25 yards further down the path and stopped near a bolder that provided a platform on which he could rest his arms as he prayed. Theo was deeply troubled because he knew that he was going to face not only an emotional and spiritual test of his will but also a physical challenge not faced by anyone that this world had ever known. Theo got on his knees and began to pray in an agonized manner. He poured out his heart to the Heavenly Father. Theo was so emotionally fervent in his prayer that great drops of sweat rolled down his face and made a puddle on the ground. Theo cried out to heaven, "Let this horror pass from me, the cruelty of those that were out to bring an end to me, and my message is coming this way even as I pray. But Father not my will but your will be accomplished. Please give me the strength to do what I was sent here to do, so that you will be glorified, and all men will have the ability to be saved from sin."

After Theo had spent about 30 minutes in intense prayer he went back to where he had left Peter, James and John and found each of them asleep. Theo surprised them and they awoke to hear Theo say, "Could you not watch with me for the 30 minutes that I went to pray."

As Theo was talking to the three close friends a group of people led by Jud-I came rushing down the trail with guns in their hands. Jud-I stepped up to Theo and embraced him as the disciples were apt to do at friendlier times. Theo accepted Jud-I's embrace but said, "Would you betray me with a hug of friendship?"

One of the men holding an AK 47 pointed it at the group of 4 men standing in the woods and said, "Which one of you is Theo?"

Theo stepped forward and said, "I'm the one you are looking for, these men with me are not the ones you need so give them a pass. I will go with you without trouble."

The people holding guns grabbed Theo and started back up the path to where their cars were parked. They pushed Theo into an SUV. John and Peter got back to the cars and followed the SUV in which Theo had been put and the whole group headed back to Nashville.

The caravan drove to the home of Fred McIntire who had a large home in the Brentwood section of Nashville. McIntire had political connections and also was well known to the Clergymen group and the Crump syndicate. McIntire agreed to allow the factions wanting to destroy Theo to use his house and grounds to hold Theo while they discussed how to get rid of him. McIntire had a home with a brick wall around the lawn and garden. The house had a gate and access to the house and grounds could only occur if you were known to the security man stationed at the gate. McIntire had told the security guard to allow those who had taken Theo to pass through the gate. By pure chance the guard allowed the car driven by Peter into the compound. John followed the gunmen holding Theo into the mansion while Peter remained with the car.

Dr. Jefferson, Dr. Jones, Bishop Chandler, and McIntire were seated in a dining room that had an overly large table, large enough to seat 40 people. Theo was brought in with his hands bound with the plastic ties used by police to restrain criminal suspects. Theo stood before Jefferson and McIntire and the others and said nothing. Soon another group of men entered the room. That group included Buddy Crump and some of his drug dealing associates. There were also several of the more radical Clergymen who were known to be of the opinion that Theo was subversive to the interest of the church and religious system as they appreciated it. Bishop Chandler appeared dressed in a red suit with a black shirt and tie. For some unknown reason John was allowed in the dining room, but he tried to remain as inconspicuous as possible.

Back at the car Peter was sitting in, one of the guards came up to him and said, "You need to move your car over to that car parking area next to the green house. By the way aren't you one of the followers of the guy they just brought in here?"

No, no you got the wrong person, buddy. I don't know what you are talking about." Peter replied.

Meanwhile, things were heating up in the house between the factions that wanted to get rid of Theo. Buddy Crump wanted to take Theo out with what he called a "brain hemorrhage." What Buddy meant by that was a 45-caliber bullet to the back of Theo's head. On the other hand, the Clergymen needed a more public display so that their group could more or less humiliate Theo in front of a viewing audience and so that people could express their hatred of everything that Theo stood for.

What none of them understood or expected was that Theo, even though he was brought to them, was actually in complete control of all that was going on in the house and, more importantly, in complete control of all that was about to happen to him.

Dr. Jefferson began to question Theo and asked, "Who are you really, do you claim to be the son of God?"

"I have been teaching publicly for all to hear who I am and where I have come from. I have not hidden anything from you or anyone else. Did you not send your representatives to take notes and make reports?" Theo said in an assertive tone.

"Son, don't you speak to me like that, I am superior to you in every way, and I deserve some respect." Dr. Jefferson said with an air of arrogance.

The next thing that happened was that one of the Clergymen came up to Theo and slapped him across his face with such a force that it left a bright red welt. Theo stood his ground and did not react.

"I said do you claim to be the son of God?" Dr. Jefferson shouted into Theo's face.

Theo stood silently for a minute or more starring straight into Dr. Jefferson's eyes as if he could read everything going on in his brain. Bishop Chandler then spoke, "Why did you have to stir up all this shit. We were getting along just fine. People bought in to our program. We were making a good living and you come in and make people think that they don't need to pay to play. The people need us, they can't make up their minds for themselves. You need to get with the program, or you need to die."

Dr. Jefferson told everyone to calm down while he consulted with his group of Clergymen about what needed to happen.

Back at the car park, Peter was again confronted by one of the Clergymen who happened to be passing by the car in which Peter was still sitting. "You are one of Theo's right hand men, I saw you with him in Percy Warner Park last night."

Peter snarled back, "I have nothing to do with the man you are speaking of and leave me the hell alone."

While Dr. Jefferson and his men were discussing how to proceed, they took Theo out of the house to where the cars were parked in order to keep him from bleeding on the carpet while Buddy and his men ruffed Theo up a bit. As they were passing by the car in which Peter was sitting a woman came up to Peter and said, "You are one of Theo's men, I saw you driving him to the TV station a few days ago."

"You are out of your ever-loving mind; I do not know him, and I wouldn't be caught dead with him."

Peter shouted at the woman just as Theo passed by the car and looked squarely into Peter's face.

Peter suddenly remembered what Theo had said to him about his denial. Peter could not take anymore. He started the car and drove out of the Brentwood mansion as quickly as he could.

It was now early Thursday April 9, 2015, morning and things slowed down as far as the trial of Theo at the hands of the Clergymen and the other factions was going on. By the time that the sun was coming up Theo had been in the hands of his captors for about 10 hours, and he had been beaten and bloodied and paraded around the McIntire estate for all the factions to gawk at.

Chapter 37

The Death of Theo Son of Mann

After Dr. Jefferson and Bishop Chandler had rested for a few hours, they decided to talk with their media consultant to figure out the best way to get their propaganda about the danger of Theo' message and teachings out to the people in and around middle Tennessee. Judy Swartz, the media consultant arrived at the mansion at 10:00 AM and began to discuss how Theo could be portrayed to the public to get the most favorable response to the Clergymen's point of view and to cause the most negative reaction to Theo and his ministry.

They decided that they needed a news conference to be scheduled immediately and that Theo needed to be shown as a radical who molested children and wanted to destroy the United States economy by allowing immigrants in through open boarders, and who wanted to deny the right to keep assault weapons in violation of the Second Amendment.

The news conference was arranged through Ed O'Neil, who was enlisted to have the news conference carried live on TV that noon.

The cameras were rolling, and the broadcast was live. People were brought in to swell the crowd that gathered at the sight of the news conference that was in a church near the Tennessee State Capitol Building. Finally, Theo was brought out with his hands bound behind him, Theo had been severely beaten and his face was a bruised and bloody mess. Newspaper journalist and photographers were in attendance as well as TV news personalities. There was also a contingency of police officers in riot gear posted in the church and just outside in case the crowd got too unruly.

Dr. Jefferson stepped up to the microphone and began with his opening statement. "Last night me and some of the church leaders that you all know, and respect invited Theo Mann to a cookout at the home of Fred McIntire a highly respected business-man who lives in Brentwood. Theo showed up at the cookout in an inebriated state with a little girl in the car with him. It was obvious that Theo was a danger to himself but more importantly to the child that was in the car with him. We inquired about the child but could get nothing out of Theo that would help us to know to whom we could take the child.

"We called Child Services to help, and they determined that the little girl had been sexually abused. When Theo was confronted with this report, he became belligerent and started a fight with the lady from Child Services. At that point a security guard employed by Mr. McIntire engaged in a fight with Theo and you see Theo now as he appeared af-ter the fight with the guard. The little girl was taken by Child Services and a medical report as to the little girl's condition will be forth coming later today.

"We called the police and when they arrived Theo again lashed out and had to be restrained. The Police found drug paraphernalia in Theo's car along with methamphetamine producing equipment. There was also a pamphlet in which Theo advocated that the United States allow unlimited immigration of Mexicans and the confiscation of all guns by the Federal government.

"We all know that Theo has a large following and many who have been duped by his anti-American rhetoric and for the sake of safety we the men of the true church and true religion, thought that we needed to bring these developments to your attention."

As Jefferson was closing his remarks a signal was given to plants in the crowd to start chanting "lock him up, lock him up, lock him up." Suddenly, as if on cue, the crowd started rushing forward with the intent of seizing Theo. The police in attendance did nothing to stop the mob as it rushed to the place where Theo stood without any impediment to the on-rushing mob of highly incensed people. Someone could be heard to say, "We ought to string him up."

None tried to restore order. Jefferson, Chandler and the media expert got exactly what they wanted, and Theo was taken by the mob out of the church. Men came up to Theo and punched him in his already mostly unrecognizable face, women came up to cursed at him and to spit on him. Someone had a rope in the trunk of his parked near-by car and quickly made a noose. The mob found a tree with a convenient branch and threw the rope into the tree. They placed the noose around Theo's neck.

By force of his own will Theo stopped the crowd. He demanded silence and without understanding why a calm silence swept through the mob. Theo said, "Father forgive them for they do not know what they are really doing. These men who accuse me think that they are bringing an end to me and the purpose for which I was sent to this world. They mean this as a justification of their belief that would put each of you in bondage to your sins. But they are wrong. By lifting me up my purpose will become clear. By my death many will be saved. They mean this as an end, in reality this is only a beginning. You may kill my body today, but I will rise again. They mean this as a way to stop the spirit of truth from going out to a sinful and dying world. Nothing could be further from what the work of the Holy Spirit will accomplish when He comes upon the saints with power.

Then with a loud confident and steady voice Theo cried out, "Into your hands I send my spirit, it is finished!"

Buddy Crump quickly stepped up to make sure the noose around Theo's neck and secure. Buddy took hold of the rope and with the help of others in the crowd Theo was pulled up. Almost before his feet lost contact with the ground, he was dead. It was as if Theo willed his body to stop its living function and his spirit departed at his own command. One of Bishop Chandler's armor bearers pulled out a 9mm pistol and shot Theo on his left side near his heart to make sure that Theo was dead. Water and blood poured out of Theo's wounded side. A cloud burst rainstorm descended on Nashville as if the very air needed to be cleansed. The earth trembled, the sky was pitch dark and people moved back to the church to get out of the storm.

People in the crowd began to look at Theo's body hanging in the tree and felt a great sense of grief at what had transpired right before their eyes.

One of the Clergymen who moments before had been caught up in the mob hysteria began to weep in an uncontrolled expression of sorrow for the part he had played in Theo's death. He shouted, "Theo was the son of God and we have killed an innocent man."

Others still caught up in the violence said, "He deserved it for what he said about taking our guns away."

Most however, felt as if a great light in a dark world had been snuffed out. They went home to their families and refused to tell anyone what they did or especially what they had seen and heard from Theo.

Later, that evening Pastor Nick O'Deamus and another man, Joseph from Arimathea, New Jersey, came and cut Theo's body down from the tree near the Tennessee Capitol and took it to the morgue that was on the Vanderbilt Hospital campus. As it was late on Friday night nothing further could be done. Theo's disciple who he loved called Mary Jane and broke the news of what had transpired. Mary Jane told John to do nothing until she could get there on early Sunday morning.

Dr. Jefferson was aware that Theo's body was taken to the Vanderbilt Hospital morgue and he and Bishop Chandler got some men to stand guard at the morgue to prevent any of Theo's followers from taking the body away and claiming that he was not really dead. Theo's body was covered by the usual sheet and his head was covered with an additional covering because it was so badly beaten.

Chapter 38

Resurrection

Everything either slowed down or stopped completely on the Saturday following Theo's death. Theo's close friends went into hiding because they feared the Clergymen and the Crump syndicate. Theo's mother, Mary Jane was on her way to Nashville from Burnsville and the Clergymen, and the Crump syndicate posted guards at the Vanderbilt Hospital morgue so that Theo's followers would not steal the body and claim that he was still alive.

When Mary Jane arrived in Nashville she was taken to the room where Theo and his disciples ate the last supper. The group also included Janet Gilmore, Rebecca, Mary from Magdala, who was brought to Theo and accused of adultery, and other women that had followed Theo during his earthly ministry.

When the morgue was open very early on Sunday morning Mary Jane and some of the other women went to the Vanderbilt morgue to see Theo's body and make funeral arrangements. When they got to the morgue, they found the guards that had been posted by the Clergymen lying flat on the floor outside of the cooler where bodies were stored. The guards were not unconscious but were visibly stunned and unable to speak coherently.

The ladies stepped inside of the cooler room and found the drawer where Theo's body had been stored was empty. A man dressed in a bright white suit was standing next to the open drawer. He said to the women, "Why are you seeking the living among the dead?"

The women did not reply because they were frightened beyond words. They ran back to their car and drove back to where the others were staying and reported to the men what they had seen and heard. The men were perplexed at what the women had excitedly told them. Only Peter and John took any action. Peter and John got to Peter's car and drove quickly to the Vanderbilt morgue. When they arrived all most before the car stopped moving John jumped out of the car and raced into the room where Theo's body had been stored. Peter being older did not run as fast but when he got to the cooler room he brushed past John and went in. John then joined Peter and they were suddenly greeted by a man dressed in dazzling white clothes. They saw the sheet that had been covering Theo's body folded neatly laying on a chair near the drawer in which Theo's body had been stored and the towel that had been on Theo's head still in the cooler drawer folded but still bloody.

The man in dazzling white greeted Peter and John and said, "He is not here he is risen and will go before you to Pickwick Lake, and you will meet him there in a few days." Just as suddenly as the man in dazzling white disappeared and Peter and John were alone in the morgue cooler with the drawer wide open and Theo not there.

They got back into Peter's car and drove back to the hotel to tell the others about what they had seen and heard. As they were driving back to the hotel, two other followers were driving down the Natchez Parkway towards Florence when they saw a hitchhiker wearing a hoodie on the side of the road and stopped to pick him up. The guy got in but because of the hoodie being over his face the men in the car could not see his face and he did not say who he was. After a mile or two they asked the hitchhiker where he was going, and he said Florence. The two followers began to talk about Theo's death and the hitchhiker was interested to know about who and what they were referring to. One of Theo's followers said, "Are you not aware of what has transpired in Nashville this weekend? We are followers of Theo and we believed that he would bring peace and love to the world, but he has been murdered by a crowd. Some of the women in our group have reported that he has risen. We just don't know what to believe."

The hitchhiker then began to refer them to the Old Testament of the Bible and to show them how the savior of the world must suffer and die for the sins of men to be forgiven. This conversation went on for many miles. One of the followers who had picked up the hitchhiker said, "Friend we are going to stop and get a bite to eat. Will you join us?"

The hitchhiker was reluctant at first but because they insisted the hitchhiker agreed to go into a Waffle House with them. They ordered and when the grits and bacon was brought to the table the hitchhiker blessed it in the same manner as Theo blessed food that he ate with his followers. The driver shouted, "It's you, it's you; you are alive!"

As he said "alive," the hitchhiker was gone and could not be found in the Waffle House. The two men jumped back in their car and drove back to Nashville and went straight to the hotel room where Theo's disciples were still staying.

Later, in the morning after the women had gone to the morgue and returned to tell the disciples what they had seen and heard, Mary of Magdala returned to the Vanderbilt morgue. As she was approaching the morgue, she was met by a man in dazzling white. "Where have you taken his body? Please tell me so I can make proper arraignments for his funeral." Mary from Magdala asked.

Something moved behind her. Her eyes were filled with tears and when she turned, she could not see clearly because she was weeping. A hand reached out and touched her hand and he said, "Mary."

She immediately knew it was Theo and she said, "Teacher."

She would have embraced Theo in the manner in which the fellowship always embraced but he said, "Mary do not hold on to me. I have not yet ascended to my Father. Go tell the others that I am alive, and I will come to them when it is the right time."

Meanwhile, back at the Clergymen head-quarters, Dr. Jefferson found out that somehow the guards who had been hired and placed at the Van-derbilt morgue did not do their job and Theo's body was missing. Jefferson called the guards in for a re-port on what had happened. The guard who was in charge related the following: "We four men were fully awake and standing at our post at about 2:30 AM on Sunday April 12, 2015. One man was in the cool-er room where the bodies are kept and we the oth-er three were just out in the hall next to the cooler room. The whole building began to shake just like an earthquake was happening. The man in the cool-er room shouted and the other three, me included ran into the cooler. The drawer where Theo's body was being kept burst open and Theo came out. Men dressed in dazzling white assisted Theo as he passed by us. Something happened to our legs, and we lost the ability to stand. To tell you the truth, I was so frightened that I could not speak. All that I could do was to lay there on the floor. It was over an hour or more until I was able to get back on my feet. By then some women had come by, they looked in the room and quickly left. As soon as we were able, we came here to give you this report we got ourselves together and drove over to meet you."

"Don't you say a word to anyone about this, you hear me. Keep your mouths shut. The less you say and the less you remember, the better. There will be a bonus paid if you don't talk when this all blows over." Jefferson told the guard.

They did as Dr. Jefferson asked them to do and nothing more was reported about the location of Theo's body by the Clergymen or more importantly by any news outlet.

Chapter 39

Theo appears to his disciples and to many others.

In the evening of the Sunday after his death the disciples excluding Jud-I, who was reported to have hung himself, and Thomas, were together in the hotel room where Theo had washed their feet and where they had the last supper together. They were deep in discussion about what Mary and the other women had said and what Peter and John had reported. Then there was the report from the men who were driving to Florence and met the hitchhiker.

The room was locked from the inside, and they felt somewhat safe from the Clergymen and the Crump syndicate. Theo appeared in the room and sat down on a chair at the large table that they had dined on a few nights earlier in the week. "I bring you peace. I am alive. Death has no hold on me. As the Father has sent me, in the same manner I am sending you." When he said that he breathed on them and said, "Receive the Holy Spirit. If you forgive anyone they are forgiven, but if they refuse to be forgiven, they remain in their sin."

When the group saw Thomas again, they told him of Theo's appearance and what Theo had told them. Thomas said, "Unless I see Theo and see the rope burns around his neck and see his bloodied face, I will not be satisfied that he is really alive and that whoever he is, he is not some impersonator trying to infiltrate our fellowship."

A few days later the disciples including Thomas were all together in the upper room where the last supper had taken place. Again, the door was locked because they were still afraid of the mob that had killed Theo. They were deciding what they needed to do next when Theo walked through the wall and came right up to Thomas and said, "Peace be with you, Thomas come over here and examine me closely so that there is no doubt in you at all that it is me. Do not be faithless but believe that I was dead but am now alive. Have faith that all that I said would happen has happened. Believe so that non-belief is driven from your mind and from your spirit."

Thomas realized that he was in the presence of God, Thomas fell to his knees before Theo, and said, "My Lord and my God!"

Theo replied, "Thomas have you believed because you have seen me and examined me, those who believe who are coming after and who will not have the opportunity to see what you have seen will be blessed."

Theo revealed himself to many others after he had been resurrected.

After he had been with his disciples in Nashville, Peter still dissatisfied with himself for denying Theo after Theo was arrested, told the others that he wanted to go fishing. Seven of the fellowship went with Peter down to Pickwick Lake and got a boat. They fished all night but didn't even get a bite. They were about to give up when they heard a shout from the beach at the State Park. The sun was behind the person shouting so that no one on the boat could see exactly who was trying to get their attention.

The man on the beach was finally heard to say, "You're fishing on the wrong side of the boat."

Peter was skeptical but the man on the beach seemed to be insistent, so they tried the other side of the boat. Every time they cast a line; they got a large catfish. They had never experienced anything like it before. Suddenly it began to dawn on Peter that the man on the beach had to be none other than Theo. Peter took off his shoes and shirt and jumped in the lake and swam the hundred yards to the beach.

The others on the boat had so many fish they didn't know what to do because the live well on the boat was full and they still had more fish to deal with. They brought the boat to the shore and found Peter drying himself off with a towel offered by Theo. Theo had built a fire and had fried some catfish for the men to have for breakfast.

Theo took Peter aside and they sat 20 or 30 yards away from the others. Theo put his arm around Peter's shoulders and said to him, "Peter do you love me more than going fishing with your friends?"

"Yeah, I love you more than fishing with my buddies." Peter replied.

"Feed my sheep." Theo responded as he looked Peter in the eye.

Theo still with his arm around Peter and pulling him closer to his chest asked, "Peter, do you love the time we have spent together and all the things that you have learned from the time we met?"

"I certainly do appreciate all that you have taught me and all that I have seen during the time we have spent together." Peter said not really knowing what Theo was getting at by asking these questions.

Theo said, "Tend my sheep."

A third time, pulling Peter even closer so that the two of them were in a full embrace with Peter's face just inches from Theo's still battered and scared face, Theo in as emphatic voice as Peter had ever heard asked, "Peter, are you willing to love me with a love that will cost you everything that you are or hope to be?"

Peter vexed by Theo's questioning and realizing the earnestness in Theo's voice, said, "You know everything about me. You know my heart and soul. You know that I do love you and will give my life in your service. You know that I am troubled by my behavior when I denied that I am your disciple, and that I know that you are the true son of the living God."

"Then feed my sheep." Theo said, while releasing Peter from the strangle hold that he had on him.

Then looking lovingly again into Peter's eyes, and with a wistful smile, Theo said, "Before we met, when you were a young man, you did what you pleased to do and went where you chose to go. But now you are undertaking a different life. You will be led by the Holy Spirit to go where the Spirit will lead you to go. You will do as the Holy Spirit will lead you to do. You may question that leadership, but you will go and do even if you are called on to sacrifice your life in my service." Theo said this to signify that Peter would become a martyr in the service of the Lord.

After he had a time of fellowship with his close

friends, they followed Theo over to Woodall Mountain the place where he had been transfigured. Theo said to all of his disciples, "All authority in heaven and on earth has been given to me. Therefore, go and make disciples of all people of every nation, baptizing them in the name of the Father, the son, and the Holy Spirit. Teach everybody what I have taught you. I will always be with you even to the end of the age."

When Theo had finished blessing those who were there he ascended into the clouds and was out of their sight. A man in white dazzling clothes appeared and said, "Why are you still standing here gawking at the clouds. Didn't he just give you your marching orders? If I, were you, I would not be lazy. I would be doing what the Lord just told you to do."

Afterwards

The book of Acts tells us that the Disciples of Jesus did as the angel had told them to do after Jesus gave his disciples his "great commission" and ascended into heaven. They returned to Jerusalem and awaited the coming of the Holy Spirit on the day of Pentecost. Peter preached a sermon after being filled with the promised Holy Spirit that appeared as a tongue of flame on all of the Jesus believers' heads. As a result of Peter's sermon that day 3000 new believers became followers of the "Way" as the followers of Jesus were referred to in the early days.

Jesus' disciples disbursed throughout Asia, the middle east and Turkey. Jewish Clergymen in Jerusalem began to terrorize the members of the Way and a Clergymen named Saul, from Tarsus, was a zealot against the followers of Jesus. Saul was given a warrant to go and arrest Jewish members of the Way in Damascus. On the trip to Damascus, Saul was confronted by Jesus as a bright light from heaven blinded Saul. Saul asked who it was that was blinding him. The voice from the blinding light said, I am Jesus, why are you persecuting me?" That changed Saul's prospective on life. Saul was converted and became a follower of Jesus. Eventually, Saul whose name was changed to Paul was recruited by Barnabas one of the followers of Jesus while Jesus was still in his earthly ministry. Barnabas persuaded Paul to go to Antioch and engage in the conversion of non-Jews. It was in Antioch that those who believed in Jesus first became known as Christians.

There was some interaction between Paul and the disciples of Jesus who were still alive that allowed for the conversion of non-Jews. Soon Paul and

Barnabas were commissioned to travel to Asia Minor and founded Christian Churches as they traveled especially among non-Jewish groups. Within a short time, Paul and a group of Christians moved their missionary efforts to Europe. By the end of his life Paul had established churches in Greece and traveled to Rome in order to spread the Gospel message of Jesus Christ. Paul was said to have even stood before Caesar to proclaim Jesus.

In letters written by Paul, Peter, and John a Christian theology was established as a dynamic movement that caused belief in Jesus as the Christ to grow exponentially throughout the middle east and Europe. The New Testament book of 1 John is extremely important in Christian thought and practice. The writings of Paul are essential to the understanding of Christian life and practice.

After Paul, Peter and many others were martyred for proclaiming Christ, others took up the Christian Faith and Christianity swept through Europe in the form of the Catholic Church. Later in the history of Christianity, a reform movement caused a division in those who claimed to be true Christians. Protestant denominations of various beliefs sprang up in opposition to the State/ Catholic coalition that was prevalent in many locations.

Eventually, The Reformation reached England and another brand of state supported religious belief caused division among followers of Christ. English opposition to certain Christian sects caused people to immigrate to the Americas. When the English colonies rebelled against the English King and Parliament in 1776 one of the reasons for the rebellion was to promote religious freedom. One of the main movers in the fight for religious freedom was the Baptist. After the United States was formed and the Constitution was ratified in 1783, the Bill of Rights to the Constitution guaranteed freedom of religion to United States citizens. In the First Amendment to the Constitution freedom of religious belief is guaranteed. The words of the First Amendment are, "Congress shall make no law respecting an establishment of religion, or prohibiting the free exercise thereof..."

Over the years the rights established under the US Constitution were also guaranteed to citizens of the states by the Fourteenth Amendment to the Constitution.

That brings us almost to the present. Religious liberty has been a focal point of mainly conservative (right-wing) religious organizations. When they present their idea of religious liberty it is always infused with conservative political issues. Whole cloth political issues have been co-opted by religious organizations to engender support for political causes such as governmental support to parochial schools, prayer in public schools, and most notably the right to life movement.

The Supreme Court of the United States in several constitutional law opinions interpreted the First Amendment ban on laws regarding the free exercise of religion or the establishment of religion. The Supreme Court established by precedent, a separation between the operation of the government and religious organizations. That wall of separation seemed to have served the Constitution and the United States for many decades. The separation between church and state has recently become more blurred by more recent Supreme Court decisions in which local government has stepped into such matters as funding of certain operations of parochial schools.

Most recently the Supreme Court has announced its opinion to uphold a Mississippi statute that almost completely bans a woman's right to an abortion. It is not a coincidence that the issue of abortion rights finds its roots in conservative religious dogma. From a conservative religious standpoint, the issue of a woman's right ends at the moment of conception. Counter to that argument, pro-choice adherents contend that a woman's choice to an abortion should be upheld until the time that a fetus is viable. The Supreme Court in its landmark ruling in <u>Roe v. Wade</u>, found that there was embedded in the constitution a right of privacy that pervades the Constitution and allows for freedom of choice by a woman in the privacy of her own conscience.

Those who support anti-abortion legislation contend that there is nothing specific in the Constitution concerning abortion, that there is no real right of privacy set out in the words or even the spirit in which the restrictions on the establishment of religion or the right to the free exercise of religion can be found. While conservative political operatives can find plenty of leeway in the Second Amendment to the Constitution to allow the purchase and possession of automatic assault rifles, they cannot find a similar right of freedom within the First Amendment to allow women a right to abortion.

Because much of this discussion centers around religious freedom and the interpretation of that freedom by the right-wing conservative movement, it is certainly appropriate to ask, "Is there anything in the message, teachings, and life of Jesus Christ that would speak either directly or indirectly to the so-called religious liberty movement in the United States?" A few years ago, I noticed that many people were wearing bracelets that had the letters WWJD on their wrist. WWJD stood for the words,

"What would Jesus do?" Asking that question remains important.

When I became a Christian and surrendered my life to the service of Christ, I felt it was most important to me that I understand, as best as possible, the commandments of Jesus. This book is an effort to examine the life and teachings of Jesus. I have used the name of Theo Mann as being a close reference to The Son of Man; a name or title that Jesus used for himself. I have studied the Gospels in order to become closer to a full understanding of the words of Jesus in the Sermon on the Mount (Matthew 5-7). Those teachings are a good starting point for an inquiry into many life situations that a serious follower of Jesus will encounter. My study of those teachings has led me to believe that as a follower of Christ I should be most tolerant of all people, to treat all with dignity, forgive every indignity, pray even for my enemy's, treat everyone as we wish to be treated, and not place undue burdens on the poor and helpless. I think therefore, that the religious right has misapplied the teachings and spirit of Christ.

It is my prayer that this book will produce in each of us a desire, to also study the words and actions of Jesus Christ to ascertain for our own selves the answer to the question, "What would Jesus do?"

June 24, 2022

Jeffrey Sakas

www.ingramcontent.com/pod-product-compliance
Lightning Source LLC
Chambersburg PA
CBHW071248300726

48975CB00002B/593